A GLADIATOR'S TALE

Leonidas the Gladiator Mysteries, Book 2

ASHLEY GARDNER

JA / AG Publishing

A Gladiator's Tale

Leonidas the Gladiator Mysteries, Book 2

This book is a work of fiction. The names, characters, places, and incidents are products of the writer's imagination or have been used fictitiously and are not to be construed as real. Any resemblance to persons, living or dead, actual events, locales or organizations is entirely coincidental.

Cover design by Kim Killion

CHAPTER I

Februarius, AD 63

"I need your help, Leonidas."

Aemilianus, once my trainer, held up a blunt-fingered hand as I paused inside the doorway to my rooms above a wine shop on the lower slope of the Quirinal Hill. I was just returning from the baths, my scoured skin smelling of oil, my damp tunic clinging to my back.

Aemil gazed at me from mismatched eyes within a sharp face, heavy scars on his half-missing ear. He sat on my stool, at my table. Cassia, the scribe who lived with me, had retreated to the doorway of the balcony and watched Aemil warily.

Aemil had trained me as a raw youth who had strength but no skill, and built me up to become *primus palus* of his ludus. I'd been a champion, the most famous gladiator of my time.

Since the day I'd been given the *rudis* at the Saturnalian games and left the Circus Gai as a free man, Aemil had made it clear that he would do all he could to recruit me to help him teach others.

As I drew a breath to sling him out, Aemil said quickly, "Not to persuade you to return. I need you to help me find someone. Three someones, in fact. Gladiators."

This puzzled me enough to halt my invective. "Find them?" I wondered if he was asking me to help him round up new fighters. "What gladiators?"

"Ajax, Rufus, and Herakles." Aemil faced me on the stool, palms landing on his large, parted knees. "Find them, as in *find* them. They are missing."

My surprise mounted. "You mean they ran away?" Aemil was tough, but his gladiators ate good food and were housed in moderately comfortable cells. He didn't practice cruelty on his gladiators, because broken men couldn't fight, though Aemil wasn't soft on them either. Few ever tried to flee him.

"Not so much ran away as are staying away," Aemil said with impatience. "They walked out of the ludus during daylight, off to do jobs, or in Rufus's case, visit a wife. Then did not return."

Not unusual for gladiators of high standing to be given leave to depart the ludus, either to work as bodyguards or go home to a paramour or wife. My closest friend, Xerxes, a very popular gladiator, had taken a wife and lived with her on a farm not far from Rome. Marcella still lived there, now that Xerxes was no more.

"They left together?" I asked.

"No." Aemil scowled. "Stop interrupting. They went, with my leave, not together, and haven't returned. I give all my men some leeway for sleeping it off before they come stumbling home, as you know, but four days is too much. I suspect they're in a stupor from drink or fornication, but it's bad for business if they aren't where I can put my hands on them."

Out of the corner of my eye, I saw Cassia quietly move to the table, open a wax tablet, and make a note with her stylus.

"The urban cohorts can find them and bring them back to you," I said without moving.

"I don't want the cohorts." Aemil made a noise of exasperation. "If they've found trouble, I don't want them dragged off to a magistrate or the Tullianum. I need them."

Aemilianus was a businessman through and through. A former gladiator, he taught his men how to entertain while fighting for their lives, and his gladiators won prizes and brought him money and prestige.

"When exactly did each of them leave?" I did not ask for myself, but so that Cassia could write it down. Her fingers twitched, anxious to record more information.

Aemil rubbed his close-shaved brown hair. He'd begun life as a Gaul, large and strong, with one blue eye and the other brown-green. A hard man, he didn't like problems that were too complex.

"Ajax, four days ago, right after breakfast. Rufus, the same day, at the sixth hour. Herakles, that night. Rufus went to his wife, Ajax to enjoy himself in the Subura, and Herakles didn't say. He'd earned a night of debauchery, so I assume a lupinarius, like Ajax, or maybe the home of some woman."

Cassia's stylus scratched in the silence when he finished.

"The vigiles should be able to find them then." I brushed leftover droplets of water from my arm. I'd indulged in the newly opened Baths of Nero and its fine marble frigidarium. Unlike Cassia, I had no interest in the bath complex's artwork or the library, but I swam in the wide pools and sweated in the broad exercise yard.

"Did you not hear what I said?" Aemil rose. Taller than most Romans, his head brushed the low ceiling. "I want you to find them, Leonidas. Haul them back to me, and *I'll* decide how to punish them."

He'd terrify them but keep them alive and well, he meant. Aemil had perfected the art of intimidation.

I had to wonder why the three hadn't turned up again, but on the other hand, I knew they'd have their reasons. All three were strong, capable men, in the top ranks of the ludus, with an arrogance that accompanied it. No doubt they were luxuriating in fine beds while women fussed over them.

"Why ask me?" I said. They wouldn't return because I told them to.

"Because you have a slave who is good at finding things out. If the men are caught by anyone but us, they'll be executed, and you know it. Ajax and Herakles aren't citizens. You want to see them crucified?"

Ajax and Herakles had been captured after a battle in a far-flung corner of the Roman empire. Aemil had bought them once they'd reached Rome, stripped them of their own names, and given them those of Greek warriors. The two men were not Greek at all, being from a tribe from somewhere in Pannonia, but the crowds at the games liked ancient heroes.

Roman citizens were allowed the dignity of execution by sword or strangulation. Those not citizens could be killed in varied and horrific ways.

I did not want to see two men I'd known well and trained with torn apart by wild beasts or made to choke on a sword or molten metal. Aemil knew I would not. As I said, he was a master of coercion.

Aemil held my gaze. "As a favor, Leonidas. To me, and to them."

Cassia made a soft sound in her throat, one quiet enough for Aemil to ignore, but I understood exactly what the tiny noise meant.

"Not as a favor," I said. "For a fee."

Aemil's mouth turned down. "So said your slave."

Cassia kept her head bent over her tablet and remained silent.

I lived in this small room, an L-shaped apartment with an alcove that held my bed and shutters that closed off the balcony at night, and paid rent to the wine merchant downstairs for the privilege. I had been freed by a benefactor who'd provided me Cassia and found this place for us, but I had to earn my own keep. According to the go-between for this unknown benefactor, I was to await instructions about what he or she wanted from me.

I'd been freed near the end of December, and it was now the second month of the year, Februarius, a day after the Nones. So far, we'd had no word.

Cassia spent the time finding jobs for me, mostly bodyguard work for merchants or patricians. She made certain the fee was reasonable and that I was paid. Often those who hired me tried to stall on payment, but Cassia, soft-voiced and modest, could pry coins from the most reluctant of clients.

"We must eat," I told Aemil bluntly.

Aemil studied the sparsely furnished room. We had a table and three stools, a bed for me, a pallet for Cassia near the balcony doors, and another table that held a shrine to those gone before us. A long cupboard near the table contained our meager possessions, and a rickety shelf above the table held a wooden sword inscribed with my name. The *rudis*, which symbolized my freedom.

Cassia had brought in a third stool recently, explaining that if clients came to us, they'd need a special place to sit while we negotiated. That stool rested at the end of the table, but Aemil had chosen to take mine.

"I don't think much of your benefactor, Leonidas." Aemil folded his arms across his barrel of a chest. "You should be lounging in silk, bathing in milk, and eating pastries and apricots coated with spun sugar. Not plopped on a rough stool gobbling down lentils." His eyes took on a cunning I recognized. "Come back to the ludus and work for me. You can live in a far nicer home and have whatever women and food you want. I'll even split prizes won by the gladiators you teach. If Leonidas the Spartan is training the men, I can command an even higher price for them."

He'd suggested this to me many a time in the last months. I continued to refuse, as I did now.

Instead of arguing, I simply shook my head.

Aemil did not appear discouraged. "One day you will accept my offer. For now, find those Hades-spawned gladiators and drag them home by their balls. I'll pay you a sestertius for each."

"A denarius," I countered. Cassia's faint nod told me I'd chosen correctly. "A sestertius only buys a flask of wine."

Aemil's gaze went flinty. "Fine. A denarius. But only if they're standing upright and ready to fight. If you bring them back dead drunk and unable to move, the fee is half."

In other words, he'd hold me responsible for sobering them up once I found them.

I shrugged my agreement.

"Good. Start right away." With this last order, Aemil heaved himself to his feet, sent me another sharp look, and stomped out.

I waited until he was down the stairs and into the street, the outer door banging behind him, before I closed the door at the top of the stairs to shut us in.

Cassia had stepped onto the balcony, a flat space that was the roof of the wine shop below. I joined her, and we watched Aemil stride down the narrow lane to the Vicus Longus at its end. Romans on errands melted out of the way of his angry bulk.

I rubbed the top of my shaved head. "I suppose I'll start at the ludus. The gate guards will know better than most where those men would go. Hopefully, I'll run them to ground before too long, and we'll be three denarii richer."

Cassia was pleased by this, I could see, but she only gave me a quiet look.

I studied her a moment, her light-brown skin, her all-seeing dark eyes, the curling black hair she caught in a tail at her nape to keep out of her way. Her tunic was the plain garment of a slave, bound at the shoulders and falling to feet clad in neat sandals, but she kept it clean and wrinkle-free, as dignified and tidy as any matron.

When my stare went on too long, Cassia's brows rose the slightest bit, as though wondering why I lingered.

I ducked inside, made certain I had coins and a knife in the pouch slung around my waist, and departed to join the teeming masses of Rome.

AEMIL'S LUDUS LAY IN THE TRANSTIBERIM, ACROSS THE RIVER to the west. I merged with the crowds on the Pons Agrippae and angled southward once I reached the other side of the Tiber.

The ludus was a large structure of barracks that encircled a rectangular training area. There was space within this makeshift arena for several pairs of gladiators to practice fighting while the novices struck posts with wooden swords, learning to jab and cut.

The wood and stone building had a gate of stout planks, guarded by hired toughs to keep the curious outside. They also guarded against those who might creep in to nobble a favorite by slipping them a draught that would make them sleepy or weak, or even kill them entirely.

The gate guards were young, burly, and fit, and while they might lean idly against the gate as though bored, they were diligent and came alert in a heartbeat.

The man on duty this afternoon was called Septimius, and he hailed me with enthusiasm. "Welcome home, Leonidas. Come to fulfill Aemil's dreams?"

He asked me this every time I arrived, and I'd ceased bothering to answer. "I'm here to see you, actually."

"I am flattered." Septimius was a thick-bodied brute of a man, with wiry brown hair that curled down his neck, dark eyes, and ham fists. He'd quietly let me slip back into the ludus long after my curfew many a time. "Missed me, did you?"

"I have, yes," I said without feigning. Septimius was good-natured and friendly without being oily, though I'd watched him beat a man to a pulp when the man tried repeatedly to climb the wall to seek out his favorite gladiator. "I want to ask you about Ajax, Herakles, and Rufus. You'd have been the last to see them go."

"Ah." Septimius leaned against the gatepost and picked at a tooth with his thumbnail. "Aemil has you chasing them, does he? I don't know where they are."

"You'd have let them out. Or maybe Plinius did."

"Naw, it was me." Septimius gazed down the street that teemed with slaves running errands for masters, men heading for the nearest popina for wine and games, and plebeian women shopping for wares. On the far corner, a thin, harried teacher tried to keep the attention of six children gathered around him who traced letters carved into boards with sticks.

"When did they go?" Aemil had told me, but I wanted to hear Septimius's version.

"Five—no, four days ago. Last day of Januarius, at various times. I remember because Plinius was ill, and I took his shift. They all had passes, and I let them out."

"But they never came back."

"They didn't." Septimius removed his thumb from his teeth and spat on the street. "If you ask me, Aemil is worried for nothing. They're most likely spending their prize money from the Saturnalian games. Rufus has been trying to persuade his wife into a better apartment, so he's probably moving her into a lower floor of their insula. I'd guess that Ajax and Herakles are sleeping off nights of debauchery. Ajax will poke anything that moves. Maybe he got punched for it."

I had to agree with Septimius. The most likely explanation was that each of the men had been caught up in ordinary circumstances—renting a new apartment or recovering from the aftermath of drink and whoring.

"Did any of them tell you where they planned to go? Besides Rufus, of course."

"No *of course* about that." Septimius grinned. "Rufus isn't exactly the model of fidelity. But as it happens, he did say he was going home to Chryseis—that's his wife. Ajax headed for the Subura. Herakles wouldn't tell me, but I think he has a highborn lover with a villa on the river."

The gate suddenly was wrenched inward by a massive hand that belonged to a huge gladiator with close-cropped dark hair and hard brown eyes. His name was Regulus, and at one time I'd called him friend. He was now *primus palus* of Aemil's gladiators, a position he'd inherited from me.

"Are you talking about those idiots who've disappeared?" he demanded.

Septimius took a step back. Regulus made him nervous, as Regulus would beat on anyone when in a pique. Gate guards were fair game to him, and as long as Regulus left them fit for duty, Aemil wouldn't stop him.

"Do you know where they are?" I asked Regulus.

Not long ago, Regulus and I had been inseparable, drinking together, visiting lupinari together, sparring for the joy of it. That had ended the day he'd begged me to kill him, and I'd refused.

"I know where they're likely to be," Regulus said in his usual snarl. "Dead, aren't they? Dead and gone to the Elysium Fields, like the selfish bastards they are."

CHAPTER 2

Regulus scowled at me as I regarded him in surprise. Even Septimius shuffled back a step.

"Why do you believe they are dead?" I asked in a calm tone.

Regulus hesitated, as though he'd expected his belligerence to be accepted without question. Months ago, I might have laughed at him, or retorted with a, *Why? Did you kill them?* accompanied by taking him for a drink.

"Herakles wants to die in glory," Regulus said. "He'd do something stupid like jump from the top of the Capitoline Hill and pretend he's flying. Ajax fights anyone he sees. Rufus will be coshed by his wife when she finds out about his mistresses."

"I'll wager she knows about them already," Septimius offered good-naturedly. "And Ajax usually wins his fights."

"Ajax is a sodding ass." I could see by Regulus's red-rimmed eyes and swaying stance that he was half drunk. "If he faces *me* in the next games, he'll be dead."

Ajax was third in the ludus, always with an eye to becoming *primus palus*. Rufus was *secundus* now that Regulus had moved up into the slot I'd vacated. It was Aemil's decision who his top fighters were, but there was always rivalry within the ranks.

Herakles, who was equivalent in talent with Ajax, had never

completely adapted to being a gladiator. He had the pride of the savage peoples who made life for soldiers on the Roman frontier exciting, and he'd never lost his air of scorn. Romans to him meant conquerors. Herakles sometimes talked about working to buy his freedom, but more often declared he'd die in the arena, taking several Roman dogs with him.

Many of Aemil's gladiators were, like Herakles, captives from outposts, but Herakles sneered at any who'd embraced the Roman way of life. He'd hated me, Roman born, on sight.

"Good riddance to them," Regulus went on.

If the three ran away or caused trouble, Aemil also would have to answer for it, either with a large fine for not keeping his slaves contained, or with imprisonment, or his life, depending on what the gladiators did and to what Roman.

"Did Ajax have a favorite woman to visit?" I directed my question to both Septimius and Regulus, ignoring Regulus's bluster.

"True—he could be smothered in some woman's bosom." Regulus waved an arm, bracing himself on the wall when he lost his balance. "Look for him in the Subura."

So Septimius had said. I turned to Septimius, noting he remained out of arm's reach of Regulus. "Who is Herakles's lady in the villa?"

"Don't know." Septimius's reply was quick, but I could not decide if he lied. "Nonus Marcianus does, I think."

Nonus Marcianus was the *medicus* who doctored the gladiators when we were cut up in the arena. Marcianus sewed wounds, set bones, and gave us concoctions that brought us back to life.

Marcianus was in the Equestrian class, maintaining a practice on the Aventine among the plebeians even while working for Aemil. He'd told me he liked healing those who had no expensive private physician at their beck and call, as well as learning all he could about anatomy and medicine by treating gladiators. He was an unassuming man, but very few disputed Marcianus.

"Is he here?" I glanced through the gate to the sunshine

glaring on the practice space. The air was cool but the sun warm on my shoulders.

"I don't know," Regulus snapped. "I'm not your errand boy." He pushed past me with a growl at Septimius. "Tell Aemil I'm off to find dinner."

Septimius glowered at his back. Aemil must have given Regulus leave to depart because Septimius said not a word as Regulus stalked away along the street.

A boy who'd escaped the tutor teaching letters darted to Regulus, wide-eyed at seeing a true gladiator. Regulus scowled at him but stopped to scratch his name on the piece of brick the boy held up. Regulus had no use for fawners, but he knew how to keep the public of Rome cheering for him.

"The *medicus* came in maybe an hour ago," Septimius told me once Regulus had gone, the boy scampering back to the annoyed tutor. "One of the tiros was hurt."

While Aemil hadn't had gladiators in games since Saturnalia, he didn't hold back on training, which could become as brutal as actual bouts.

I gave Septimius a nod and moved through the gate into the ludus.

As usual when I entered the place, a feeling came over me that I'd never left. The practice yard was full, mostly with the younger, rawer gladiators battling away at the posts. Two more experienced gladiators were practicing throwing the weighted nets.

My feet wanted to take me to the rack where the wooden swords waited, my hand remembering the weight and heft of them. I'd pick out a newer gladiator and force him to face me, teaching him how to survive by coming at him without mercy.

Afterward, I might take the limping, bleeding lad to the nearest popina and relieve his pain with drink, but I wouldn't go soft on him in the training yard. They either learned to fight back and hard, or they'd die on the day of the real games.

I made myself not assess the net throwers on their skill or

the swordsmen on their thrusts. I had been a secutor, fighting with a short sword, my left arm swathed in padded armor, but Aemil liked to train everyone in multiple areas in case a fighter was needed to replace a fallen one, so I'd had some experience as a retiarius.

I strode into the dim interior of the building that held the gladiators' cells. Most cells were empty, the men in the practice yard or lounging in the sun watching the training.

I paused in front of a grated door that was closed and pushed it open.

This had been my cell. I'd lived here the last two years I'd been with Aemil, and I knew every cranny of it. Regulus had taken over once I'd gone, and his spare tunics hung on pegs driven into the stone wall.

I glanced at the ceiling. My best friend, Xerxes, had drawn erotic stick figures there as a joke one day, roaring with laughter when I'd laid down to sleep and the flame of my lamp had flickered over the drawings. I'd shouted, and Xerxes had nearly pissed himself with hilarity.

I saw that Regulus had scratched most of them out. Only one remained, a gladiator with a large phallus chasing a maiden in the far corner, the rock there too rough for the marks to be easily erased.

Anger burned in my stomach. I was slow to wrath, but any pity I'd had for Regulus vanished. He'd erased what Xerxes had made, destroying a part of the man I'd loved like a brother.

I shouldn't have looked. I slammed the door and strode on in rage.

"Leonidas?" Marcianus called out to me as I passed the cell he used as his workshop.

I halted, remembering my errand. Inside, Marcianus wrapped the splinted arm of a broad-shouldered young man who had the blond hair and large frame of those from the far north.

"Praxus took a direct hit on his arm," Marcianus said cheerfully. "Broke it clean through."

Praxus, who had joined the ludus after I'd left, was large and very young, with the vast confidence of a youth who thought nothing could defeat him. He winced as Marcianus tightened the bandage but kept up his air of bravado.

"It's not bad." Praxus's accent was thick, his Latin barely intelligible.

"Train more with a shield or arm guard," I advised him. "A broken bone will get you ejected from the arena. You won't have a chance at prize money, and Aemil might make you haul water or slops until he thinks you've learned your lesson."

Praxus gazed at me in all seriousness. "Then I will practice, as you say."

"Not for some weeks," Marcianus continued in his sunny tones. "This bone has to set. No training for you for a while. Why are you here, Leonidas? Come to assist me?"

"To find the gladiators who've run off," I said, not responding to his jest. "Did they mention to you where they were going? Ajax and Herakles, I mean." I would simply look for Rufus at his home with his wife.

Marcianus lost his smile. "I imagine it's their business."

Marcianus did not approve of gladiators being penned in like animals. He enjoyed his job of patching them up, but he avowed that all gladiators should voluntarily join the life and be free to leave it when they wished. Many, like Rufus, did join as free men, hoping for fortune and fame, but most were bought at auction or given to the ludus in lieu of execution, as I had been.

"Better I find them than Aemil," I told him. "Or the urban cohorts."

"They haven't been gone all that long, and there are no games scheduled," Marcianus pointed out.

"If they're simply dicing or drinking, then Aemil can decide what to do." I paused. "He seems worried."

Marcianus snorted. "If you are painting Aemil as a concerned mother hen, don't. And leave the men be."

As I cast around for a way to pry the information from Marcianus, Praxus broke in.

"Look for Herakles at a villa north of the Pons Agrippae," Praxus said. "He told me of a great house there with a wine cellar the size of a theatre."

Both Marcianus and I turned to Praxus in surprise. The lad must be all of sixteen, tall and bulky, but with the lankiness of one who'd just grown into his body.

"How do you know that?" Marcianus demanded. He finished tying off the bandage, his movements gentle, though I could see he wasn't pleased with Praxus for giving me the information.

"Herakles told me. He doesn't talk to many, but he does to me. Probably because I'm not a Roman."

Most gladiators were from outside Rome, but Herakles must have taken to this young man from northern Germania, both of them coming from the very edges of the empire.

"Where exactly is this villa?" I asked him.

Praxus propped one foot on the bunk, leaning against the wall behind him. "Across the river from the *trigarium*. One of the big houses on the hill on the western bank."

The *trigarium* was a track for chariot races. It was nowhere near the size of the Circus Maximus but was a place for training and smaller races.

Marcianus's face pinched in disapproval, but he said nothing as he folded away the rest of the bandages and mixed a concoction for Praxus to drink. "This will help with the pain," Marcianus told him.

Praxus scoffed. "I am fine."

Marcianus held the cup under his nose. "Maybe you are now, but when the shock wears off and you want to sleep, this will help. More sleep will heal you faster."

Praxus shrugged but took the cup. I'd drunk Marcianus's potions before, and I was usually asleep within minutes.

Praxus downed the liquid in one gulp. "Tastes foul." He

managed to give the cup back to Marcianus before slumping onto the bunk.

I watched with detached interest as Praxus's big body deflated, and his eyes closed. In the next moment, a snore emitted from his open mouth.

Marcianus wiped out the cup and returned it to the shelf. "Hunt for Herakles and the others if you must, Leonidas. But say nothing to Aemil until you find out what they're up to. No need for him to flog them if they're only visiting their lovers."

"I would leave them to it." I hesitated, wondering why I needed to explain myself to Marcianus. "But I need the fee Aemil has said he'll pay."

"Your benefactor hasn't showered you with riches yet?" Marcianus's good humor began to return.

"Not yet. If he—or she—ever will." I had a few ideas about who my anonymous and rather stingy benefactor might be, but so far, I'd found out little. "I haven't had a job in a few weeks, and if Cassia says our funds are dwindling, I believe her."

Marcianus's face softened. "Cassia is a wise young woman. Give her my best, Leonidas."

Marcianus and Cassia had formed a friendship—both of them spoke fluent Greek and were well-read in the sciences and medicine. I imagined that Cassia found relief in speaking with Marcianus after days of living with an illiterate gladiator.

"I'll say nothing to Aemil until I know what's become of them," I promised. "If they simply show up for training tomorrow, he might go easier on them."

"Let us hope so. Good day to you, Leonidas."

I returned the goodbye and left Marcianus, who was always cordial. Behind me, Praxus snored on.

I walked along the colonnade, avoiding my old cell, and departed through the gate. Septimius bade me a good-natured farewell, his annoyance with Regulus gone.

The gate clanged behind me with finality. Inside was a life and routine I'd known for years. Outside was uncertainty, the scramble to make enough money to feed myself and Cassia. My new life, like the one I'd left, could end just as suddenly.

I was not certain which was better.

I DECIDED TO SEARCH FOR AJAX FIRST, TURNING MY STEPS toward the brothels of the Subura. I knew the Subura well, having spent plenty of time there at a lupinarius run by a woman called Floriana. That house was empty now, the women gone, but I knew of other places.

The Pons Agrippae was busy as I crossed it, people hurrying both away from Rome or into it, wanting to be indoors when darkness fell. In Februarius, the sun set near the twelfth hour, and by the looks of the sky, it was close to that.

I glanced upstream as I went. Villas lined the Tiber, with terraced gardens flowing down toward the river. Which had Herakles gone to?

The current of Romans took me with them to the Campus Martius. During daylight, I would have simply cut through the Campus to avoid the crowds in the forums, but at night, it was better to stay in more congested areas.

It was already twilight by the time I turned south past the Theatre of Pompey and the Campus Flaminius. I continued with the throng around the Capitoline Hill, the crowd thinning somewhat as I neared the Forum Romanum, as business there had concluded for the day.

Usually, I'd make my way northward from the Forum up the hill to the small lane where I lived. Cassia would be home, laying out things for our supper, making notes on her tablets, singing some ballad under her breath.

Our life had settled into a routine—Cassia fetched water and food for our meals, then spent time after breakfast going through our accounts and deciding how much I needed to charge on my next job. I'd go to the Forum and skulk about, looking for men who might need a guard. Sometimes I was successful, sometimes not. I'd then adjourn to the baths and to exercise to keep myself fit, as I had today, before returning to find Aemil at my table.

I wanted more than anything to go to the apartment now, to eat my lentil stew and greens and any sweet treat Cassia had found on her way home. I'd listen to her talk about who she'd spoken to that day and what was happening in Rome—Cassia always seemed to know.

My compulsion to tramp that way made my limbs ache as I turned away and continued along the base of the Quirinal to the Subura.

Most people feared walking here in the dark, but I'd done so many a night. I passed the building that used to contain Floriana's lupinarius. Most of the house had been pulled down, and the shops replacing it were still under construction.

Passing Floriana's made me think of my friend Gnaeus Gallus, an *architectus*. He'd once offered to take me on as his assistant, but I hadn't accepted. First, because I doubted he could pay more than the bodyguard work, and second, I wasn't certain about returning to the remnants of my old life—the one before the ludus. Walking onto a building site was bittersweet for me.

A painting of a nude woman pursued by a satyr adorned the wall of the next lupinarius along. Men gathered outside the door, clumping together nervously as they waited their turn.

"Leonidas! Who are you choosing tonight?" A burly man I'd seen many times at Floriana's hailed me in recognition.

I shrugged, which made him laugh, probably thinking I'd line up the ladies and pick who I wanted. I threaded my way through the men and ducked under the low lintel and inside.

"We're full." A woman in a garish red wig, curled like the best patrician matron's, skewered me with a glare. "Oh, it's Leonidas. I haven't seen you in these parts for months. Too good for us now, are you?"

She snapped her retort in all seriousness. I'd been a well-paying customer, though I'd preferred Floriana's.

"I'm looking for Ajax." I saw no reason to lead up to my question.

"Not here."

The woman turned away, finished with me. I caught her arm, which earned me a scowl and a hand raised to slap before I released her.

"It is important. Has he been here in the last four days?"

"Of course, he has. Couldn't be rid of him, but at least he paid. He left last night."

"Do you know where he went?"

"No." Her kohl-lined dark eyes narrowed in suspicion. "Why should I? Why are you asking?"

I decided not to explain. "If Ajax returns, tell him I'm looking for him and to come to me on the Quirinal."

"I'm no one's messenger."

The woman turned away again. I caught her once more, but this time, I held a sestertius in front of her pinched face.

"Tell him." I pressed the coin into her hand and let her go.

I would have asked which lady he'd spent the most time with, but the cubicles were all occupied, and from the ecstatic shouts and groans drifting from behind the curtains, busy.

I left the house, aiming for the next one.

"That was quick," the burly man called out with a laugh. "Well met, Leonidas." I answered him with a wave of my hand.

I had a similar result in the next lupinarius. Ajax had visited it two nights before, but no one had seen him since. Here, I was able to talk to the women who'd been with him. Ajax had been his usual robust self, the ladies told me, then declared he was going to another house when he departed, as he had plenty of energy still.

Probably he'd gone to the first house I'd checked. I thanked the women, distributing a few *as* to them and to the madam who ran the place, and left them.

I continued my walk. It was fully dark now, and I had no light to guide me, except the few feeble oil lamps that flickered here and there in doorways. Pinpricks of light guided higher-born men through the area, but most of the respectable were either at home or taking supper at the house of another well-born family. Those in the Subura either were here for the brothels or hurrying through on their way someplace else.

One such party, led by a wary guard with a lantern, came up behind me. Lictors carried bundles of short spears over their shoulders, hardening their faces to all. Two plump-bodied patricians, purple stripes on their togas, walked surrounded by their retinue, talking loudly as though not afraid of passing through these streets after dark.

I had to step into a side passageway to let them by. The lane was narrow and inky, and I pressed myself into a wall to wait.

My sandal landed on something that gave a faint metal clank. It could be anything—a discarded cup, a spent lantern, a stray bit of coin.

Unusual for the Subura. Anything metal, especially coin, was snatched up, hoarded, or sold at the nearest market.

As the lantern-bearer swept by, the beam of his flame glanced across what was at my feet.

I went very still. The lantern-bearer rushed on, the lictors and patricians leaving a breeze in their wake.

I'd seen, in that brief moment, the gleam of light on the bronze helmet of a gladiator, the grating on the eyeholes dark and silent. Next to it lay an arm gripping the small shield of a secutor. Behind that, I'd seen two legs encased in bronze shin guards decorated with the reliefs of a fighting man. None of these limbs were attached to the trunk which bore a loincloth and nothing else.

The lantern light vanished, and darkness fell like a shroud. A gladiator lay here with me, but one in many pieces.

CHAPTER 3

I barreled out of the lane, shoved my way into the nearest lupinarius, snatched up the first lamp I found, and was out again before any could ask me a question.

In spite of my agitation, no one followed me. They did not want to know what I was chasing in the darkness. In the Subura, it was not healthy to be too curious.

I flashed my light over the floor of the passageway—a small space between two buildings that narrowed into a wedge shape, ending at a building on the street behind it.

The gladiator who lay at my feet was Ajax. I recognized the large round scar on the inside of his right arm, put there by a retiarius' spear.

His body had been cut into precise pieces—arms, legs, head, torso. Those were not strewn haphazardly but had been laid neatly in the small space. His head, encased in its helmet, rested next to what had once been a man's body.

I stood transfixed, staring down at what remained of Ajax.

In my career, I'd witnessed gruesome deaths. Part of the games involved executions, where criminals were sent off in creative ways. Professional gladiators could be hacked to pieces in their fights, and animal hunters mauled by the wild beasts they stalked. Bodies and parts of bodies were dragged from the arena all day long, blood drying on the sand.

There was not much blood here, and the pieces had been laid tidily like bones in a charnel house.

I should have been accustomed to the many ways a person could become a body. But for some reason, the food I'd had for lunch roiled in my stomach. I turned away and retched it onto the stones.

I REMAINED IN THE LANE A LONG TIME, MY ARM HEAVILY ON the wall, until the oil lamp flickered out, its fuel spent.

Ajax was dead. Not only dead but carefully dismembered. Someone had then brought him to this place and laid him out. No blood coated the stones, which told me he'd not been killed or cut up here.

Why? And why bring him *here*? If a person wanted to cover up a crime, they'd throw the body into the river or cart him a long way into the countryside and bury him. Not leave him neatly in the Subura for an unlucky person to stumble over him.

I stood up, an ache pounding behind my eyes. No one passing glanced into the alley, none wondered why I waited here. Safer to keep one's gaze forward and notice nothing.

What to do? If I called out, drew attention, someone would run for the vigiles. I knew one of the vigiles for this district, a lad called Avitus. He might aid me.

No, he would have to report this to his watch captain. I'd be questioned. Aemil would be as well. Perhaps all the gladiators, including the new man, Praxus, would be suspects—the magistrates might claim the men wanted to eliminate an opponent they'd never beat. Or Aemil might be forced to close the ludus, the gladiators dispersed to other schools. One or more could be executed, the magistrates needing someone to pay for the crime.

Gladiators might be famous and lauded, but their lives were forfeit in the end.

Trash lay in the lane, discarded and broken pottery vessels and a cloth so dirty and tattered even the rag men didn't want it.

I snatched up the cloth and draped it the best I could over Ajax's body. I moved shards of pottery with my foot, building up a pile that would hide him from the street.

Only when I was satisfied that nothing could be seen in the darkness did I quit the lane. I strode back into the lupinarius to return the lamp and then I set off for the ludus.

My journey this time was quicker, as the streets were more deserted. Most people were indoors for safety, though the wine bars and dining shops overflowed. The delivery wagons hadn't yet descended on the city for the night, but they would soon.

Septimius was still at his post. "Back already, Leonidas?" he began, but he trailed off when he noted my grim expression.

"I need to see Aemil. Let me in."

Septimius did so without argument, peering at me in curiosity.

Aemil was taking his evening meal in his office with Marcianus. He'd shoved aside ledgers and tablets to make space for the bowls of greens, savory meat, beans, and apricots.

"I found Ajax," I said without preliminary. "He's in the Subura."

Marcianus froze in the act of lifting an apricot to his mouth, honey dripping across his fingers. Aemil scowled.

"Is he? In what brothel? I'll drag him out—*after* I've finished my supper."

"He's dead," I said. "I found his body." I turned and started out of the room. "You'll need a cart."

Aemil spewed colorful language both in street Latin and whatever Gallic dialect he used as he stooped over Ajax's body, the light from Marcianus's lamp flickering across the scene.

I'd pulled the cloth from Ajax and then positioned myself at the end of the lane to hide what we did from the main street. Again, any passers-by simply scuttled on, not wanting to know.

"You are right that he was killed elsewhere," Marcianus said softly. "No blood at all. He was washed as well. I'd say the greaves and helmet were put on after death, but I'd have to examine him to be certain."

Aemil continued his cursing, lending nothing to the discussion.

Marcianus spoke in clear, calm tones, as he always did, even when dealing with the most serious wounds or while easing the pain of gladiators as they died. His face, however, held shock, which mine must have done when I'd burst in on his meal.

Aemil at last rose, a grimness in his eyes I'd never seen before. Aemil was a hard man, but I realized he tempered a ruthlessness he chose not to unleash.

"We take him back." Aemil, the same height as I was, glared straight into my eyes. "Discover who did this, Leonidas, and bring him to me."

I hesitated. I had no business hunting murderers, especially one as mad as whoever had done this to Ajax, but I nodded. I did not like that a killer wandered Rome who could bring down a fighter as skilled as Ajax.

"And find the rest of my be-damned gladiators," Aemil snarled.

He marched past us to the street, leaving Marcianus and me to place Ajax's body into the cart, covering him again with the tattered cloth plus another Marcianus had brought.

"He's been dead at least a day," Marcianus said to me. "By the feel of his limbs. Again, I can be more certain when I look at him."

"He was at a lupinarius down the street last night, so the woman who runs it said."

"Well, that narrows things down." Marcianus turned to Aemil, who waited at the mouth of the passageway. "Are you sure you want him at the ludus, Aemil?"

Aemil's scowl grew harsher. "Where else would we take him?"

"My office? I have more instruments there and can examine him more thoroughly."

"What good will that do?" Aemil snapped.

Marcianus met his belligerence with his usual clear-headedness. "I might ascertain how he was killed and what was used to cut him apart. Whether he was in this garb when he died, or someone dressed his corpse. All useful information."

Aemil only growled and spun away.

"Marcia still lives with you," I said in a low voice. Marcia was a young woman Marcianus had taken in out of pity, and who had since become his assistant. "She shouldn't see this."

"Marcia is resilient and is a very efficient helper," Marcianus said, unbothered. "She can also be discreet."

Meaning she wouldn't scream and run for a cohort when she beheld a dismembered corpse.

Marcianus went on. "My house is also closer, and we won't have to cross the river or go through a gate." Guards could stop us at either place and inquire about our business, or worse, look under the cloth.

Aemil grunted. "Fine. We'll go."

He conceded to heft one side of the hand cart while I took the other. We followed Marcianus as he stepped lightly down the street in the direction of the Aventine.

We reached Marcianus's small house where he ran his practice without mishap. Once we'd carried the wrapped parts of

Ajax's body to his back room, Marcianus instructed me and Aemil to go away.

"Nothing more you can do," he said briskly. "I will let you know how I get on."

Aemil gave another of his grunts and walked out.

Marcia, as Marcianus had predicted, while she blenched when she saw what was under the tarp, proceeded to lay out Marcianus's tools on a side table and fill a basin with water from a jar without a word. In her plain ankle-length tunic, her hair scraped into a bun, she looked like a young housemaid rather than the brothel girl she'd been.

I could think of nothing to say to either her or Marcianus, so I left them and strode after Aemil.

"You ruined my supper." Aemil barely slowed his steps as I caught up to him, then he suddenly halted. Beside us, a fountain with three bronze fish spewed water into a bowl in a quiet trickle. "Hercules defend us, Leonidas. Who would do such a thing?"

I studied the corroded green bronze of one fish's mouth. "Someone who hates gladiators?"

"Well, I hate magistrates." Aemil glanced behind him through the darkness to the light in Marcianus's window. "But I wouldn't murder one, chop him up, and dress him in a toga."

"Someone who hated Ajax in particular," I suggested, for something to say.

"Well, find him. Use that slave of yours who writes everything down. And find Rufus and Herakles. And Regulus. He's now beetled off too."

"I watched him leave. He said he had permission."

"Well, he's a liar." Aemil let out a sigh. "True, I give Regulus a loose rein when there are no games on. He usually just goes to a popina near the ludus, but he hadn't returned by the time Septimius locked the gates."

"I'll search for him," I promised.

"I know you two have become sworn enemies." Aemil's lip

curled. "But bring him back without bruising him too much. He's valuable, my biggest draw now, may the gods help me."

Aemil looked me up and down as though he wanted to blame me for Regulus's bad temper, but then he shook his head.

"Good night, Leonidas." Aemil strode off into the darkness, his boots crunching over loose pebbles on the street.

I watched him until his tunic faded into a pale smudge, then I turned my steps toward the forums and the road to the apartment I now called home.

CASSIA HAD SET OUT STEW AND BREAD BY THE TIME I REACHED the room above the wine shop. A cool breeze flowed in from the balcony, but the shutters had not been closed, as they were too heavy for Cassia to lift.

Cassia sat at the table, bent over her tablets, waiting for me before she ate. Her hair was neat and in place, curls tamed on her forehead, her pale linen tunic without stain. She glanced up as I entered, after making a careful note of the time of my return.

I halted in the doorway and gazed without interest at the food.

"Did you find out anything useful?" The avidness in Cassia's voice at any other time would have amused me. Her stylus hovered, she ready to transcribe anything I had to say.

"I found Ajax." My voice was heavy, falling numbly into the room. A mule and cart clattered to a halt in the street below, the drover calling out to the wine merchant.

"So soon?" Cassia rose, her eagerness fading as she beheld my expression. "What happened?"

I told her. All of it, sparing no detail. The color drained from her cheeks as I spoke, and she slowly resumed her seat.

Murder was not unusual in Rome. The dark streets could teem with brigands who would knife a man for a few sestertii—robberies that turned violent accounted for many deaths. Likewise, quarreling men in the popinae could strike each other down in drunken rages.

This had been very different. A deliberate killing, almost like a sacrifice.

When my words trailed off, Cassia quickly poured wine from a jug into a cup and pushed it at me.

I dropped onto my stool across the table from her and drained the cup in one go. I barely tasted the wine, which then lay in a heavy pool in my stomach.

"Horrible." Cassia's voice was barely a whisper.

I seized the jug and poured myself more wine. "Ajax deserved better. It was as if he was being mocked."

"Tell me about him." Cassia quietly lifted her stylus. "I mean, was Ajax a proficient gladiator? Would someone have been able to kill him easily?"

"No, they would not." I sipped the wine this time instead of gulping it and carefully set down the cup. "He was one of Aemil's best. In order, after Regulus, it's Rufus, Ajax, and then Herakles. Ajax has only lost a few bouts, and even then he wasn't badly injured. A skilled fighter."

"Who would be able to kill a skilled fighter?"

"Another skilled fighter." My mouth flattened to a hard line. "A gladiator, or a soldier, one very good at hand-to-hand combat."

"Like one of the Praetorian Guard?"

"Yes." I didn't like the direction of her thoughts. "Are you saying he was invited to fight, as in an exhibition? Paired with an experienced Praetorian to see what would happen? Up on the Palatine?"

The *princeps* of Rome, Nero, adopted son of Claudius, might think such a battle was a grand diversion. He would not stop the exhibition from ending in death if he did not choose to.

"Possibly." Cassia regained some of her composure. "Though the *princeps* likely would have sent Ajax's body back to the ludus, perhaps with a note or a gift to make up for killing one of

Aemil's best fighters. Even if Nero didn't think of that, his majordomo would. I was speculating that it was a private matter gone wrong. But Marcianus believes the fighting gear was put on him after he died?"

I recalled Marcianus muttering something about that. "He thought so. He will be sure once he looks Ajax over."

"The poor man." Cassia did not specify whether she meant Ajax or Marcianus. "Ajax must have been taken unawares. Or plied with drink beforehand."

I'd lifted my cup for another gulp but set it down abruptly. "Why would someone get Ajax drunk, or slip him herbs to make him sleep, and then kill him? And then ..." I waved my hand so I wouldn't have to describe it again.

"Yes, it is very odd." Cassia began marking her tablet, the stylus making little noise on the soft wax.

"What are you writing?" I asked in mild irritation.

"A list of possibilities. None are more probable than the others at this point." Cassia raised her head, the end of her stylus at her lower lip. "Did you find any hint of where the other two gladiators are? Herakles and Rufus?"

"And now Regulus. Aemil thinks he has gone missing too, though I doubt it. Regulus will keep himself away to be annoying. I haven't had time to look for the others. Herakles has a highborn lover on the west bank of the Tiber, and Rufus has a wife and apparently mistresses. They should be safe enough with them." So I hoped. "Ajax had been visiting various lupinari for days. He might have met someone there who lured him out to kill him."

"Or he might have been killed *in* one of the lupinari."

I thought back on my encounter with the ladies inside the two I'd visited and shook my head. "The women would have been far more nervous about my questions. They were annoyed at my interruption but not worried over where Ajax had gone."

Cassia returned to her notations. "Then we will assume he

met someone either in one of the houses or as he departed the last one. Someone who took him elsewhere."

"Invited him elsewhere," I suggested. "And he went willingly. If he'd resisted, there would have been a fight, and people would have remembered."

"A good observation." Cassia wrote this down, approval in her tone.

"Aemil has instructed me to find his killer. He doesn't want the cohorts involved."

"No? What will he do with the culprit when we find him?"

I noticed she said *when*, not *if*. I also noted the *we*. "I don't know. Give him to the magistrates himself, maybe."

"That would rather depend on who this murderer turns out to be."

True. If the killer was a bandit or brigand, Aemil would simply execute the man himself and toss the body in the river. Magistrates would frown on Aemil taking matters into his own hands but not care too much. No one had much sympathy for bandits, who preyed on any they could.

But if this murderous madman was a highborn person, or even of the Equestrian class, the situation would be very different. A patrician or Equestrian would have family, money, and advocates on their side.

But why would a patrician or Equestrian murder a gladiator and leave him in pieces in a back lane in the Subura? Carefully redressed in his gladiator gear?

"It makes no sense," I said, coming out of my thoughts.

"I agree with you." Cassia's nod was decided.

"Gladiators always fight as warriors," I mused, half to myself. "Legendary ones. Thracian, myrmillo, provacatur. The retiarius is a fisherman, or sometimes Poseidon, who hunts the secutor. During the Republic, gladiators were dressed as people the Roman army had conquered—the Thracians are from that time. So Marcianus has told me." I ran my fingers across the scarred tabletop. "We are real fighters, but everything about the battles is staged. The costumes, our names, our combat style. We fight in an arena, before an audience, not on a battlefield." I paused again, trying to decide what I wanted to say. "Ajax's body was like that. Staged. Unreal."

"But all too real at the same time," Cassia said softly.

She understood, to my relief.

The speech had made me thirsty, and I drank my wine. Swallowing two cups in quick succession added to my drowsiness—my refuge from too much shock was sleep.

I was also hungry. As shaken as I was about the death, my body, used to taking strain after strain and then getting on with things, nudged me to eat.

I scraped my bowl to me and downed the stew. I barely tasted it, but I'd emptied my stomach in the alley, and needed to fill it up again.

"We had better find the other gladiators to make certain they are well." Cassia observed my slumped shoulders and softened her tone. "Tomorrow, I mean. Do you know where this highborn woman Herakles meets lives?"

I thought back to what Praxus had said. "North of the Pons Agrippae on the west bank. Near a large winery."

"Oh." Cassia's eyes widened. "The Villa Flores."

I set down my spoon. "You know it?"

"I do." Her gaze turned nostalgic. "My mistress and her husband visited it often when she traveled to Rome. My father and I accompanied them from time to time. I know the villa well and the people in it." A remote smile tugged at her mouth. "I believe I will have no trouble gaining entrance and discovering what has become of Herakles."

CHAPTER 4

Cassia made this announcement as though gaining entry to the villa of a wealthy woman would be no trouble at all.

"How?" I demanded.

Cassia eyed me without distress. "I will tell you all in the morning. You have had a shock, Leonidas, and you should sleep. I cannot go on the moment, so the discussion will keep."

I stared at her in frustration, though I knew she was right. I was bone-weary, my eyes sandy, the tiredness that accompanied any agitation coming over me. Cassia went back to marking in her tablets, humming a little tune in her throat.

I heaved myself to my feet, set the shutters' boards into their slots in the floor, and went to bed. I'd pry from her what she meant when I woke again.

Cassia was no stranger to villas, I reflected as I shucked my sandals and settled into my bunk. She'd been raised on a large estate in Campania, away from the harsher world of Roman streets. Her father had been the family's scribe and accountant, and though a slave, would have lived in better circumstances than most. The man had obviously been able to have a family, though Cassia had never spoken of her mother.

I drifted off to Cassia's light voice as she sang something in

Greek. I dreamed of her walking in her careful way through the ambulatory of such a villa, high on a hill, with the bay of Napoli spread before her in its blue glory. In this dream, she owned the house and dressed in a matron's silks with the gold earrings a grateful patrician had given her earlier this year glittering against her hair. A gladiator who looked like me tried to gain entrance to this house and was repulsed by a sneering majordomo, while Cassia looked on serenely.

When I jerked from sleep, morning had dawned, sunlight pouring through the tiny window above me. Marcianus was helping Cassia open one of the board shutters to the balcony.

I peeled myself from the bed, scrubbing at my face. Marcianus leaned the unwieldy shutter against the wall with some difficulty.

I'd slept in my tunic, which I straightened as I padded toward Marcianus in my bare feet.

"What did you find out?" I asked him.

"A joyous good morning to you too, Leonidas," Marcianus said without rancor. "May your ancestors bless this house."

I grunted but gave him an apologetic nod. "Didn't sleep well."

"I understand. Ajax was quite a shock."

Cassia quickly poured Marcianus watered-down wine and waved him to the stool reserved for guests. A new spray of flowers reposed on the shrine to our ancestors, the water jug was damp with a fresh draw, and sunlight gleamed on the bronze sculpture of a hand studded with blue stones, a gift from the same patrician who'd supplied Cassia's earrings.

"I know you want to learn what I found," Marcianus said in his unruffled manner as he took a sip of wine. "I was correct that Ajax had been dressed in his costume after death. The way the straps left marks—or did not—on his skin, and so forth, tells me this."

He paused to drink before he went on. "It appears that he was felled with a blow to the head, There is a large gash in his skull, the bones beneath broken. He might have obtained the wound falling against something hard, including a stone floor, but I do not believe so. It is not a sword wound but made by something long and narrow. His stomach held the remains of a meal, a rather rich one. Meat and apricots, dates, a few other things I could not identify, and interestingly, flecks of gold."

Cassia flinched but she dutifully wrote down his words. I, the hardened gladiator, took a quick gulp of wine as I tried not to picture Marcianus rooting around in a man's stomach, picking over its contents.

I swallowed and eased out a breath. "Someone fed him a good meal and then hit him when he turned to leave it?"

"That is entirely possible." Marcianus nodded.

"Flecks of gold?" I asked.

Cassia answered, "Gold leaf. Cakes or fruit can be gilded as decoration. So a hostess can serve her guests golden food."

"Gold is poisonous," Marcianus said cheerfully. "Though the tiny dose of gilt in one meal won't cause too much harm. In any case, there wouldn't have been enough time for him to die of that. He was killed before he even was able to digest it."

"He dined with a wealthy woman then," I said. "Or man. After he left the last lupinarius in the Subura?"

"A lavish supper, or a breakfast." Marcianus opened his hands. "He hadn't lain in that alley long—he was still quite clean, and the lane was a mess—but I'd say he met his end night before last or as late as yesterday morning. Poor fellow." Marcianus let out a breath. "Ajax was not the most congenial of men, but he did not deserve this."

Ajax had been arrogant, as most champion gladiators were, every bout survived serving to pump more confidence into him. He'd also, like Herakles, held himself above Romans, saying his tribe, called the Quadi, was far more savage than any of us could hope to be. Ajax had loved flattery and basked in his fame.

"I can imagine he'd have easily accepted an invitation to dine," I said. "Ajax liked being celebrated."

"And suspected nothing," Marcianus went on. "As I say, he likely rose from his meal and was hit right away. There is nothing to indicate he fought or struggled."

A deliberate murder then. Not a bout gone wrong, not Ajax attacking someone in a pique and being hit too hard in return.

"Not an accident," I stated.

Marcianus shook his head. "It is a slight possibility that he wasn't meant to be killed. Slight. Someone could have hit him with a length of piping as a joke and exerted too much strength. Or was furious with him and simply wanted to hurt him."

Cassia glanced up, her stylus poised. "If we discover where he had the meal, we will likely find who killed him."

"Very likely." Marcianus poured more wine for himself before Cassia could reach for the jug. "He might have been struck down in the street when he emerged from whatever house he was in, but it's more probable he met his end inside it. His body was clean—a domus or villa would have the space or outbuildings in which to wash him."

A chill crept down my spine. "What you mean is someone invited Ajax to dine—or to spend the night with them if the meal you found was breakfast. They fed him well, then as he turned to leave the table or the triclinium, hit him hard enough to kill him. Then they removed whatever clothing he wore, cut up his body, dressed him in gladiator gear, and carted the pieces back to the Subura, where they lined him up as though placing bones in a tomb."

I finished, my mouth dry. Cassia and Marcianus had stilled as I'd spoken, the appalling crime becoming more real with my words.

"Who would do such a thing?" Cassia asked in a quiet voice. "And why?"

Marcianus pushed away his cup. "This is why I prefer being a *medicus*. I see the body and what happened to it. I don't worry myself about what morals a man would lack to be this strangely cruel."

That ability to separate his job from the reality of life was how he managed to work for the ludus, I realized. Marcianus focused on sewing up our wounds, mopping away the blood, and setting broken bones, not on the terrible theatrics of the games.

Cassia's stylus made a soft click as she set it down. "The question is—did this killer have such anger at Ajax that they would mock him in death? Or is their focus on gladiators in general?"

I should have felt great fear or dread as Cassia's question sank in. Someone in the city of Rome could be hunting gladiators, using this odd method of murder. They might not distinguish between current gladiators and former ones.

But just as stepping into the arena had a numbing effect on me, as I fixed on survival alone, I felt strangely empty as I returned Cassia's and Marcianus's stares.

"I will hunt down Rufus and Herakles," I said. "And Regulus." Regulus, with his great pride, might readily fall into a trap of a banquet put on for him. Though I wondered if Regulus would be foolish enough to turn his back on another. He was pompous but careful.

"You should," Marcianus agreed, his briskness returning. "I will report to Aemil and cart Ajax's body to the ludus for a burial."

The organization of gladiators—our *collegia*—would see that there was a marker for Ajax. We paid into a fund, which footed the cost of burials and small pensions to surviving wives and children. Xerxes' widow had received a few sestertii from the cache when he'd been killed. Ajax would be buried outside the city walls in the space Aemil had purchased for members of the ludus.

"I will inquire at the Villa Flores about Herakles," Cassia said, as though this were a reasonable suggestion. "Leonidas will find Rufus's wife and make sure Rufus is safe with her."

I rose. "No."

Cassia sent me a perplexed frown. "I know the people at that villa, as I told you last night. I will be able to find out more on my own."

"At a villa where a gladiator could have been given his last meal?" I rested a balled hand on the table. "No."

"I have to agree with Leonidas," Marcianus said. "It will be dangerous for you, in any case. You might not be admitted, or even ejected bodily if your questions infuriate the mistress or master. If Herakles is the lover of the lady of the house, or Ajax was, she will never impart such information to you."

Marcianus said the words I wanted to but could not form.

Cassia regarded us with a patience I'd come to know meant she comprehended far more than anyone else in the room.

"I do not intend to question the lady of the house at all," she said. "She'd never answer a slave, and as Nonus Marcianus has stated, would have me turned out of the villa. But I know her servants, some of them quite well. I will not speak to the lady—she will never know I was there."

Very likely the lady would not. As a gladiator, whenever I was invited to a patrician's domus I was admitted to the public rooms, expected to show off my skill, discuss bouts, or take one of the highborn women to bed. I'd never skulk about the kitchen or back rooms of the house with the servants.

Though a scribe ranked far above a gladiator in the hierarchy, Cassia would be expected to remain in the background with the other household staff, unless requested specifically. I had fame without status, and she had status without fame.

"It is still dangerous," I rumbled. "Slaves must tell their master and mistress anything they command, such as why a scribe who worked for their friends in Campania came to interrogate their servants."

"The master of the Villa Flores died a few years ago." Cassia lifted her stylus, one thin lock of hair falling from her knot. "The mistress, Domitiana Sabinus, still lives in the house, though her son in Hispania technically owns it. She has been taking lovers from the ranks of actors, charioteers, and gladiators. So say her servants. They are rather ashamed of her behavior, and I am confident they will say nothing to her about me. She has lost their respect."

Cassia's firm lips told me this was the worst thing a lady of a household could do.

"Ah." Marcianus relaxed. "If you have friends to speak to, things might be well." He turned to me. "She will go only to ascertain whether Herakles is there or has been there, and where he is now." As I started to speak, Marcianus held up a slim hand. "I will accompany her."

"There is no need," Cassia said quickly. "I can be unobserved on my own."

"Nonsense. A physician is always welcome in a patrician's household. I can say I heard someone was ill or hurt, but perhaps I was sent to the wrong home. The lady will then talk about her own aches and pains or faulty digestion without compunction."

Marcianus chuckled, as though we'd find this amusing. Cassia smiled politely but I could see she was annoyed with his insistence.

"He will go with you," I declared. "Or I will."

Cassia opened her mouth to argue, but she took in the hard set to my jaw and subsided. "Very well. I agree that Nonus Marcianus will be more inconspicuous."

"I excel at being inconspicuous." Marcianus leaped to his feet. "We should go at once. Ajax might have been targeted specifically, but if gladiators are the true quarry, then they must all be accounted for."

"There are other ludi in Rome are there not?" Cassia asked, her worry returning. "Perhaps a warning should be sent to them."

"Aemil will do so," Marcianus said. "And if he does not, I will. Rufus's wife lives in an insula on the Aventine, Leonidas. Go toward the river on the street that runs in front of my house—the insula is beyond where an arch of the Aqua Appia intersects the road. I've walked home with Rufus a few times and said good night to him on his doorstep."

I wanted to reason that Marcianus would be better to visit Rufus if the two had walked from the ludus together, and I should stay with Cassia.

But she was right that a hulking gladiator would be obvious at the villa, while she would be able to slip into the servants' area and out again with the family being none the wiser. Marcianus, while a quiet and modest man, had a firmness about him that few argued with.

"There and straight back," I told the two of them. "We will meet again at Marcianus's and I will help deliver Ajax to Aemil."

"Excellent." Marcianus drained his wine and thumped the cup to the table. "Shall we, my dear? I obtained some new mathematical treatises from Athens that might interest you. I dabble in geometry, but some of it has quite fascinating applications to medicine. We can discuss them on the way if you like."

Cassia brightened. She loved to read, and it would be a treat for her to converse about civilized matters with a learned man. If Cassia had been male, she'd have been a sought-after scribe and tutor by now, who'd have curated a library of scrolls for some fortunate patrician. She'd have been much happier. I saw that in her face as she regarded Marcianus.

The three of us left the apartment together, trudging down the stairs to the street. The wine shop was doing brisk business, the wine merchant lifting an amphora into a hand cart for a burly slave who would trundle it to his master.

The wine merchant, a slightly built, bald man with thick dark eyebrows, nodded to me as I passed. He seldom spoke to us but quietly accepted our presence and our rent.

I parted ways with Cassia and Marcianus at the crossroads shrine where the Alta Semita and Vicus Salutis met, I to make my way to the Aventine, and they to travel across the Campus Martius to the far side of the river.

I decided, but did not tell them, that I would hasten through my visit to Rufus's wife and venture to the villa to keep my eye on them. I could stay out of sight but be on hand to rescue them if needed.

Marcianus bade me a breezy farewell. Cassia sent me a suspicious glance when I waved them off without argument, then hurried after Marcianus, already asking him about the treatises he'd read.

At the bottom of the hill I turned to walk behind the Forum Augusti, its great wall shielding the colonnaded building from the shabby street. An archway led to the forum for those who wished to enter it, but I wanted to avoid the crowds that would be there as well as in the Forum Romanum.

I strode through the Carinae and the low valley in the shadow of the Palatine, glancing at the hill and its several domii on top as I went.

I had not heard from the *princeps* since my last adventure in his opulent home, but I was neither surprised nor uneasy that he'd not sent for me since. Nero's focus fixed and then moved on, his obsessions changing from month to month.

I continued between the Palatine and Caelian hills, past the end of the Circus Maximus, and so to the Aventine.

The lower slopes of this hill, like most in Rome, were covered with cheap insulae and shops, the shops now thronged with freedmen and slaves buying supplies and food for the day.

I followed Marcianus's directions, passing the fountain of the three fish, then his own place. One shutter of his house was open, and I glimpsed Marcia fluttering about inside.

I wondered briefly if Marcianus saw Marcia as anything but an efficient assistant and unofficial apprentice. Marcianus was not a man of bodily appetites—at least he was not obvious about it—reserving his interests for books, medicine, and languages. But I wondered.

The street narrowed a few buildings past Marcianus's, bending to make room for the pillars of the aqueduct soaring above me.

The insula past this intersection was tall, five stories at least, with two shops on the ground floor, one selling baskets, the other metal boxes and copper vessels. The coppersmith sat at his bench, his hammer striking metal in even strokes, clanking like an out-of-tune bell.

The basketmaker's shop was much more quiet; he and his wife and daughter frowned at the reeds in their hands as they wove them with dexterity.

I paused on the basketmaker's doorstep and addressed the man. "I'm looking for a woman called Chryseis."

The basket weaver regarded me blankly as though he didn't understand my words. His wife answered for him, in a heavy accent. "*That* one. She's been shouting at everyone all day, snarling and swearing out of the window. Why do you want *her*?"

"She's the wife of a friend," I extemporized.

"Oh, yes, the gladiator." The wife's lip curled. The husband and daughter continued to weave, eyes on tasks, in complete silence. "He's been in and out of here for days, the two of them bellowing at each other. He finally shut up, but she keeps yelling. On the fifth floor, dear. Fortune go with you."

A small statue of the goddess Fortuna sat at their front door. I touched it for luck, thanked the woman, and ducked into the cool darkness of the insula, beginning my ascent.

CHAPTER 5

The staircase to the insula's first floor was well made, the steps outlined in tile. A mosaic depicting a hunting scene lay on the landing between two polished wooden doors with bronze hinges and round knobs in their very centers.

The decor deteriorated as I rose through the next levels. No more tile graced the stairs, and the stone crumbled as I stepped on it. The walls to either side of me had letters scratched into them, crudely done by those with an idle moment. A sketch of a man entering a lady from behind dominated the third-floor landing.

At the top of the fifth flight, I found two doors, both with worn boards, their hinges and knobs black with age. One of the doors was open, the other fixed with a pristine new lock.

I paused on the landing. The stairs went on for another level, and an icy draft poured from cracks in the roof on the next floor.

"Chryseis?" I asked into the open door.

The door behind me slammed open, and a woman of great beauty appeared on the threshold. She had black hair, naturally curled—the thick mass was no wig—that framed the face of a goddess, one a sculptor would want to capture. Dark eyes like hard onyx glared at me.

"What do you want?" Her voice was sharp, brittle.

"Are you Chryseis?" I asked her.

"Who's asking?" She looked me up and down. "Oh, gods, it's Leonidas, isn't it? The one who was freed?"

I nodded. "I—"

"If you're after Rufus, he isn't here." She leaned against the doorframe, one arm above her head, a seductive pose, but her gaze was flinty. Her stola was fastened at only one shoulder and skimmed a body of sultry curves, but Chryseis herself was anything but inviting. "You didn't come to apologize for him, did you? Save your breath. Tell him he can have his tarts, but he doesn't get a soft bed here at the same time. Understand? Tell him."

"I haven't seen him," I interjected when she paused for breath. "No one has. When did he leave here?"

Chryseis didn't appear in the least worried that her husband might be missing. "Last night. Do you mean Rufus hasn't returned to the ludus? I'll wager Aemil will beat him something awful." Her eyes gleamed in anticipation, but her mouth remained a straight line.

"He didn't," I said, uneasiness rising. "When exactly did he leave? Did he tell you where he was going?"

"He didn't have to, did he?" Chryseis snapped. "He's got two tarts in the Transtiberim, above a wine shop off the Via Aurelia. He thinks I don't know where they live, but I do. They share the room, and he has both of them. He says he'll stop, but he never does. I don't know what he sees in those flat-chested, gnarled-haired nobodies. Tell him if he doesn't drop them, he'll never see *this* again."

She slid the loose stola from her shoulder and caught it at her waist, baring her plump, perfectly round breasts, dark nipples stark against her skin. Sculptors would want to capture those as well.

I pretended not to notice. "It is important I find him."

"Is it?" Chryseis took a step toward me, but her voice was no softer. "Would you like me, Leonidas?" She glanced into the apartment behind her.

I remained rooted in place, and her eyes flickered in surprise.

"Do you prefer men?" Chryseis restored her stola with quick, efficient movements, clasping the fabric at her shoulder with a gold fibula. "If you are after Rufus, good luck. He won't look at you. He can't pull himself out of those two whores."

I did not answer, letting her believe what she wished. I'd had little interest in women—or men for that matter—in the last few months, my wenching days over. The numbness that had settled over me after winning the *rudis* had made my bed only for sleeping.

But even if I'd been as randy as the youth I once was, Chryseis wouldn't tempt me. She had great beauty, radiated it, but at the same time, her coldness cut like an obsidian knife. She was the sort who wouldn't enjoy a lover for his own sake but for how she could control him and what she could make him do.

I'd met women whose faces were plain to the point of ugliness, but they'd been warm and caring, and I ceased noticing they were not lovely. They'd been far more alluring and desirable than Chryseis, who might as well be carved of marble. All the beauty and none of the warmth.

"If Rufus returns, tell him to go to the ludus at once," I said.

Chryseis's perfect brows rose. "Aemil is that angry, is he? Perhaps I'll go with Rufus, to see what Aemil does to him."

"Just so he reaches it." I debated telling her about Ajax, but I wondered what good it would do. She might wish the same fate on Rufus, or she might panic and run for the cohorts.

"Good day, Leonidas." Chryseis folded her arms, her bosom pressing the translucent fabric. "If you want to have me, come back, and then I'll tell Rufus all about it."

I had no wish to be a bone between this woman and Rufus. I gave her no farewell, only turned from her for the stairs.

The open doorway across from Chryseis's darkened, and a girl of about ten summers peeped out. The smell of something boiling wafted behind her. The girl had flyaway hair and a too-thin body, and she blinked rapidly when she saw me.

I gave the girl a polite nod and started downward. Behind me, Chryseis made a snort of disgust and slammed her door.

The girl was still watching me when I reached the next landing, staring at me with curious dark eyes. I nodded at her again then descended, my footsteps falling in with the rhythm of the coppersmith's hammer below.

I thanked the woman in the basket shop, her husband and daughter remaining hunched over their work, and walked on, heading for the Transtiberim, in search of Rufus's mistresses.

The Pons Sublicius, an ancient bridge, crossed the Tiber near the Porta Triemina, a gate through which I'd departed Rome on a journey to Ostia Attica not long ago, escorting a retired senator.

The bridge had pilings of stone but the structure itself was made of wood, rickety and old, often repaired. As I crossed, I had a good view of the Pons Aemilius not far upstream—an arched stone bridge that was far more substantial.

The Transtiberim swallowed me as I stepped off the other end of the Pons Sublicius. Its many buildings blocked the sight of the river, and also of the nearby Naumachia, a manmade lake for the staging of mock naval battles.

The popina just off the Via Aurelia had lettering on its outside walls and what was meant to be a Greek painting of battling heroes. A tiny staircase led upward beside the open counter, and I climbed it on the chance it directed me to the right apartment.

I heard squealing female laughter as I reached the first floor, and I knocked with my fist on the rickety door.

Footsteps pattered toward it. "Who's there?" a woman cried, far more eagerly and curiously than Chryseis had.

"Leonidas. Friend of Rufus."

The flimsy door shook as it was pulled open, and a small young woman with uncombed brown hair grinned at me. "It really is Leonidas the Spartan," she all but shouted as she opened the door all the way. "Welcome, Leonidas. Our humble home is honored."

The home was truly humble. One room with uneven stone walls and a slanted stone floor greeted me, the only light and air coming from a window set high in the wall. In this dim interior were a table and stools and a single wide pallet.

Another young woman with similar features to the first jumped up from the table, and a slim young man sat cross-legged on the pallet, a jug in his hand. I saw no sign of Rufus.

"Welcome," the second woman said. "Gaius, turn loose that wine and pour Leonidas a cup."

The first young woman took me by the arm and led me to the table. "We have bread, freshly baked. And grapes if Gaius hasn't eaten them all. He is our cousin but thinks he's our paterfamilias, the brat."

I allowed her to sit me down. The second woman poured me wine from the jug Gaius had readily handed her while the first shoved a much-mended plate of bread at me and a basket that held a few grapes.

"I am looking for Rufus," I managed to say.

The first woman's face blossomed into a smile. "Did his wife send you? If so, we won't tell. I'm Merope, by the way. She's Martolia, my sister." She jerked her thumb at the second young woman who gave me a good-natured nod.

I took a polite sip of the wine, which was sour and oily tasting. "I visited Chryseis, but she did not know where Rufus was."

The two girls burst out laughing. "You met Chryseis? Do you understand now why Rufus likes to stay with us? He'll break himself to pieces on her."

"I think he likes variety," Gaius said quietly from the pallet.

Martolia threw a shriveled grape at him. "Misery-maker. Rufus arrives morose and leaves much happier."

"He's a good man, is Rufus," Merope told me. "When Gaius was run down by a cart and broke his arm, Rufus carried him to a physician and paid the man to set his bone and give him concoctions to make him sleep. Show him your arm, Gaius."

Gaius obediently lifted a thin arm that looked whole and healthy. "I never said he wasn't kind. Just that he could leave his wife if he was that unhappy with her."

"He doesn't, because she has money." Martolia resumed her seat at the table and leaned toward me. "Much, much money."

Chryseis had described the sisters as *flat-chested, gnarled-haired nobodies*. The two were thin, showing that a feast of bread and grapes was rare, and their hair hung in unkempt hanks. They wore tunics that were far more modest than Chryseis's stola but much mended, like their plain ceramic plate.

For all that, the sisters bathed me in smiles and offered me what little they had. They were as excited to see me as if I'd been a wealthy patrician gracing their tiny home.

"Chryseis has money?" I asked in bewilderment as Martolia poured me more wine. "She lives high in an insula on the Aventine. Rufus has been trying to persuade her into a better place."

"Oh, she doesn't like to *spend* money," Merope declared. "She likes to keep it. She owns a warehouse in the Emporium and is part owner of a ship that runs spices. She has a fortune tucked away. Why do you think Rufus wanted to marry her?"

"Why did she want to marry Rufus?" I thought that the more baffling question. Rufus was not the best-looking man, his granite-like face having been caved in too many times, and his voice loud and grating. Chryseis had beauty.

Gaius broke in, "She wanted a gladiator at her beck and call. Wanted to boast to her friends about it, I suppose."

I thought of the brittle woman in the doorway of the apartment, and the chill wind coming down the stairs from the floor above. Chryseis likely did want to brag that she'd tamed a vicious gladiator, and Rufus had probably thought he'd landed in soft living.

Rufus, as a free man who'd made a contract with Aemil, could marry if he liked—perhaps he'd chosen Chryseis to pad his retirement. Then maybe Rufus had, too late, realized she was tightfisted, and too late Chryseis realized she couldn't control Rufus at all.

"How did you two meet him?" I asked the sisters.

"Gaius did," Merope said. "Rufus came into the popina, and Gaius works there. Gaius became his lover first then he introduced him to us."

"Gladiators stink," Gaius declared, then flushed as he caught my eye. "At least Rufus does. So I foisted him off on my cousins."

"We like him," Martolia said. "We send him off to the baths and then he smells fine. Why do you need to speak to him, Leonidas? Can't you talk to him at the ludus?"

I pondered what to tell them. I hated to introduce the tragedy of Ajax into this lighthearted room, but I also wanted them to be aware of the danger.

"Aemil is looking for him. He didn't return when he was supposed to."

The two women appeared puzzled. "Then he's with Chryseis," Merope said. "He has to spend *some* time with her so she won't disinherit him."

"She has not seen him, and I am concerned," I said. "So is Aemil."

Merope lost her cheerful smile. "What is it, Leonidas? What has happened?"

I let out a breath, choosing my words carefully. "The gladiator, Ajax, was killed last night. Murdered."

The warmth drained out of the room with a swiftness of a winter storm. Merope and Martolia drew nearer to me, and Gaius went silent, his gaze on mine.

"Someone killed him?" Merope whispered. "In a fight?"

"No." I did not want to tell them the details, so I closed my mouth.

Merope and her sister had quicker minds than the wealthy Chryseis. Merope's lips quivered. "And you are afraid this has also happened to Rufus?"

"I don't know. I will feel better if I find him."

The young women exchanged fearful glances. Rome was a dangerous city. The desperate preyed on any they could, and a group could bring down even the toughest man.

Merope swallowed. "We will search for him."

"No," I said at once. "Tell me where he liked to go, and I will search."

"The three of us can do it more quickly," Merope countered. "We know every place Rufus might hide, places you will never find. We will look and send word to the ludus."

"Send word to me on the Quirinal." I explained to them the location of the wine shop and the apartment above it. "Tell me or Cassia."

Martolia's curiosity flickered above her alarm. "Who is Cassia?"

I cleared my throat. Explaining Cassia was never easy. "A scribe who works for me."

"Scribe?" Martolia repeated. Both girls and Gaius turned to me with interest.

"She's a friend and very smart." I rose. "Thank you for the wine. If you find Rufus, keep him here if he won't return to the ludus, and inform me."

The young women nodded, and Gaius watched me in concern.

"We will begin at once," Merope promised. "Thank you, Leonidas."

I paused at the doorway. "Thank me for what?"

Merope gave me a tiny smile. "For coming to us. For not dismissing us because we aren't rich shrews."

I gazed about the small room with its crude furniture and few carefully kept belongings. The sisters huddled together, and Gaius cracked his knuckles, as though trying to keep himself from fearing the worst.

I did understand why Rufus preferred this place. It held laughter, affection, and caring, instead of miserly chill.

"You deserved to know," I said. "Please be careful. Someone very dangerous is out there."

The three sobered again and agreed.

I had an idea they would be very resourceful, but I also felt a qualm as I left them. I hoped I could run Rufus to ground so the two spirited ladies and their cousin could receive him here in peace.

As I made my way northward toward the Pons Agrippae and the villa Cassia and Marcianus were visiting, I checked every popina and eating shop to see if Rufus was enjoying food or drink in them or sleeping in one of their back rooms.

No one I spoke to had seen him. Rufus was a frequent guest at these places, but he had not visited any in the last few days.

I told myself that Merope and Martolia were correct that they'd know more hidden places Rufus might retreat, and left the Transtiberim to them.

I followed a path alongside the river, joining farmers and merchants who headed for their villages. More and more farmland had been bought up closer to Rome so the rich could have vast villas with plenty of space, driving the farmers farther and farther out. But now those villas were becoming cramped themselves as developments in the city grew.

The Villa Flores had so far managed to stave off the invasion of insulae, shops, popinae, and other domii. It sat by itself at the top of a low hill, and several tiers of gardens stepped down toward the Tiber from its rear walls. I spied an ambulatory—a colonnaded walkway—that led from the garden and disappeared around the far side of the house.

The garden contained rows of trees and shrubbery, bare now for winter, but in the summer, the lush growth would more or less hide the entire house from the road that led to it.

I approached a gate in a wall that lined the street. The wall was plain on the outside, dusty from the sand thrown up by the feet of travelers both human and beast. Its gate was tall, a grill closed off by a hatch. Trees showed over the top of this wall, promising quiet, soothing pathways within.

Before I could decide what I should say to the door slave after I knocked on the gate, bolts drew back and the ponderous wooden structure swung open.

Three men I recognized walked out, their beefy bodies and knives in their belts proclaiming they were bodyguards.

Behind them strode a man I also knew. His name was Sextus Livius, and he'd once declared to me that he was one of the wealthiest men in all of Rome.

Dark eyes under thick black hair widened when he saw me. "Leonidas?" he asked in surprise. "What by all the gods brings you *here*?"

CHAPTER 6

I wanted to ask Livius the same question. "Business," I answered quickly.

Livius's gaze skewered me. As when I'd met him a month ago, he wore a plain tunic made of fine linen with a cloak draped carelessly over his arm and wristbands of beaten gold.

"What business is that?" he asked good-naturedly, but I could see he expected me to answer. Wealthy men liked to be obeyed, even ones who'd started life as slaves.

I glanced behind him at the wide garden and the columned path that led to the villa, and decided to confide in him. He'd been helpful before and had resources that I never would.

"In truth, I am seeking another gladiator," I said in a quiet voice. "I heard he might be here."

"The one called Herakles? He is indeed within. The lady of the house claimed he had come to entertain guests, but I believe he entertains her personally." His grin told me what he thought of the woman's flimsy deception.

I deflated in relief. At least I wouldn't find Herakles cut to pieces and left stacked in an alley.

"I need to speak to him."

Livius's interest grew. "I admit I am curious as to why. As you will never gain admittance without an invitation, I will escort you inside."

I was too eager to see Herakles to question his generosity. "Good of you."

"Not at all. You did me a good turn, and I told you I was happy to repay you."

Livius jerked his chin at his guards, who turned without expression. Two preceded him through the gate, and the third waited for him to walk ahead of him.

I entered with Livius—not much else I could do.

The gate led to a long walkway lined with marble columns interspersed with carefully trained and pruned trees. Shrubs separated the path from beds on either side of it, where rich earth had been turned, waiting for the nights to grow warmer before planting began.

We tramped along, our way paved with mosaics depicting garden scenes and an inevitable one of Bacchus on a chariot with his cornucopia of abundance, amphorae of flowing wine, and scantily clad women dancing around him.

The villa, encircled by the garden, which itself was enclosed by walls except on the river side, rose before us. Two great doors, painted red and gilded, stood open to the atrium.

The doorman was more watchful than many, and he came to attention as Livius and I strode to him.

"Sir." The door slave bowed low then squared his shoulders under a very white linen tunic.

"Tell your mistress I wish to ask her about one final thing." Livius spoke easily, without haste. A coin appeared in his hand, though I had not seen him reach into a pouch for it.

The doorman accepted the coin with a humble bow of his head. "Yes, sir. Thank you, sir. I will inquire, sir."

Livius took no notice of his obsequiousness. He strolled into the atrium as the doorman dashed off, a room three times the size of the entire apartment Cassia and I lived in.

In the middle of this atrium was the impluvium, the square

basin that caught rainwater. This one had been fitted with a burbling fountain in the form of a maiden pouring water from a jar, her long hair spilling over one bared breast.

The house rose two stories above me, a balcony encircling the atrium, its balustrade made of elegantly carved wood.

The walls on the ground floor held vividly colored murals of gardens with elegant people wandering through them, or hunting scenes with lifelike deer running from men with bows. Another depicted a man and woman gazing longingly at each other through a hole in a garden wall.

"Pyramus and Thisbe," Livius said at my elbow. "They fell in love speaking to each other through a crack in the wall. Publius Ovidius Naso told the tale, which I read as an incorrigible youth. The two die tragically, of course, as in any good love story."

I turned to him quizzically, ready to ask him why tragic death made any story good, when the doorman returned and signaled us to follow.

He led us through a pedimented doorway into a long corridor. To our left was an enclosed peristyle garden with another fountain, this one oblong, with Neptune in his chariot racing through it.

To the right was a stairway leading to the next floor, cool darkness above. Under the stairs was a narrow passage that probably led to the servants' area and the kitchens. I thought I saw a slim figure in a long tunic in the shadows, but I could not be certain.

The doorman escorted us through an open doorway at the end of this hall to the main gardens. The first terrace, balustraded, held a large mosaic floor and a swath of trees and greenery at either end. The next terrace, down a shallow flight of stairs, sported fountains amidst blocks of hedges. To the right of the terraces was a vineyard, the bare vines waiting for spring.

Before us, the sparkling river wound lazily around the hills of Rome. From here I could see the stables and practice area for the chariot teams on the other side of the Tiber with the round swell of the Theatre of Pompey in the distance.

On the second terrace, a woman reclined in an alcove set into the wall that formed the upper terrace. Red and gold hangings lined the niche, ready to be pulled closed against wind or chill.

The alcove held three couches, the middle one occupied by the woman. Herakles lounged on the couch to her right, his torso positioned elegantly, one knee drawn up, on which he rested a negligent arm. He reminded me of a resting leopard, a beautiful animal that could in a moment change into a wild and unpredictable predator.

On the couch on the lady's left was Nonus Marcianus. He held a gold cup between his slim hands and wore his usual jovial expression.

"I have indeed patched him up several times," Marcianus was saying with a nod at Herakles. "That scar across his forearm—I had to cut into it to set the bone and align the ligaments, and then sew it back up again."

Herakles obligingly turned his arm over to show a sharp white line across his inner arm.

"Did he scream?" the lady, who must be Domitiana Sabinus, asked in curiosity. No eagerness, just interest.

"Not so much screamed as cursed and shouted at me, threatening to kill me and all my progeny." Marcianus chuckled. "Of course, most of what he said was in whatever tongue they speak in Pannonia, so I have no idea what plagues he willed to rain down upon me."

"That's my brave boy," Domitiana said, drawing a languid hand across Herakles's thigh.

She was middle-aged, perhaps in her forties, but she'd kept herself youthfully slim, her face unlined, unless the lines were hidden by clever cosmetics. She wore a wig of blond curls carefully styled, done artfully enough that it looked natural.

"I was in much pain," Herakles spoke in a deep voice, his accent just thick enough to reveal he came from a land far away yet not so thick that his paramour would have difficulty understanding him. "I cannot feel shame for berating Marcianus. I am now grateful." He made a seated bow to Marcianus that was anything but humble.

Domitiana caught sight of her servant and then Livius with me behind him. She straightened her stola, which was of shimmering red silk.

"Sextus Livius, you've returned," she said brightly. "Bringing me another gladiator?" She regarded me with dark eyes that were not as hard as Chryseis's, but nowhere near as friendly as those of Merope and her sister. "You are Leonidas the Spartan, are you not? *Were*, I should say."

I bowed, hoping I looked more polite than Herakles.

"I apologize for the intrusion," Livius said smoothly. It was clear Domitiana did not mind—Livius was young, attractive, and wealthy. "We have need of Herakles."

"Oh, do you? I would insist on knowing the reason, but it is not my business." Domitiana flashed a smile that made her appear years younger. "Very well, Herakles, you may go. Remember, my banquet is two days before the Ides. I will speak to Aemilianus if he is too stubborn to let you come."

She meant she'd pay Aemil, if necessary, to allow Herakles to attend her.

Domitiana waved a slim hand, gold and gemstones flashing in the sunlight. "It was good to meet you Nonus Marcianus. Tell my majordomo to give you a token on the way out."

Marcianus rose as Herakles heaved himself reluctantly from the couch. "No need for that, your ladyship," Marcianus said.

"Nonsense. I bleated on to you about my digestion, and you are a professional physician. It is only right I pay a fee for your time. Good day to you."

She snapped her fingers. Three servants materialized from the upper terrace to bring her wine, adjust a cushion, and hold out scented water so she could bathe her hands. Domitiana reclined more deeply on her sofa and closed her eyes, finished with us.

A fourth servant led us away as the doorman had scurried back to his duties. I glanced at the view as we climbed to the higher terrace, marveling that distance could reduce the dirt and stink of Rome to a shimmering, hazy beauty.

None of us spoke as we followed the servant back into the house past the peristyle garden, and into the atrium. There the servant spoke quietly to a tall, thin man who handed Marcianus a pouch that clinked. Marcianus murmured his thanks and pocketed the coins.

Once the servant had ushered us to the dusty path outside the villa and pulled the gate closed, Herakles, tall with golden brown hair and hazel eyes, scowled at me.

"Thanks to you, Leonidas, I must trade a soft pallet for a hard slab. What are you doing here?"

I did not want to discuss Ajax on the open path with others passing, but Marcianus, his countenance serious, faced Herakles.

"There is danger about," he said. "You need to be at the ludus."

"What danger?" Herakles demanded.

"Ajax is dead," Marcianus said flatly. "But this is not the place to talk about it."

He started along the path, leaving Herakles and Livius stunned behind him. I strode after Marcianus.

"Cassia. We can't leave her."

"And we will not. She will appear about ... here." Marcianus halted next to a nondescript door in the villa's outer wall.

Not a moment later, the door creaked, and Cassia ducked out, settling her cloak over her head.

"I think you should explain, Leonidas." Livius had reached us, his bodyguards hanging back at a flick of his hand.

Herakles gathered close to Livius, his expression sour. There was nothing for it. In quiet tones, I told them what had happened, Marcianus adding details. Cassia kept a fold of her cloak over her face and said nothing.

Herakles's jaw had gone slack by the time I finished. "Jupiter and Minerva. What sorcery is this?"

I hadn't thought of it until Herakles said the words, but it was true that the way Ajax had been killed could have been the result of a gruesome spell.

"Sorcery or madness," Livius said.

Marcianus looked him up and down. "May I inquire who you are, sir? You came to call upon Domitiana Sabinus, but I was not certain of your name."

"This is Sextus Livius," I broke in before Livius could answer. "A friend."

I was not certain Livius would appreciate me calling him a friend, but I did not know how to account for him. *Very, very powerful and wealthy secret son of a man I once did business with* seemed an inadequate explanation.

Livius did not dispute the label. "I am a freedman who has been extraordinarily lucky."

"And I am Nonus Marcianus, *medicus*."

Livius gave him a nod that was more of a bow. "I am honored, sir."

Marcianus as an Equestrian outranked a freedman many times over. Livius, no matter how much money he acquired, could never hold high office or marry into certain classes or be considered anything but a former slave. Yet Livius wore more gold on his wrists than Marcianus would make in a year, even from patching up expensive gladiators.

Herakles shifted impatiently. "Can we return to Ajax being cut up like firewood? You said he'd supped with a wealthy man. One like *him*?" He glared at Livius in suspicion. "It would be just like a Roman dog to gut one of my countrymen."

"Or your lady of the villa did," I told him.

Herakles snorted. "Domitiana? She wouldn't hurt a fly. She'd fear to mar her manicure."

"Wealthy women can hire men to do the difficult deeds for them," Marcianus pointed out. "I suggest we discuss it elsewhere rather than beside her door."

"Agreed." Livius gestured us onward. "I will lend myself and my bodyguards to escort you to the gate of your ludus. You will be safe with them."

"Possibly Ajax was told the same thing," Herakles muttered, but he started with us along the path southward toward the ludus.

I let the bodyguards pass me as they surrounded Livius, Herakles, and Marcianus. Cassia hesitated as well until we were a dozen or so paces behind the others.

"Were you all right in there?" I asked her.

I could see only Cassia's eyes in the folds of her cloak, but they crinkled as though she smiled. "Yes, indeed. As I said, I know some of her servants well. They will not mention my name to her."

"You are very certain," I stated.

Cassia slowed her pace. "Do you have friends you trust beyond logic? Nonus Marcianus, for instance."

"Yes." The answer came without hesitation. I would trust Marcianus with my life and had several times. In a way, I trusted Aemil, though I knew he was self-serving. But he was honest.

"These are people like that," she said. "I've known them most of my life."

"They told you much?"

"All about Domitiana Sabinus and Herakles, yes. I will tell you more when we are private. Did you find Rufus?"

"No." One of the guards glanced over his shoulder at us and slowed his pace, and I gave Cassia a cautioning glance. "When we are home."

Cassia agreed, and we caught up to the party.

Septimius stood at the gate again this afternoon. He straightened quickly when he saw us coming, then put his hand on his sword, glower in place at the bodyguards and the man they surrounded.

Marcianus stepped in front of the guards. "Let us in, Septimius, there's a good fellow. I will vouch for Livius and his entourage."

Aemil was already jerking open the gate. "Herakles," he bellowed. "Thank all the gods. In your cell—*now*—or feel my wrath. Leonidas, why did you bring a mob with you? Did you find Rufus?"

Shaking my head, I said, "I spoke to his wife and his mistresses then searched where I could on this side of the river, but there is no sign of him."

Aemil let out a curse in his Gallic language. "At least you found one of the strays. What about Regulus? Where in Hades is he?"

"I haven't seen him either."

Aemil scowled at me as though I were to blame for his troubles as Herakles slid through the gate and strolled toward the arched line of cells.

"Can I help?" Livius asked, his voice full of smooth strength.

"You can indeed," Marcianus answered before Aemil could. "I have a cart to bring here and I could use the assistance."

He meant for Ajax's body. I'd planned to offer to help but Livius's guards would be able to do the job swiftly.

"I would be happy to," Livius said. "If I learn anything about this horrible business or find what has become of the other two men, I will send word to you, Leonidas."

We inclined our heads cordially at each other. Livius even nodded to Cassia, whom he'd met in our rooms at the end of our last adventure. Then he and Marcianus moved off toward the Aventine, the guards closing in around them.

I turned back to Aemil. Herakles's mention of sorcery had stirred an idea. "Do you know if you've been cursed? Or maybe the ludus itself has?"

Aemil folded his thick arms. "I thought of that this morning.

I've looked for scrolls, but found nothing, though we haven't had time to make a thorough search yet."

Anyone could pay a priest or a vendor of such things for a curse—they supplied the leather or papyrus scroll, stylus, and the words of the incantation, assuring the purchaser that the magic would work if they followed a certain formula.

The curses weren't always successful—if the incantation was done wrong, or the god called upon wasn't pleased, nothing might happen. But many families had been ruined or businesses failed because of curses.

"Go away, Leonidas." Aemil rubbed his forehead, drawing his broad hand down to his chin. "Thank you for finding that vermin, Herakles. Now if we can lay hands on Rufus and the blasted Regulus, so much the better."

He turned away without a good-bye, striding toward the cells, chivying men with his shouts.

Cassia and I were left relatively alone. "Should we retreat or continue searching?" she asked.

I thought of the two young women and their cousin Gaius who vowed to leave no stone unturned until they found Rufus. I had the feeling they could search the Transtiberim better than we could.

As for Regulus ...

A chill touched me when I thought of him, but at the same time, I didn't really believe anyone would be able to kill him. Ajax could have been lured to his banquet, promised riches, or patronage, or sex. Seduced. Regulus never would be. He was suspicious of everyone and liked to have the upper hand in any situation. An assassin would more likely be laid low by Regulus than he by him.

"Home for now," I told Cassia. "You can write down all we've learned."

Her eyes crinkled again.

"Leonidas."

Herakles approached from the cells on swift feet, glancing

over his shoulder, but Aemil could be heard berating unfortunate men in the far wing.

"*You,*" Herakles barked at Cassia. "Wait outside."

Cassia did not move until I gestured to her. She bowed her head and slipped out the gate, though she was anything but meek.

I braced myself for Herakles to berate me once more for wresting him from his cushy accommodations, but he put his hand on my shoulder and turned me aside.

"I'd watch that slave of yours." His hazel eyes held vicious glee. "She's in thick with Domitiana's menials. One of them is her lover."

CHAPTER 7

I regarded Herakles stonily. He was inebriated from whatever wine he'd imbibed at the villa and angry at me for bringing him to the ludus to face Aemil's wrath. My skepticism must have been obvious, because Herakles leaned closer, his breath pungent.

"I saw them together," he said with conviction. "She's sleeping away, Leonidas. With a spindly nobody. I'd take a strap to her."

With that, he sent me a derisive sneer and sprinted back to the cells.

I exited through the gate, answering Septimius's farewell. Cassia hovered a few paces down the road, having stepped against the wall to stay out of the way of passers-by. No one paid much attention to her, an unmoving slave in a plain cloak.

She fell into step behind me as I moved on. I couldn't turn in this narrow passageway and demand to know what Herakles meant unless I wanted us to be amusement for the street. I clamped my mouth closed and led the way home.

We went over the bridge to the Insula in the middle of the Tiber, shuffling along with those crossing back into Rome. From there we skirted the Theatre of Marcellus, passed the temples to

Fortuna and Mater Matuta, and moved under the towering Temple of Saturn toward the Basilica Julia and the forums.

The crowds had dispersed from the Forum Romanum, as most men headed for the baths in the afternoon, informally continuing business they'd begun in the Curia or the basilicas. The roads became relatively quiet as we left the flat areas around the forums of Julius and Augustus and wound our way to our apartment.

The wine merchant raised a hand in greeting as I unlocked the door—I'd managed to install a new bolt not long ago—and we went inside and up the stairs.

Cassia disentangled herself from her cloak in the dim coolness of our rooms, then reached for a jug of wine and one of water to mix a refreshing drink for us.

"Who was the man you were speaking to at the villa?" I asked as Cassia set the water jug next to the wine. "Was he your lover?"

Cassia jolted, nearly spilling the water. "Gracious, no. Why would you believe that?"

"Herakles told me this." I could never be anything but blunt.

"I see." Cassia arranged the jugs neatly on their shelf and handed me a cup. "Herakles is wrong. I have several acquaintances in Domitiana Sabinus's home. One is called Helvius, and I know him fairly well. He is also a scribe—Domitiana's secretary."

I conceded that Herakles had exaggerated to stir up trouble, but a small knot formed in my stomach. Cassia had a quick mind and a talent with numbers and writing. It would be natural for her to be drawn to another scribe, a person who shared her interest in literature and languages.

Why this should cause me to flinch, I did not know. I had no such annoyance when she spoke with Marcianus about the same subjects.

She could not go to another man without permission in any case. Unless she was freed, she could not marry or form any relationship against our benefactor's will.

She might, of course, save to buy her freedom, but I'd never seen any evidence of that. Perhaps, as I had when I'd been a gladiator, she'd concluded that her price would be unreachable.

I would inquire of Hesiodos, the slave who was our go-between for our benefactor, exactly what her price was. An idea was forming in my head, so new it made me rub my temple with callused fingers. But I could do nothing until I spoke with Hesiodos.

I gulped the watered wine, letting the liquid wet my parched throat. "This Helvius would be in a good place to know what goes on inside the villa."

"Exactly my thinking." Cassia took a delicate sip and set the cup aside. I'd noticed that ever since she'd been poisoned by a draught of wine, she'd been very careful not to drink too much at one time.

She was waiting for me to take a seat, so I scraped out a stool and thumped to it. Cassia brought out leftover bread from breakfast and placed it in the exact center of the table.

"Helvius knows quite a lot." Cassia smoothed her tunic as she sat. She did not reach for the bread, but I knew she expected me to. I broke a chunk from the wedge and dunked it in my wine, and only then did Cassia set a smaller morsel on her own plate. "Domitiana Sabinus was married to a consul called Severinus who left her very well off. She also inherited money from her own family. Domitiana is a very wealthy lady."

"Perhaps that is why Livius was there," I offered. "The wealthy befriend each other."

"He is a freedman, no matter how much he is worth. But handsome, and that might be Domitiana's interest. She apparently likes young and comely men."

"Is Herakles comely?" I asked skeptically. He was hard-faced and ungainly to me.

"To many, yes, I suppose he is. Herakles is strong, and though not as pleasing of countenance as you are, he is unusual. The barbarian coloring fascinates some women. Notice she wore a wig to resemble a woman of the north. I know of one *domina* who will only have red-haired slaves or freedmen working in her house. She enjoys looking at them, she says."

"Like pet birds," I said in distaste.

"Yes, though hardly as pampered. She's not a kind mistress."

I said a silent prayer bidding the ancestors of these servants, whoever they were, to watch over them.

I realized in the next instant, that Cassia had said *not as pleasing of countenance as you are*. She spoke of me only in comparison to Herakles but for some reason, her observation trickled a tiny bit of warmth through me.

I took another large bite of bread. "Livius might tell me why he'd visited her, if I ask. Or he might not."

"If it was private business, he most certainly will not." Cassia returned to her wine for another minute sip. "Helvius explained to me more about the household. I knew a little from my previous stays in the villa, but he filled in the gaps. Domitiana's son is a praetor in a small city in Hispania where he enjoys his power. He rarely comes home as he doesn't like his mother, so he leaves her to her own devices. Domitiana also has a daughter."

The way Cassia's mouth tightened signaled to me that this fact was significant.

"Does the daughter live at the house?" I asked. "Perhaps Livius's visit had something to do with her."

"Helvius did not think so. The daughter, Severina, is married to a man called Tertius Vestalis Felix and has her own villa on the Caelian Hill. She met her husband, a retired proconsul, when she and her mother visited her brother in Hispania a few years ago. Severina is also horribly spoiled. According to Helvius, she's found fault with everyone since the day she was born. I've never met her myself." Cassia set aside her wine cup. "She'd been sent off with governesses to her father's relatives from a young age—her mother had little to do with her."

I'd known patrician parents who were very close to their children—a man named Priscus, for example, loved his adopted son without shame. Others couldn't be bothered with them. As one who'd never known his father and barely remembered his mother, I didn't much understand either situation.

"If her husband is a retired proconsul, he must be much older than she is," I said. A man with a political career went from aedile to praetor to senator, and usually was not elected consul or given a proconsulship until later in his life.

"Oh, yes. Quite a bit older. Helvius said Severina loves to host banquets, the more lavish, the better. Usually when her husband is away."

I stilled. "Does she invite gladiators?"

"Gladiators, charioteers, actors, musicians ..." Cassia chewed a tiny portion of her bread. "Severina enjoys being entertained as much as her mother does."

I turned my wine cup on the table. "I have known one or two women—gladiators—who'd be able to kill Ajax and saw up his body. But I am guessing the pampered wife of a proconsul could not."

"Helvius says Severina is a rather small woman. I asked."

"But she could hire men to do it for her."

"She also might coerce some of her lovers to do such a thing. Severina is apparently quite beautiful."

Ajax had been vain and pompous. It was not difficult to imagine a beautiful, rich woman enticing him to her side and stuffing him with a sumptuous meal before signaling her hired men to kill him—but for what reason? Was it simply another form of entertainment for her?

"We must find out if Ajax visited her," I stated.

Cassia reached for her tablets, which were never far from her hands. "It will not be easy. I do not know any servants in Severina's house, though perhaps Helvius could sneak me inside."

"No," I said immediately.

Cassia didn't bother to look up. "I thought you would object."

"If this Severina likes gladiators, then I could somehow gain an invitation to her home."

Now Cassia pinned me with her stare. "I believe that a dangerous idea. She might like to *kill* gladiators."

"Or perhaps she wished only to kill Ajax," I argued. "He might have angered her. Maybe Severina grew annoyed with him for going to lupinari in the Subura. For betraying her, in her eyes. She punished him, and left him in the Subura to humiliate him. If she simply enjoyed murdering gladiators, I'm certain we would have heard of it before this."

"That is true," Cassia conceded.

I finished off my bread and washed it down with more wine as I pondered. "What if her husband killed him out of jealousy? Came home too soon and found Ajax there?"

Cassia tapped her stylus to her cheek. "Helvius told me that her husband doesn't pay much attention to Severina. She's his second wife—he married her for her money and her family connections, as he didn't have much wealth of his own. As long as Severina stays close to home, the husband gives her free rein. Or so it seems."

"Still, a man walking into his wife's chamber and finding her in bed with Ajax would make even the most indifferent husband angry," I said. "He could have struck Ajax down in fury, realized he was dead, and decided to leave him in the back street like discarded trash."

"Except the husband is small and elderly," Cassia said as she bent her head to write.

"He probably has a large bodyguard to do such deeds for him."

Cassia's stylus moved decidedly. "That is certainly something to inquire about. But you have no need to rush into danger. I can tell Helvius to find out whether Ajax went to Severina, and if the husband discovered them and has a strong bodyguard."

I reflected that I'd heard Helvius's name too many times in this conversation. "And if he is caught and the truth beaten out of him? Wrath will fall on *you*, and I might not be able to protect you. Patrician families are dangerous."

The stylus paused, and Cassia glanced up. "I know. I grew up in a patrician household."

"And now you are here."

Cassia's cheeks pinkened. "Yes, I take your point."

"Inquiring is dangerous for both of us, but less so for me."

Cassia studied her tablet again, but her hand did not move. "Very well, we will think on how best to gain her household."

I growled. "No rushing out when I'm at the baths and having Helvius smuggle you into her house in a rolled-up carpet."

This drew a laugh. "Like Cleopatra with Julius Caesar? I am dubious about that story, though it does make a good tale."

"Promise me, Cassia."

Cassia lost her smile and heaved a small sigh. "Very well, I promise. Neither of us will enter what might be a killer's household without a good plan in place."

Neither of us, she said. Trying to bind my word with hers. I wasn't certain whether to be amused or exasperated.

"What about the brother?" I asked to move us past the sticky question. "Are you certain he is in Hispania? A husband can grow furious at a wife's wantonness, but so can a brother."

"Helvius is certain, but yes, we ought to—"

The door banging open downstairs cut off her words. I was on my feet in a flash, my hand reaching for my knife.

The wine merchant must have admitted whoever it was. If it had been anyone dangerous, the wine merchant would have tried to stop them, but if they were *truly* dangerous, he could not have.

Several pairs of feet rushed up the stairs, and I wrenched open the inner door.

"Leonidas—good, we found the right place."

The speaker was Merope, out of breath from her scramble up the steps. She wore a threadbare woolen sheath, her hair pulled into a knot that half escaped its bonds. Behind her came her cousin Gaius, a tunic over his thin body, sandals on his overly large feet.

Cassia rose, lips parting at the abrupt intrusion, but I relaxed, lowering my knife.

"This is Merope and Gaius," I told her. "They are ..."

"Rufus's bit on the side." Merope laughed as she delivered these words, and Gaius rolled his eyes.

"Ah," Cassia said. She made a note and closed her tablet. "May I offer you wine?"

Gaius flashed a grin. "Wouldn't say no."

Cassia drew two more cups from the cabinet and mixed wine and water.

"Thank you kindly," Merope said as she accepted the beverage. "Searching for Rufus is thirsty work." She took a slurp from the cup, and Gaius swallowed his wine in one go.

"We haven't found him," Merope continued sorrowfully. "Martolia is still out looking, but we've seen no sign of Rufus, and we've searched everyplace we could think of." All smiles gone, Merope's eyes filled with tears. "I'm very much afraid, Leonidas, that he has ended up in the river or been buried in a deep hole by that wretched woman."

CHAPTER 8

That wretched woman, must be Chryseis, Rufus's wife.

"Do you believe Chryseis killed Ajax too?" I asked.

Merope nodded vigorously. "Of course. To make it look as though someone is killing gladiators so she could rid herself of Rufus."

"She could simply divorce Rufus," Cassia pointed out gently. "From what you tell Leonidas, Chryseis has much money and property. If she was tired of her husband, she could easily eject him."

"Chryseis is a vindictive harpy." Merope turned to Cassia without compunction. "If she wanted to be rid of Rufus, she'd murder him. She'd do it so he couldn't come to us. Vengeance on all of us at the same time."

Gaius sighed sorrowfully in agreement.

"You truly believe she would kill Rufus?" Cassia asked.

Merope nodded vigorously. "Yes. She's awful. You met her, Leonidas. Don't you think she'd kill a man simply because he peeved her?"

I thought of the beautiful woman with cold eyes and luxuriant hair who'd curled her lip at me from the doorway of her apartment.

"Only if she'd gain by it," I said slowly. "I think she's a woman who wouldn't make an effort unless it was well worth her time."

"She'd gain by being a bitch for the fun of it." Merope scowled, unconvinced.

"Where did you look for Rufus?" Cassia asked them.

"Everywhere." Merope threw open her arms, a graceful movement. "Didn't we, Gaius?"

"All over the Transtiberim," Gaius agreed. "Every popina in every street, every lupinarius we could find. Up to the temple of Jupiter and back to the Naumachia. Crossed over to the Aventine and scoured it as well. Merope said we'd better tell you what we did—or rather didn't—find, so we came here. We searched in many more popinae along the way."

Cassia quickly wrote down every word. "I am growing very concerned for Rufus. Perhaps we'd better discover if he's returned to the ludus or to Chryseis."

"We'll check with Chryseis." Merope beamed us a wide smile, her eyes lighting with mischief.

"Better not," Cassia advised. "If he is hiding with her, or if she has him trapped, she will never let you see him. You could ask at the ludus, and Leonidas and I will speak to Chryseis. She knows Leonidas now."

"She did not warm to me," I warned.

"She couldn't warm to anyone," Merope said decidedly. "Oil hardens in her hand."

"Then it's settled," Cassia said. "Merope and Gaius will journey to the ludus and inquire about Rufus while we seek Chryseis."

She spoke as though there was no more argument to be made. Such was the firm power of her reasoning that Merope and Gaius nodded, if reluctantly.

"Talk to Septimius, the gate guard," I said. "Tell him I sent you."

"And let us know what you discover," Cassia said. "Leonidas and I will seek you in your rooms after we speak to Chryseis."

Merope wasn't happy that she couldn't confront Chryseis, but Gaius appeared to think it wise. An encounter between the two women would only lead to shouting or even violence, and we'd be no closer to locating Rufus.

We left the apartment together and parted at the bottom of the stairs. Gaius steered Merope toward the river and the Transtiberim, and Cassia and I descended the Quirinal and started our trek toward the Aventine.

"I understand why Rufus likes Merope," Cassia said as we walked. "She has fire. Most Roman women are raised to be subdued and obedient, no matter what class they come from. I can see him responding to that."

"*You* are not subdued and obedient," I said.

Cassia blinked up at me from under her cloak. "How can I not be? I was born into servitude."

"You are soft-spoken and duck your head, but you also do exactly as you please. Including accompanying me to a dangerous part of town to confront a dangerous woman."

Her stare was perplexed. "Not exactly as I please. I do what makes the most logical sense. My father taught me that."

"What makes the most logical sense to *you*," I countered. "Even when you're ordered not to."

"You did not order me to stay behind today."

"No." I took a few strides, turning sideways to move through a knot of men with baskets of produce hoisted on their backs. "It made the most *logical sense* for you to accompany me."

Cassia pulled a fold of cloth over her mouth to hide her expression and bent her head to study the large stones at her feet, still hesitant on the uneven streets of Rome.

I led us across an increasingly deserted city and around the Forum Bovarium—the cattle market—past a shrine to Ceres near the Circus Maximus and onto the Aventine. I wondered if Marcianus had returned home. We could call on him after we met with Chryseis, if the woman even proved to be in. It wouldn't take much longer to speak to Marcianus before we met up with Merope and Gaius again.

The lower streets of the Aventine were more crowded than the heart of Rome, as people sought home in the late afternoon sunlight. Clouds formed on the horizon, and I tasted a bite of chill in the air—it would rain tonight.

The basketmaker's wife was nowhere in evidence when I peered into the shop on the ground floor of Chryseis's insula. Nor was the daughter, but the basketmaker himself was there, tidying away unsold wares.

Baskets of all sizes, from tiny bowl and plate shapes to wide two-person baskets for hauling wood, hung from the walls or rested on the floor or the benches the basketmaker had just brought inside from the street.

The basketmaker glanced briefly at me then went back to stacking small woven mats on a shelf. When I asked whether Chryseis was above, he only shook his head and waved my words aside, as though he did not understand them, muttering a few syllables of his own.

Cassia stepped out from behind me, slid down a fold of her cloak, and began addressing the man in a language that sounded Greek, but not quite the same as what I'd heard her speak with Marcianus.

The basketmaker jerked his head up, an expression of pleased astonishment unfolding across his face. He set aside the mats, and once Cassia finished, responded with enthusiasm. As Cassia continued the conversation, the basketmaker became eloquent. The two corresponded a long time, the basketmaker waving his hands for emphasis, while I, the ignorant Roman, watched in incomprehension.

Finally, Cassia gave the man a smile and said a few final words, turning away after the basketmaker had answered. He was grinning as we departed, lifting a hand in farewell.

"Chryseis is not at home," Cassia told me as we approached

the staircase that wound upward through the insula. "But he will say nothing if we go up and search her apartment."

She started for the tile-lined stairs, but I stepped in front of her. "A very long conversation for only that."

"He doesn't speak much Latin, and usually lets his wife do all the talking. He was happy to converse with someone who understood his language."

"Greek." I turned and started up the stairs. "There are plenty of Greeks in this city."

"*Aeolian* Greek," Cassia said as we climbed. "It's a different dialect from Ionic, which is what you mostly hear in Rome. Aeolian is spoken in Pergamum and on Lesbos."

"Is that your dialect?" I asked. "Aeolian?"

"My father spoke both, as well as Doric and Achaean. He was very well-read. He came from Smyrna, which straddles the border of Ionia and Aeolia."

"Smyrna." This was the first I'd learned of her heritage. I'd guessed her family came from the eastern end of the Mare Nostrum, but she'd never mentioned exactly where. Cassia's father had already been a slave in a Campanian household when Cassia was born.

"Yes," Cassia answered without hesitation. "My father's family is still there."

I had not heard Cassia's entire history—how had her father been brought into captivity? What had happened to her mother? Did Cassia long to return to her father's home, or had she given up the idea that such a thing would ever happen? Or had she adapted to Rome as so many of us had, and had no intention of living elsewhere?

We could not discuss these things now as we climbed the many floors, the stairs deteriorating as we went. I added the ideas forming in my head to the ones I'd had earlier this afternoon.

The upper landing where Chryseis lived was quiet, her door

shut. The door opposite hers was open, but I saw no sign of the little girl I'd encountered there, nor heard anyone in the apartment beyond. They must fear no theft of their belongings while they were out. A glance inside revealed one low table and that was all. Perhaps they didn't fear thieves because they had nothing to steal.

Chryseis's door had a lock, as I'd observed before. It was a sophisticated metal one with tumblers, very new. None of the other apartments we'd passed bore such locks.

What I noticed most about it today was that it was unfastened, which made me uneasy. I doubted Chryseis would leave her door unbolted and wondered at the lapse.

I cautiously opened the door, peering inside before I signaled Cassia to follow me. I saw no one, but I did not relax.

The room we stepped into was square, with an ill-fitted door in the wall leading to a small balcony. A table and stools were the only furnishings, with a cabinet along one wall hiding its contents behind a coarse linen curtain. An unlit lamp reposed on the table beside a stack of unevenly made ceramic plates. I found nothing that indicated a woman of means lived here.

Another room, a smaller square, was tucked behind the first. A bed reposed here—a wooden pallet with a straw mattress and blankets. Pegs held a line of tunics and stolae, well-made but unadorned.

When I returned to the front room, I saw that the curtain had been folded partway back from the cabinet, and Cassia had pulled out a box of scrolls and tablets.

Without a qualm, Cassia laid out the tablets and began to unroll and examine a scroll. I lifted the cloth from the other end of the cabinet and found cups and a small jar with one piece broken off—the missing piece lay beside it as though Chryseis meant to have it mended. She had towels both new and threadbare, and several baskets, most of which resembled those made downstairs.

While Cassia read through the scroll, I stepped idly to the balcony.

The wooden platform was just wide enough for me to stand on. The insula had been built on the side of the Aventine Hill where it began to be steep, and this balcony looked out over the rooftop of the insula next door.

I could see down to the valley that held the green oval of the Circus Maximus. Chariot teams were just finishing training for the day, horses being led slowly away and practice chariots wheeled off by assistants to the great drivers.

I thought I understood why Chryseis had chosen this apartment. Her belongings told me she was frugal to the point of meanness—with her wealth she could easily buy another jug to replace the chipped one. So high in the insula, these rooms would be cheap, but the view was marvelous, Rome rolling into the mists.

Cassia gasped, and I turned quickly to the room. "What is it?"

Cassia had opened the scroll all the way, her fingers holding down the papyrus as she read. "Chryseis owns this entire building. Why on earth does she live up *here*?"

The view aside, I wondered as well. "She could have a large residence on the first floor, you mean."

Cassia let the scroll roll up on itself before she set it carefully back into its box. "From what I am reading, I'd guess because she can charge a high rent for those first-floor apartments. Why occupy them when tenants will pay for them? She doesn't need much space, and she can collect rents on the more expensive rooms."

I recalled the furtive glance of the little girl across the hall. It must be unnerving for a poor family to live right next to their landlord, and by all accounts, Chryseis was not a compassionate woman.

"Is there any clue there to where Rufus might be?" I asked. "Chryseis might have another house where he could be hiding."

Cassia closed the last tablet. "There is no mention of Rufus at all. Chryseis does own properties throughout the city—the warehouse and part of the ship Merope mentioned, two more insulae, and a few shops in the Subura."

I studied the shabby room with the cracks in its walls and no sign of comfortable furnishings. "Rufus must have thought he'd landed in luxury with her. A horrible disappointment for him."

"He might not be hiding from Aemil or a murderer, but from Chryseis herself," Cassia said. "If she is not a warm woman, as you say."

I suppressed a shudder. "Not warm in the least. But if he hid from her, why not seek out Merope and Martolia?"

"Because Chryseis would know how to find him there. She told you she knew where they lived." Cassia began to lift the box of scrolls, but I took it from her and lugged it back to the cabinet myself. "Or perhaps Rufus does not care. He might be happy that his lady has looks and money, assuming that one day he will inherit that fortune."

I shoved the box where Cassia indicated and reached for the tablets she handed me. I opened one on impulse and studied the lines in the wax that appeared as random scratches to me.

"Could you teach me how to read?" I asked abruptly.

Cassia started, the hem of her tunic moving with her misstep. "You wish to learn to read?"

By her tone, I might have told her I wanted to flap my arms and fly.

"Why not? If Gnaeus Gallus ever requests me to work for him, it might be useful."

Gallus had been impressed that a gladiator had known so much about building sites. I'd been trained by a master builder long ago, before that master had been killed.

Cassia lost her shock, her eyes lighting. "I would be happy to, Leonidas. I hadn't thought you keen, but if you truly wish to learn ..." She trailed off as though musing on the possibilities. "Certainly. You leave it to me."

I tucked away the tablets and rose as I lowered the curtain.

"Let's call on Marcianus," I said. The way Cassia studied me was unnerving, and I began to regret my impulsive request. "He might have more to tell us."

I doubted it, but speaking to Marcianus was always soothing. He could put a reasonable and clear-thinking perspective on most events.

We left the insula and made our way to his home past the fountain of the three fishes. Marcianus was not in, but Marcia was there.

She admitted us, though she'd been locking up for the night. "He's still at the ludus with poor Ajax," Marcia told us. "Aemil and the gladiators will give him a funeral—no one else to do it. If Ajax had family, they are far from here."

"Did Marcianus discover anything else about how Ajax was killed?" I asked.

Marcia shook her head. "Marcianus says you are suspecting a highborn woman of luring him in and killing him, but Ajax didn't like highborn women. I remember him from when I worked in the Subura. He preferred plebs or slaves, he said. He didn't want to be involved with senator's wives—too dangerous."

"None of the lupinari he visited in the last days could have given him such a meal," I pointed out.

"No, but a highborn *man* could have," Marcia said. "Ajax did like patricians—or rather, patrician's sons."

"Do you know which ones?" I thought of the many domii and villas that marched up Rome's hills. Difficult to search them all, if we even could.

"He never mentioned names—he didn't want to land them in scandal. More likely to keep himself from punishment than to spare the young men dishonor."

The information did help, I supposed, if only to tell us we needed to look beyond women like Domitiana and her daughter.

"If you hear of anyone who favored him, please tell us," I said.

"Of course." Marcia spoke with conviction, a strength she'd grown into.

"But be careful," I warned. "This person is ruthless."

Marcia flashed me one of her rare smiles. "I am no fool, Leonidas."

True, she had proved competent and calm. I comforted myself that Marcianus would keep her from harm and left it for now. We departed after Cassia bade her a gracious good night.

The sky was darkening, residents of the neighborhood heading indoors. The cloud bank began to devour the sinking sun, plunging the street into gloom.

Our route home took us past Chryseis's insula once more. The basketmaker's shop was shut, as was the coppersmith's, boards bolted across the counters and over doors to lock out intruders.

Something made me turn and enter the building. Cassia pattered after me without question, but I threw her an explanation.

"I want to check one more time. Chryseis might have come home, and we can shake answers out of her."

I said *we*, but of course I would do the shaking and Cassia would make notes.

We climbed the many stairs toward the top of the insula. The door across the hall from Chryseis's apartment was still open but again, I sensed no one inside. Even the odors of food I'd smelled last time were gone.

I opened the door to Chryseis's rooms and halted so abruptly that Cassia ran straight into me. She untangled herself, peered around me, and sucked in a sharp breath.

On the floor was Rufus. He was dressed in a plumed helmet, arm guard, and shin greaves, a sword on the ground next to him. He, like Ajax, had been cut into neat parts, all of them stacked tidily, with his head perched on top of the pile.

A curse left my mouth, one so foul it blackened the air. Cassia, after her initial intake of breath, went very, very quiet.

A footstep sounded behind us. In the next instant, a woman's shrill and horrified scream rent the silence, echoing up and down the long staircase and all through the insula.

CHAPTER 9

I swung around to behold Chryseis, her lush hair tumbling across her shoulders, her beautiful eyes wide in her chiseled face. Her mouth was open, red and gaping, as she screamed and screamed.

Voices sounded on the stairs, Romans braving the gathering darkness to discover what madness occurred above them. Chryseis continued to scream, the sound like a blade straight into my brain.

Cassia swung from me and seized Chryseis firmly by the shoulders. "Stop!"

Chryseis gasped, the noise ceasing, but her eyes remained fixed on Rufus, her breathing ragged.

More voices, and then hurrying footsteps. Residents stared into the apartment, including the small girl from across the hall. I stepped in front of her to block her view of the grim scene.

Astonished and horrified babbling began, those who couldn't make a noise staring in shocked fascination. Too many people crowded the landing, those on the stairs below demanding to be told what was happening above.

"It's that gladiator," one man called down to his neighbors. "He's all cut to pieces."

"Rufus?" another man demanded. "Hades." His gaze fixed on me. "Is that Leonidas the Spartan? Did *you* kill him, Leonidas?"

"No," I said tersely.

"Leonidas never did this," another man scoffed. "That woman took an ax to him, I'll wager." He pointed at Chryseis.

Chryseis broke from Cassia, fell to her knees, and began keening.

"Let me pass. Let me pass, pox take you." The growling voice of authority came to us as a burly man with a breastplate over his tunic pushed his way to the landing. "*Isis* ..." He breathed as he beheld Rufus, his ruddy face losing color.

The man was a vigile, probably a captain of whatever house was on the Aventine. Behind him came another slim vigile I knew, by the name of Avitus.

"Jupiter's balls." Avitus took in Rufus and swiftly turned away.

The watch captain recovered himself. "Did she do it?" He pointed at Chryseis as her wailing continued.

"I don't think so," I said. "She did not expect to find him like this."

The captain pried his gaze from the corpse and Chryseis and fixed it on me. "What are *you* doing here? You're Leonidas the Spartan, aren't you? I thought you'd retired."

"I came to speak to Chryseis." I debated what to tell him—would Aemil thank me for spreading the tale that his gladiators were being hacked to pieces and left in artful piles?

Avitus stepped forward. He wore no breastplate, only a tunic and sandals. "Leonidas didn't kill him," he said with confidence. "He wouldn't."

The captain frowned but apparently took another vigile's word for it. "Send my men up here," he ordered Avitus. "We'll take her away with us."

"She had nothing to do with it," I tried. I looked around for Cassia, but she'd slipped out in the melee.

"Doesn't matter. She's a witness, and I can't have her

screaming in here all night. I'll give her to the captain of the cohorts. If she's innocent, she'll be able to prove it."

I knew that wasn't necessarily true, but I couldn't stop him without fighting the other vigiles now streaming up the stairs, plus all the tenants who appeared pleased that Chryseis would be led away in shackles. I'd have to let the captain take her and decide how to help her in the morning.

Chryseis's reaction had not been feigned. Whatever she'd felt about Rufus, she'd not expected to see him dead.

Another shriek sounded over the impatient snarls of the vigiles as they swarmed up the stairs, responding to Avitus's summons.

"You killed him." It was Martolia, her words cutting into the room. "You killed him, you filthy bitch."

Martolia easily twisted past the men closing on Chryseis and seized the woman by the throat.

I grabbed Martolia around the waist and hauled her from the still-wailing Chryseis. Martolia kicked and fought, but she was no match for my strength.

"Someone shut her up," the watch captain said in disgust, gesturing at Chryseis.

One of his men sent a tight punch to Chryseis's face. Her head lolled, her mouth closing as blood seeped from it. Chryseis didn't fall senseless, but the blow dazed her, and she did not resist as two vigiles pulled her up and half dragged, half marched her to the door.

Martolia collapsed in my arms and began to cry—heartrending, lamenting sobs.

"Everyone out," the watch captain bellowed. "Get this door bolted. Leonidas ..." He turned to me, uncertainty in his eyes. "If that woman didn't do him in, I'll find out who did. Shouldn't be difficult. Someone would have noticed him being carted in. Not enough blood for him to have been killed here."

The floor was quite clean, as was the body, just as Ajax's had been.

I disagreed that the vigile captain would find ready witnesses who'd seen Rufus's body carried up the stairs. Romans saw nothing they didn't want to. Whoever did this must have come in when Cassia and I had gone to Marcianus's—a small part of an hour had passed at most. He'd have had to be quick, silent, and secretive.

The basketmaker's shop had been firmly shut when we'd returned, but the basketmaker might have witnessed the killer entering as he closed down for the night. My heart went cold. If he'd seen, and the killer realized it ...

I wanted to press back downstairs and make certain he and his family were well, but the staircase was crammed with the curious. Voices echoed in a constant babble.

Martolia slipped away from me and collapsed before the remains of Rufus's body, hugging her knees to her chest, rocking as she cried. Chryseis had been panicked by Rufus's murder, but Martolia grieved.

I stepped into the bedroom, lifted the covering from the bed, and draped it over Rufus. Hidden, he became innocuous lumps under cloth.

The vigile captain sent me a troubled glance as his men tried to herd the residents out and back downstairs. "Bad business. Very bad. And on my watch."

"This isn't the first such murder," I said in a low voice.

The guard captain's eyes opened wide, revealing dark brown depths. "You mean someone else on the Aventine's been chopped to bits?"

"No." I spoke quietly to the captain and Avitus. "Another gladiator, in the Subura. I found him in pieces, like Rufus."

Avitus's mouth dropped open, revealing young and whole teeth. "You mean someone is killing gladiators? For what purpose?"

They'd die just fine in the arena, he meant. "I don't know," I had to say. "My lanista is very worried."

"Isis help us," the captain exclaimed. "That means there's a madman loose in Rome."

I could argue that plenty of madmen existed in Rome, but I understood his meaning. One killing could be explained by someone who hated Ajax personally. Two meant a grudge against gladiators in general. Or, alarmingly, it could mean the person would extend his pleasure at killing to the general population.

"He needs to be stopped," I said.

"Obviously." The watch captain snorted. "What are you doing here, Avitus? This isn't your patch."

Exactly the question I'd pondered.

Avitus flushed. He was young, slim, strong, and easily flustered. "Not my patch for patrolling, no. I live nearby. Next insula over. It's my night off."

I recalled the building I'd gazed upon when I'd stood on Chryseis's balcony earlier. I wondered if Avitus had spied me there and had come to discover what I was up to.

I fixed a stern gaze on him. "You didn't see anyone carting the body here, did you?"

"No." Avitus raised his hands. "Was home, sleeping most of the day. I came over when I heard the noise. And saw *you*." He pointed at me. "You're good at finding trouble, Leonidas."

Avitus had been present at another death in the Subura earlier this year and a suspect for it.

"Trouble is good at finding me." I turned to the watch captain. "What will you do now?"

He sighed and rubbed his head, which was thick with dark curls. "Interview everyone in this building, discover if they saw anything. Do you think the wife will want his body? If she isn't found guilty of murder."

I doubted it. I did not imagine Chryseis as the grieving widow putting up a long inscription to a beloved husband.

"I'll take him back to the ludus," I said.

Relief flickered in the captain's eyes though he strove to hide it. "Good of you. I'm Marcus Vatia, captain of the Aventine vigiles."

He was a stocky Roman, hard with muscle, his face one of a man who brooked no nonsense.

"You pray to Isis," I observed, recalling his exclamation on seeing the body.

"Why not? She's the most powerful goddess of them all. Faced the underworld, defeated evil, raised the dead, *and* is a good mother. I want her on my side."

The room had finally emptied, the last vigiles planting themselves on the stairs to prevent spectators from returning. The residents, realizing they'd see no more, drifted home, but not silently. They babbled to each other about Rufus, Chryseis, and the murder, embellishments to the stories beginning to take shape.

I noted the girl from across the hall didn't retreat there but took the stairs up to the apartments at the very top of the insula. Curious.

The one person I did not see was Cassia.

A soft noise sounded across the hall, in the other apartment, and I moved there swiftly.

This set of rooms was identical to Chryseis's. Other than the table and a few plates and a jug in the corner, I saw nothing more.

The bedchamber beyond contained several pallets pushed together, filling the tiny room. The family must huddle together on them like dogs, using each other for warmth.

No one was there now, except Cassia. She'd pulled one pallet from the wall, half piling it on the next one, as she examined the floor closely.

"His body was kept in here," she announced as I entered.

Vatia and Avitus had followed. Vatia pushed past me and gazed where Cassia pointed. "Blood," he announced. "Not much. Dried."

Cassia addressed her words to me. "I suspect Rufus was

carried here, already dead and ... dismembered ... and kept in this room until the building quieted. Then was arranged in Chryseis's apartment."

I stilled. "How long in here?"

"I don't know. Nonus Marcianus might be able to discover this."

I worked through what she meant, my words coming slowly. "Then he wasn't brought upstairs in the short time we were gone."

"No," Cassia said. "I suspect Rufus was already here when we arrived looking for Chryseis."

"Which means the killer was in this room, while we were ..."

"Searching her apartment, yes." Cassia spoke calmly, but her face was ashen, her eyes wide.

"A pity you didn't nab the fellow," Vatia said, but he cleared his throat uncomfortably.

"A pity?" Avitus demanded in surprise. "They were lucky they weren't for the knife themselves. A man who can fell a gladiator won't be easy to bring down." His declaration faded as Vatia frowned at him. "Sir."

Vatia studied the splotches of dried blood. "Those could have been here for days." He shrugged. "Or, you might be right, and the body was indeed stored here. Poor fellow." He shook his head and left the bedchamber, Avitus and I on his heels. "Who lives in these rooms? Or are they vacant?"

I thought of the small girl I'd seen in this doorway when I came to visit Chryseis earlier today. She'd ascended tonight after the mob dispersed instead of returning here.

I kept this fact to myself. If the girl and her family had nothing to do with this, I didn't want Vatia hauling them to the watchhouse to be locked away. I sensed he simply wanted someone to turn over to the cohorts for the crime, and he might not be too particular who it was.

Even if the girl's family did have a part in this killing, I didn't want Vatia near them until I discovered the truth of it. They might have been bribed or forced to help, unwilling participants in a murder, and they'd face execution if so, the little girl included.

Vatia had turned from me to Avitus. "Come to the watch house with me, Avitus. I want your report on what you saw here to go with mine. I need a reliable witness."

Avitus hadn't seen much more than Vatia had, but while Avitus scowled in displeasure, he couldn't disobey.

Vatia gave me an abrupt *good night* and marched out. Avitus went with him, still scowling. We heard Vatia snap at someone on the stairs and then scuttling footsteps as the curious person retreated.

Cassia bent and lifted a small object from the floor.

"What is that?" I went to her, the scent of her simple woolen cloak soothing in this place of death.

"A feather." She held up a white broken quill that had long ago graced the wing of a bird. "From his helmet, I think."

I thought about the helmet that covered Rufus in the other room. It had a crest of white and black feathers, and now I realized what was wrong with it.

"The helmet is a Thracian's," I said. "Rufus was a myrmillo."

Cassia's brows went up. "Is the costume significantly different?"

Her question told me she'd never been to gladiatorial games. "The helmets both have crests but are not exactly the same. The swords are quite different—the myrmillo carries a straight *gladius*, but the Thracian's sword, the *sica*, is curved."

"Perhaps the killer did not know that. Or decided one costume was as good as another."

I rubbed a finger under my lower lip. "If he has fixed on gladiators, I'd think he'd be ardent about the games. He'd know the difference, and exactly which of Aemil's gladiators took what role. I was almost always a secutor. Ajax also was a secutor, and his body was dressed correctly."

Cassia tucked the feather into her cloak. "Which makes me wonder where this person obtained the gear."

"If it is a man or woman wealthy enough to serve gilded food, they'd be wealthy enough to collect gladiator gear. But I still wonder why the mistake."

"When we find him, we will ask him." Cassia stepped past me and out of the apartment, returning to Chryseis's.

I didn't bother to tell Cassia she'd be nowhere near this killer when he was caught.

Martolia huddled by Rufus's now-covered body. When we entered, Martolia sprang up and hurled herself at me, latching on to me and burying her face in my chest.

"Who is she?" Cassia asked softly as I awkwardly patted Martolia's back.

"Martolia. Merope's sister."

"Ah." Cassia came to her, gently unwinding her arms from my body. "I'm so sorry, Martolia. We will see you safely home."

Martolia turned to Cassia and flung her arms around her. Cassia started, but then gathered Martolia to her. "There now," she murmured.

I gestured for Cassia to wait with Martolia, and I left the room and took the stairs upward to find the family who'd once lived across the hall from Chryseis.

CHAPTER 10

Cold came at me as I reached the top of the building. The roofs on many insulae were full of holes, letting in wind and rain in the winter, heat in the summer. A chilly winter day meant icy dankness on the upper floors.

Both apartments were occupied, I could tell by the noise behind the doors. I thumped on one of them.

A woman yanked it open, sending me a belligerent glare that turned into a fearful recoil as she beheld me. I gazed past her at the family huddled around a flickering oil lamp but I did not see the girl among them. I held up my hand to reassure the woman and pulled the door shut for her.

I stepped across the landing and rapped on the other door. No one answered, so I pushed it open.

A smaller family gathered here. A woman and a man held a boy and the girl I'd seen at their sides, watching me as though they expected me to seize the lot of them and drag them away.

I noticed they had no furniture, nothing at all in the single room. The apartment below had held a few sticks of it, and the pallets in that bedroom had been enough for a family of four.

"When did you move up here?" I asked into the silence. The fact that they'd left their belongings below told me they meant to return, or else the move had been so recent—perhaps today—that they hadn't had time to carry the furniture upstairs.

The man cleared his throat. "A few days ago. The rent is cheaper."

He lied but I did not argue with him. "I saw your daughter downstairs earlier this morning."

The woman tugged the girl closer to her. The girl herself regarded me without alarm, as did the boy, but their parents were clearly terrified.

"She does not understand we no longer live there," the father said rapidly. "It is strange for her."

I pretended I accepted the answer. I could smell the parents' fear, which was more than that of people worried I'd come to rob them. They'd abandoned the apartment downstairs swiftly for some reason, and I could guess why. That reason put them in great danger.

"The building next door is even cheaper." I indicated the shuttered window, which blocked the view of the insula down the hill. "You should move to it, perhaps tonight. I have a friend there—name of Avitus. Tell him Leonidas sent you, and that he should find an empty room to put you in."

I held the gaze of the man until I was certain he understood me. I was not good at being subtle, but I sensed that if I baldly told the man the killer who had paid or coerced them to leave their rooms below would return for him and his family, he and his wife would panic. Better for all that they calmly did what I suggested.

The man nodded ever so slightly. I left them and went back downstairs.

Cassia had led Martolia into the stairwell. Martolia had recovered somewhat but still held on to Cassia.

I searched Chryseis's apartment until I found keys then I joined Cassia on the landing, shut the door, and locked it, securing Rufus inside. The killer must have already picked the door's lock before we'd arrived, preparing to haul Rufus's body over, which was why we'd easily gained entrance.

I started the long journey down the stairs, Cassia and Martolia behind me. At the bottom of the steps, I stopped and pounded on the shuttered window of the basketmaker's shop. He and his wife and daughter would have seen more than anyone who'd come and gone that day. Even the coppersmith, whose back had been to the street as he'd beaten on his wares, would not have witnessed as much.

After much hammering and banging, the exasperated wife at last pulled open the side door.

"We've seen no one," she answered testily to my question. "We've been asleep since we shut up shop. This is the first we've heard of any trouble at all. Murdered, you say? The gladiator?" She shook her head. "What that woman gets up to is beyond me."

She adamantly refused to say whether she'd seen anyone carrying anything inside the building. Once they closed the doors for the night, she proclaimed, they took to their beds in the back and were oblivious to whatever went on beyond their walls. They'd been awake when Cassia and I had arrived the first time, which meant they also would have been when the killer entered before us, but I recognized it would be futile to argue with her.

The basketmaker peered from the shadows in the back at Cassia, a flicker of uneasiness in his eyes, before we departed and walked away into the now-dark street.

We crossed to the Transtiberim to take Martolia home. Once inside the tiny apartment, I watched Merope and Gaius, who'd returned from the ludus, transform from excited welcome to shock to grief in the space of a moment.

The three gathered into themselves to weep, holding on to one another for comfort.

Cassia asked to remain with them while I went to the ludus to break the news to Aemil. "I can do more good here," she explained. "I will walk back home with you when you are finished."

I left her puttering about the room, pouring wine and straightening things, while the three clung to each other in bewildered sorrow.

I found Marcianus at the ludus. His face fell when I told him about Rufus, and Aemil flushed dark red with rage.

"Who in the name of all the gods is doing this?" Aemil roared. "Are they seeking vengeance on me? News of this will be all over Rome in the morning. I'll be shut down. Look what happened in Pompeii."

Not really the same thing, I wanted to point out, but a glance at Aemil told me to keep my silence. In Pompeii, a riot between rival towns had begun in the stands during gladiatorial games, which had resulted in the deaths of innocents. The official who'd planned the games had been exiled and gladiatorial combat banned in Pompeii for ten years.

"If the consuls shut me down, I'll be ruined," Aemil moaned. "The spring games are in a matter of weeks."

He blustered, but I could see that the loss of his gladiators upset him, and not only because he could no longer sell their services. Aemil considered himself a paterfamilias, feeling a responsibility to all of us. I'd learned that over the years, but of course Aemil would never openly admit it.

We again pulled his hand cart across the river, this time to the Aventine and the now quiet insula. A few of the curious inside peered around door frames but left us to the unnerving business of hauling Rufus's body, covered in whatever of Chryseis's blankets and linens we could find, down the stairs.

Marcianus requested that we take Rufus to his office so he

could examine him. Aemil growled that there was no point, but Marcianus, in his quiet way, won the argument, as usual.

Aemil and I carted Rufus there, Marcia coming out to meet us. She cleared the space in the back room where Marcianus examined patients and helped Marcianus position the body parts without a qualm.

Marcianus pointed out that Rufus too had been struck down from behind, before he ushered us out unceremoniously and began shuttering his windows for the night.

Aemil rested an arm on his cart outside, disconsolate. "How do we stop this, Leonidas? Most madmen run about tearing at their hair and shrieking, and you step aside to avoid them. But this murderer is secretive and brutal. How do you avoid a person you can't see?"

Not waiting for an answer, Aemil lifted the handles of the cart and prepared to trundle it back to the ludus.

"Is every man locked in?" I asked him as he started off.

"They are. Snarling and foul-mouthed, but yes. Except for Regulus." Aemil shot a glare back at me. "Find that bastard, Leonidas. Before *he* ends up a stack of bones."

Aemil stamped away, pulling the cart behind him, its wheels grating on the street.

Cold wind swirled around me. I very much feared that Regulus was already dead, my old comrade and now my enemy the next victim in the killer's crazed vendetta.

WHEN I REACHED MEROPE'S ROOMS IN THE TRANSTIBERIM, Cassia came down the stairs and out into the darkness to meet me.

"They are asleep," she murmured. "I mixed herbs in the wine to tire them. They'll rest at least."

"Probably easier than Chryseis will." I peered toward the river, wondering if the vigile captain had locked Chryseis in a room in his house or taken her to the Tullianum. "I am certain she did not kill Rufus. Her shock when she saw him was too great."

"Then we will have to find out who did." Cassia's voice held confidence, but then that confidence ebbed. "If we can. They are very cunning, whoever they are."

"They?"

"It must be more than one person, don't you think? Quite a task to kill a man and saw up a body and then carry it to another part of the city." Cassia shivered and drew her cloak closer about her. "It's horrible. How can they?"

"If the murderer has paid men to help him or her, those men will be hardened brigands or mercenaries. Used to anything, I imagine." I glanced down the empty street. "Let's get indoors."

The walk home was disquieting. I didn't like moving around dark Rome at the best of times, but tonight I felt additional unease. The open spaces of the city were treacherous at night, but the inky-dark lanes behind them were worse, so I pulled Cassia through wide streets, keeping well away from the pillars and dark doorways.

We reached the Quirinal in safety. The wine shop was shut up and our door was bolted, courtesy of the wine merchant.

Upstairs, we divested ourselves of cloaks, and Cassia laid out a cold meal, which we ate in silence. I knew I should be out scouring the streets for Regulus, but at the same time, I realized such a search would be futile. Either he was holed up in a lupinarius or with a lover and relatively safe, or he was already dead.

Sleep usually crashed upon me easily, as though my mind drew a cloak between myself and the world. Tonight, however, as I lay on my pallet, I couldn't close my eyes without seeing Rufus's blank stare behind the grated holes of the helmet.

Again, the question haunted me—why dress him as a Thracian instead of a myrmillo? Did the killer truly not know the difference? Or had he dressed the body in what he had on hand?

Cassia's clear thinking could help me, but I heard her soft, even breathing from her pallet across the room and knew she slept. As we'd eaten, she'd written down everything that had happened tonight, continuing to write even as she yawned uncontrollably. She was exhausted, and I didn't have the heart to wake her now.

At last, I drifted to sleep. In my dreams, I saw Regulus, his body in pieces like the others, but his eyes full of life as he snarled at me.

"I once told you to kill me," he sneered. "And now you can't save me."

I jumped awake to dim morning light and a banging on the outer door. Cassia stirred under the covers across the room, sunlight trickling through cracks in the shutters.

I dragged on a tunic and shuffled down the stairs. I opened the door at the bottom to find a very annoyed Hesiodos on the threshold.

He stared up at me, his dark hair perfectly combed, his tunic straight and unsoiled, elegant shoes of fine leather on his feet.

"You've been sent for," he said sharply.

I rubbed the sleep from my eyes. "By our benefactor?"

Hesiodos managed to exude scorn and keep his face straight at the same time. "By the *princeps*. He is furious. You are to come *at once*."

CHAPTER 11

We were out the door and on our way across Rome in a remarkably short time. The clouds that had darkened the horizon yesterday afternoon had moved in during the night, and now rain spattered down, wetting the streets. A faint mist rose, smelling of refuse.

Hesiodos, who had made it clear that Cassia was to accompany me—no argument—led us along the Sacra Via past the temple of the deified Julius Caesar and the temple of Vesta before we turned up the road that took us to the top of the Palatine Hill.

I could see that more work was being done on the Domus Transitoria that would unite the homes of Augustus, Tiberius, and Nero into one rambling building. Barrel vaults with beautiful friezes and marble floors would take Nero and his guests from one domus to the other, each being refurbished on a lavish scale.

The lauded Augustus had lived simply, I'd been told, his home large enough for his family and retainers but modestly sized and not much decorated. His successors had found his domus small and inadequate. Tiberius had built a grand structure, which Gaius and Claudius had used and Nero now restlessly enlarged.

I longed to break from Hesiodos and wander to the work site where I could speak to the builders and learn exactly how they'd finish the colonnaded walkway. Far more peaceful than facing an unpredictable *princeps* and trying to guess how he wanted me to answer his questions.

We were met by a functionary, who silently gestured us to follow him. The last time we'd entered Nero's home, we'd been escorted to an elegant anteroom and given wine. This time, we were marched straight across courtyards and through halls pierced by arched openings, deeper and deeper into the domus.

Hesiodos had vanished as soon as the functionary took charge of us, as he had on other occasions. I wondered whether Hesiodos worked for Nero's household, or if Nero's majordomo or head guard simply found Hesiodos a handy person to send on errands. I'd never learn this from Hesiodos himself, I knew, who was close-mouthed and held himself high above Cassia and me.

We were ushered into a small room with a floor tiled in a geometric pattern. The design made it appear as though we stood atop a maze of walls with staircases that sloped out of sight. An illusion in mosaic.

The chamber ended in an open balcony with columns of pink marble and a view toward the west and the Circus Maximus. Nero himself stood on the balcony, dressed in a simple linen tunic with a purple toga over it.

He turned abruptly as we entered the space, glaring so hard that Cassia immediately dropped to her hands and knees on the floor. I lowered myself as well, my palms landing on an image of steps that looked real.

Sandals whispered as the functionary who'd brought us here beat a hasty retreat. I noted other shoes in the corners, sandals and boots of attendants and guards for the leader of Rome.

"What did I wake to this morning, Leonidas the Spartan?" Nero flung the name at me in derision. "Gladiators murdered, their bodies mutilated, left in a heap to make a mockery of them. Of *me*. In *my* city." Nero swept a hand toward the open balcony. "It is all over Rome, this tale. The ordinary man is horrified, and the jaded are placing bets on which gladiator will be next."

The *princeps* approached me. I quickly bowed my head, and a pair of large feet in supple leather sandals halted before my nose. I expected one of those feet to kick me at any moment.

"Gladiators live or die at *my* whim," Nero snapped. "Do you understand this?"

I said nothing—if he wanted my answer, he'd demand it. My truthful tongue might point out that gladiators died in the arena all the time without Nero's permission, and then I definitely would be kicked.

"Who is doing this, Leonidas? Answer."

I didn't lift my head. "I do not know, lord."

The left foot twitched. I noted that Nero had someone to trim and buff his nails, which were even and neat.

The sandals then moved to Cassia. "You. Slave. You are far more intelligent than your master. Who is bent on defying me?"

Cassia remained a huddle of cloth, but her voice came forth clearly. "I do not believe the deaths are aimed at you, sir. Someone is angry at gladiators. Perhaps someone they loved died in the games."

"Hmm." The icy anger ebbed from Nero's voice. "And this is their vengeance?"

"Possibly," Cassia said.

Nero pivoted on the ball of one foot and stamped to the window. I did not dare turn my head and gaze directly at Cassia, lest one of the guards did the kicking on Nero's behalf.

Nero's voice drifted to us. "They leave one body in the Subura, another on the Aventine. Are they mocking the plebs who love the games?"

"All attend the games, from plebeians to senators," Cassia was brave enough to say.

I wished she would not speak. I wasn't certain what I'd do if a guard struck her down for her boldness. I'd likely seize his sword and kill him, and then I'd be thrown from the balcony, down, down, toward the circus where I'd fought in bouts that had made me a champion.

My mind dredged up the memory of the day I'd been pitted against Xerxes in the Circus Maximus. I'd gone easy on him and had been wounded by the gleeful Xerxes, who'd then taken me out drinking all night afterward. Aemil had shouted at me long and hard as Marcianus had stitched up my wounds, for letting Xerxes get past my guard. Xerxes and I had never been opponents again, but I still remembered staggering home with him after drinking off the bout, holding each other up. He'd met his wife that night.

Nero walked back toward us, his steps less abrupt. "You are perhaps right. This has been done by someone who wants to disrupt the games, maybe to rid himself of those gladiators who might kill his champion." Nero let out a breath, now sounding more like an ordinary person having a conversation than a ruler demanding answers. "Or it is a madman, conducting executions himself for his own crazed reasons. Well, it must stop." Some steel returned to him. "Do rise, Leonidas. I cannot talk to you with your head on the floor."

I slowly pushed myself up but remained kneeling, my backside on my heels, not wanting to anger Nero by towering over him. Cassia adopted a similar posture.

"You uncovered an assassin after me before." Nero rested one hand on his hip, his wrist encased in a jeweled armband. "Did what all my Praetorian guards and my personal servants could not." He flashed a derisive glance around the room, and I heard feet shift uncomfortably. "I command you to do so again."

I decided not to argue that there was no evidence this killer targeted Nero, but then again, we did not know for certain. It might be, as Nero said, an attempt to make the *princeps* look incompetent and in a roundabout way, rid Rome of him.

Nero wanted an answer, so I inclined my head. "I will do my best, sir."

"You will do more than your best. You will find this killer and bring him to me. The courts will decide his fate, which will not be pleasant. Shall I assign a man to assist you?"

I hesitated. I did not want an agent of Nero's breathing over my shoulder, arresting any person I spoke to or had already spoken to. That meant Chryseis, Merope and her family, and possibly Herakles's lover Domitiana, the basketmaker, and the impoverished family at the top of Chryseis's insula.

"No need." I tried to sound humble and deferential. "But it might help to let me talk to Rufus's wife. She was arrested last night, but she did not commit this crime. She might have seen who did, even without realizing it."

"Rufus was a good swordsman," Nero said nostalgically. "Didn't have the form you did, but he was spirited and fought with all his heart." He trailed off in sorrow. Many patrician Romans disdained Nero for his vast enjoyment of the gladiatorial games, chariot races, the theatre, and musical entertainment, but the lower orders liked a ruler who shared their enthusiasm.

Nero snapped back to the present. "I will have her released. But question her closely. Better still, have Cassia question her."

Nero had been taken with Cassia upon their first meeting, when she'd admired his musical selections. He'd recognized immediately that Cassia had a quicker mind than I did.

I bowed my head in acquiescence, as did Cassia. Nero returned to me, feet close together in a perfect line.

"If I am waspish today, Leonidas, it is because I do not like disorder in my city. To discover that a killer has been wiping out gladiators—strong men and trained fighters—does not please me. That you did not tell me of this right away does not please me either." His toes curled in the sandals, tight sinews of irritation. "Find this man, and tell me immediately who he is. Find him before he kills again. He might even target *you*."

Nero barked a laugh, and I ventured to glance up at him. He wasn't looking at me but at the far wall, his lips twisted in ironic mirth.

"I shouldn't like to lose you, Leonidas. I might have need of you ..."

He trailed off, then took a smart step back. "Leave me now." His tone returned to brisk annoyance. "Do not return until you bring me the killer."

Nero marched out between Cassia and me as we returned our faces to the tile. The hem of his toga brushed my shoulder, bathing me in the scent of sweat-touched wool.

Cassia and I remained abased while the guards marched out around us, followed by the scurrying attendants. We didn't raise our heads until Hesiodos's voice told us dryly that everyone had gone and it was time to leave.

———

BEFORE WE DESCENDED THE PALATINE, I TOOK HESIODOS aside and asked him what I had thought about regarding Cassia. Hesiodos frowned at me but I made him promise to inquire.

Cassia eyed me curiously once we rejoined her, but I waved her off, telling her it was not important. Hesiodos deserted us at the bottom of the hill, and Cassia and I returned home.

Once there, Cassia glumly hung up her cloak. "If we do not find this killer we might have to flee Rome." She paused reflectively. "I suppose life in exile wouldn't be so bad, depending on where we go."

I tried to feel mirth at her statement, but Cassia watched me in all seriousness. She did not joke. The *princeps* might well punish us if we did not do what he wished.

"*How* do we find him?" I dragged my stool to the wall, plunked myself onto it, and stretched out my legs. My sandals were coated with mud from our walk, nowhere near as pristine as Nero's, which had probably been made to be worn only indoors. "He flits through the Subura unseen and lurks in a crowded insula with no one the wiser."

"The family that moved upstairs ..." Cassia pulled out her

tablets and read through them until she found her notes on what we'd discovered last night. "They must have been told to vacate the apartment. They've seen the killer or at least whoever transported the body."

"They might tell me about him, if they are frightened enough." I curled my toes, unable to imagine sitting still while someone buffed my feet. "I hope they took my advice and sought Avitus and another home."

"They have children—I imagine they'll do what they must to protect them."

"Maybe." I did not explain to Cassia about poor and wretched parents who sold their children into slavery or to lupinari in order to pay paralyzing debts.

"Chryseis too might have met this killer," Cassia said. "Perhaps some of her fright at finding Rufus is because of such knowledge. We should question her, as the *princeps* commanded."

"True," I conceded. "I also must find Regulus."

I worried very much for the idiot. Regulus believed himself indestructible, but I did not want to find his lifeless eyes peering at me through a provacatur's helmet.

Too many things to think about and to do. I wasn't sure where to start.

"We should visit Chryseis first," Cassia said as though understanding my befuddlement. "Find out what she did all of yesterday. She might have seen something or someone without understanding that person's actions." A crease appeared between her brows. "I must wonder why the killer chose to leave Rufus's body in her apartment. To terrify her specifically? There was no love between the two if Rufus constantly sought solace with Merope and her sister. There was real affection for Rufus in Merope's house, even love. I could see that when I was with them last night."

"Maybe the killer didn't know Rufus strayed. Or he wanted to upset Chryseis personally." I touched a callus on the palm of my hand, finding dust from the floor of Nero's domus on it. "She is not a kind woman."

"That would mean he did not know much about Rufus and Chryseis at all," Cassia said. "Apparently it was common gossip that he had other lovers. Which brings me back to the question —why take his body to her?"

"As Nero stated, he's a madman killing gladiators for sport." I finished dusting off my hands and pressed them together.

Cassia perused her notes once more. "Merope and Martolia are dancers," she said. "Gaius plays the drum for them. They're hired for suppers and other celebrations."

I hadn't known this. "They said Gaius worked in the popina below their rooms."

"He does. But he takes the night off when the girls are hired, and gives the popina owner a small amount of what they earn as compensation."

Rich men—and women—could afford to employ dancers at a supper. "Whenever I was commanded to appear at a villa or domus, there would often be musicians and dancers there as well."

Cassia raised her head. "I wonder if this person who fed Ajax his last meal had dancers at the supper."

"If so, those dancers might be in danger," I said in concern.

"Perhaps not. I doubt the killing happened before an audience, or we'd have heard about *that* by now. I wonder if Merope or Martolia could discover if any dancers were present at the supper, which would lead us to the exact house." Her stylus moved again, quick marks on the wax. "We should also inquire around the Subura. Ajax might have boasted about where he was heading to on his last night."

"Not we," I said in a mild tone. "I will ask around the Subura and talk to Chryseis when she is released. You will stay here and bolt the door behind me."

Cassia's head came up, the stubborn flash I'd already come to recognize in her eyes. "You heard Nero. He told me to question

Chryseis and for us to find this killer—quickly. I cannot help you if I am confined indoors. I would be right beside you, in any case, not racing off to inquire in brothels or the homes of murderers by myself."

"You were eager to rush alone to Domitiana's villa," I said.

"Only because I know Helvius and other of her servants. I hadn't intended to confront the lady herself. *You* did that." She sent me a pointed glance. "And besides, Nonus Marcianus went with me."

"Because he believed you foolish for going alone." My statement ended in a growl.

Cassia laid down her stylus. "You going alone to all these places is a bad idea as well. This killer is after gladiators, remember? And you are the most famous one in Rome."

"Used to be." I looked up at the wooden *rudis* on the shelf. "Now I am only Leonidas." And I wasn't truly Leonidas but had another name that had faded into dust.

"The murderer might not make that distinction."

I spread my fingers. "I am a trained fighter. If a wealthy man suddenly springs hired thugs on me, I will be able to defend myself. What could you do?"

Cassia had helped me in a fight once, smacking my attacker with her bag of scrolls. It had almost been her end.

"I can scream for help, or run for a cohort," Cassia declared. "I would also be a witness."

"A witness who could end up dead. Silenced forever." I came to my feet, anger and worry roiling together. "You will stay here, and I will question. I command it."

Cassia only ever gave me blank stares on the rare occasion I gave her a direct order. I'd been a slave a long time, and before that, a lowly apprentice, more used to receiving commands than giving them. I had not learned the skill of authority.

"Very well." Her answer was meek, suspiciously so.

I did not wait for her to argue. Cassia was excellent at arguing, talking me into her way of thinking before I realized it. Had she been a man and free-born, she'd have found a fine career as an orator and advocate. She'd have talked rings around the great Cicero, and it was only because of Cassia that I knew who the man had been.

I left her before I could ruin the moment and thumped my way downstairs and out into the rainy street.

ONCE ON THE AVENTINE, I ASKED THE WAY TO THE HOUSE OF the vigiles and arrived to find the captain had gone to bed when his shift ended hours ago.

When I inquired after Chryseis, the vigile who'd admitted me to the house shuddered. "That woman Captain Vatia brought in last night? Beautiful as a goddess, heart of a basilisk?"

"Is she still here?" I demanded.

"Word came not long ago that we had to release her. Thank all the gods." The vigile shrugged. "She lit out without a farewell, though we gave her the best bed and fed her dinner. Ungrateful bitch. She went home, I'd guess."

I thanked the young man for his information and departed the house.

Chryseis's insula was noisy with neighbors shouting to one another, or families arguing behind closed doors, and children shrieking or laughing. The basketmaker, his wife, and daughter sat in their places, eyes on their tasks. The coppersmith hammered away, bent over his anvil. Nothing at all might have happened here last night.

The basketmaker's family did not glance up as I peered in. Either they did not notice me or they wanted nothing further to do with me.

I climbed the staircase I'd gone up and down so many times last night until I reached the landing on the fifth floor. The door to the apartment where the girl had lived was firmly shut, and I heard nothing from above.

Chryseis's door was open. I paused on the threshold.

Open crates filled the front room, piled with Chryseis's belongings. She charged out from the back room followed by a thin young man with overly long curling hair, his arms full of fabric.

"I told you to put them in *there*," Chryseis snapped at him. She caught sight of me and came to an abrupt halt. "What do *you* want? Haven't you caused me enough trouble already?"

"Who is he, love?" The young man scrutinized me curiously. He had a narrow face, long limbs, and dark eyes that held no guile.

"Another gladiator," Chryseis snarled. "I'm done with gladiators. Go away, Leonidas."

"Leonidas, eh?" The young man dumped his load of cloth into an open crate and good-naturedly took me in. "I've heard of you. I'm Daphnus. Chryseis's husband."

CHAPTER 12

"Husband?" I stared, dumbfounded, then turned to Chryseis. "I thought Rufus was your husband."

"*Was,*" Chryseis said decidedly. "He's dead now. After today, my husband will be Daphnus."

Daphnus sent me a grin. "Fortuna smiles upon me."

Chryseis stamped past him for the bedroom. I stepped closer to Daphnus and asked in a quiet voice, "Are you certain you want to marry her?"

His grin widened. "Why not? She's rich, she's beautiful ... My father thinks I'm good for nothing, but now I'll be worth more than he is." He let out a happy cackle.

"How long have you known her?"

"Six months," Daphnus answered without hesitation. "Met her at a chariot race, like any good student of the *Ars Amatoria*." He beamed at me as though I understood what he meant. "She kept telling me she'd divorce old Rufus someday but that she liked having a handsome gladiator on her arm. Served as a bodyguard for her too. But now he's gone, poor fellow."

"Did you kill him?" I remained solidly in front of the door so he could not run, but the question amused him.

"I? Strike down a large gladiator? I am more apt to write an elegy for the man than fight him. If I'd tried to engage him, I'd be a pool of nothing on the bottom floor of this building." He chortled.

"Where were you yesterday?" I persisted.

"While the foul deed was being done? It was rather awful, Chryseis told me. Scared her senseless." Daphnus touched his lower lip. "Let me think. I spent the morning quarreling with my father, as per usual. He has a fine house on the Viminal, where he pretends he is a patrician. He is not, of course. He's a freedman, but he has much money, courtesy of the man for whom he used to be a slave. Ran the man's silk cloth import business for him, and now my dear pater has his own. I am a useless blot on his life, apparently, and have been cut from my inheritance. We argue about this regularly. My mother, bless her, has been gone these last dozen years, or she'd have something to say about how my father treats me. *She* had something to say about everything. After my father and I decided we'd never speak to each other again—as we do every day—I went to the baths. Later, I met Chryseis in the hole that I call my home, and we ... well, you know. She ran off when she was finished with me, which was at sunset. Then I hear, via my one servant, who is a useless blot on *my* life, that Chryseis had been arrested—for the murder of Rufus. But happily released, and now we can be together forever."

Daphnus wound down from this speech with a contented sigh.

If he told the truth, then Chryseis had gone to him late in the afternoon, after she'd spoken to me. She'd been returning from his flat, wherever it was, when she'd walked in and seen Rufus dead.

"Not if you don't get in here and help me," Chryseis yelled from the bedroom. She appeared in the doorway, having heard every word. "Begone from my insula, Leonidas, before I summon the cohorts to drag you out."

"Did you kill Rufus?" I asked her abruptly.

Her scowl deepened. "Of course I didn't. I wanted to be rid of the lout, yes, but I had simpler ways to dispose of him. He was only a gladiator. Easy to have the marriage legally ended in the courts. I can afford it."

I believed her. She had no need to commit a gruesome murder to end her marriage, and no reason at all to kill Ajax in the bargain. She did not strike me as a crazed woman murdering gladiators for sport. Angry and cold, yes, certain that everyone she spoke to was far less intelligent than she was, yes, but not a madwoman.

I turned from her and addressed Daphnus, "I wish you the best on your marriage."

"Thank you." Daphnus's grin returned. "The wedding feast will be one of great decadence. Perhaps, love, we should invite Leonidas to give an exhibition bout at the supper. The guests would enjoy it."

"No." Her one word cut off any possibility. "Good day, Leonidas."

Daphnus sent me a helpless shrug but turned his gaze admiringly to Chryseis. I silently fished out the key I'd taken from this apartment the night before and dropped it into the glaring Chryseis's hand. I wondered if she'd had a spare key to enter today, and if she'd left that key with Daphnus. Or perhaps the basketmaker, a man she might trust more.

I silently wished Daphnus and Chryseis well in their marriage and departed.

I CALLED IN TO SEE MARCIANUS BEFORE I LEFT THE AVENTINE. He was more subdued than usual. He'd examined Rufus and found that he too had been fed a luxurious meal, including gold leaf, before he'd been felled from behind. Marcianus was on his way to the ludus now to tell Aemil he could come fetch the body.

I left him in disquiet and moved on with my next errand.

The Subura was a different place by day. More businesses were open, including a few entire buildings dedicated to shops. The lupinari were quieter, but it was late enough in the morning that several were open.

I entered the one Ajax had last visited before he went off to his fate.

The lady in charge was even less happy to see me today than she had been two nights ago. This time, however, the lupinarius was less busy, and I persuaded her to let me speak to the young woman who had been with Ajax.

I had to pay twice the going rate, because, the madam snapped, I was not a customer, just a nosy man. Thankful that Cassia kept my coin pouch full these days, I handed over the price.

The young woman yawned on a bunk in her cubicle, as I'd interrupted her sleep. A tunic slid down her arm, baring a grubby shoulder. She'd been to a hairdresser recently, but the black curls of her coiffure were greasy and drooping.

"Poor Ajax," the young woman said mournfully. "He wasn't the gentlest of men, but he didn't deserve *that*. Gives me chills, it does, thinking about it. And me with him just before."

Her pity was genuine. "Did he say where he was going when he left here?" I asked, keeping the urgency from my voice.

The young woman shook her head, curls that had been pinned into a tight cone atop her head dancing. "Only that he was off to have a splendid meal in a place far better than this hovel. That could mean anywhere."

"Did he mention a name? Or whether he went to see a man or woman?" I recalled Marcia telling me that Ajax enjoyed the company of highborn men, preferably senator's sons, when he wasn't with ladies in the Subura.

"A woman, I think, though I'm not sure why I say that." She drew her knees to her chest, her short tunic baring her legs to her hip. "No, wait, I do. He said that it was worth the annoyance to lie on *her* dining couch. I imagine he expected a large reward for his trouble."

"He did not like the woman he was going to visit?"

"Not a matter of liking or not liking. Ajax was no different from me, I suppose—or you. He did what he had to in order to put a few sestertii in his coin purse. Except, in this case, it would more likely be denarii. Ajax was saving to buy his freedom. He wanted to go back to Pannonia, to see if any of his family were still alive. I don't know where Pannonia is, but a long way from here I think."

"A very long way." Not as far as some of the regions in Germania, or where Cassia's father had lived in Smyrna, but it was in the wild part of the empire, with plenty of crazed barbarians ready to swoop down and murder those Romans who had been posted there.

"Ajax didn't mind being a gladiator," the young woman went on. "Liked his fame. But really, he wanted to go home."

I thought about the man I'd known only slightly, full of bravado, a fighter who always won. Ruthless, with a killing instinct. Aemil had to constantly tell Ajax to put on a show and not simply go for the throat. Ajax had reined himself in with difficulty.

Now he was dead, struck down without a chance to defend himself.

I wondered if the food and wine he'd been given had been poisoned. A concoction that would weaken him or make him sleepy would give the murderer a great advantage.

I couldn't imagine Ajax being unaware of an attacker coming up behind him no matter how drunk he might be. Rufus even less so. The helmets we wore blocked our view except straight ahead, so we were trained to sense where our enemy was at all times. The whisper of breath, the scrape of a foot on sand, even the creak of a joint as a man bent his knee, betrayed his position. I'd been aware of the brush of air as my opponent moved or the warmth of his body as he neared me.

Ajax, trained by Aemil, and one of the better gladiators in the ludus, would never have let himself be hit from behind if he weren't dosed with something to make him insensible.

The young woman looked sad for Ajax. I handed her a sestertii, whispered to her to keep it for herself, and left the house.

I returned to our rooms to find Cassia laying out a meal, complete with fresh bread.

"I did not take your command to remain indoors to mean we should not eat," Cassia said as she serenely ladled stew into bowls. "I went only to the baker's and the popina."

I hung up my cloak without a word and plunked myself down on my stool, reaching for a hunk of bread. I had known Cassia wouldn't cower here obediently, but I also knew she was—usually—sensible.

I tore off a hunk of bread and chewed, enjoying the airy texture and slightly sour taste. Cassia always managed to procure fine loaves, mostly because the baker was afraid of her. He was afraid of me too, but mostly of Cassia.

As I chewed, I told her what Marcianus had found from examining Rufus's body. While Cassia duly noted this down, I added, "Chryseis is married. Or is getting married. Today."

"What?" Cassia blinked wide eyes, her stylus halting. "To whom?"

"A witless man called Daphnus. Father is a wealthy freedman." I related the conversation I'd had with him.

"Did he tell you the name of his father?" Cassia asked when I'd finished. "I wonder how wealthy he truly is. Though I imagine Chryseis knows exactly how much the young man is worth."

"He said his father has cut him off." I slurped stew, sopping it with bread. Rushing around Rome and interviewing people, coupled with the sadness of the reason, had made me hungry.

"Marrying a wealthy and comely wife might restore him to his father's graces," Cassia said. "Chryseis no doubt hopes for this—or maybe she knows that she can talk his father around.

From how you describe her, she does not strike me as a woman who would marry for the sentiment of it."

"No affection in her," I agreed. "Daphnus is dazzled by her, and I imagine Rufus was too."

"Rufus was a freedman, is that correct?"

I nodded as I stuffed stew and bread into my mouth. My stomach kept growling, even as I filled it. "He came to Aemil voluntarily. He was in much debt and sold himself to Aemil to pay off his creditors. Then he earned enough in prize money to buy back his freedom but negotiated with Aemil to stay on even after that. He liked being famous."

"That fame attracted Chryseis to him, no doubt. Not to mention the prize money."

I shrugged. "Rufus could never have made as much as a freedman's son whose father owns a large silk importing business."

Silk was costly. It was brought in from lands far to the east that no one had ever seen, as pale, rather thick cloth. Importers had the cloth unwoven into silk threads, then rewoven and dyed into colors Romans preferred—red, gold, deep blues, and greens. Only the very wealthy, like Domitiana, could afford to wear silk.

"Chryseis must have discovered too late that Rufus didn't have as much as she believed," Cassia said. "He probably exaggerated his worth." Rufus had been a braggart, so that was entirely possible. "Even if she didn't need his money, having much herself, she likely wanted to add to her coffers. Perhaps she simply craves wealth."

"She is a cold-hearted woman," I said when my mouth was finally clear again.

"But very beautiful." Cassia watched me, her eyes still.

I considered this. "She is like a statue, perfectly sculpted and painted. I enjoy looking at statuary in gardens, but once I walk away from them, I forget all about them. Chryseis is like that, except with a sharp tongue. The young woman I spoke with in the lupinarius was not pretty at all, but I was far happier talking to her than Chryseis. She felt sorry for Ajax—did even before he died. He was homesick, she said."

Having stated my views, I returned to my stew.

After a moment, I realized that Cassia had gone very silent. I glanced up to find her regarding me with soft eyes, a smile on her lips.

"You are a good man, Leonidas."

So she'd said before. I did not find much remarkable in myself, so I continued my meal without comment.

When we were finished, Cassia cleared the plates, taking them to the balcony to wash them. I never saw the point in this as we'd just use them again, but I did not argue.

She brought the plates inside and stacked them on the cabinet. "Perhaps we should have a peep at Chryseis's warehouse," she said. "A warehouse would be an excellent place to hide a corpse."

"But Chryseis did not murder Rufus, we agreed."

"Yes, but what if she killed Ajax?" Cassia traced the cover of one of her tablets in thought. "Or had him killed by men she hired? Suppose she didn't pay the men, or she angered them. She's a demanding and unpleasant woman. What if they decided to take their revenge by killing her husband in the same fashion as they killed her first victim? As a warning? It would explain why she was so horrified, as all facts show she never cared for Rufus."

"A cruel thing for Rufus," I said feelingly. "We still have the same problem—how did the killers strike him down? Rufus was an even better fighter than Ajax."

Cassia's gaze went remote as she thought. "Suppose Rufus took part in the murder of Ajax. The ruffians would not only use Rufus's death to terrify Chryseis but also to rid themselves of a witness."

"Possible. But then we come back to why Chryseis should want to kill Ajax."

Cassia heaved a sigh. "I know we do. These murders make no

sense. A madman, I conclude, as Nero has, but one very calculating and precise. I can think of no compelling reason for a person to kill either Ajax or Rufus."

"We can't know why," I said. "We should concentrate on finding out who. Why doesn't matter."

"But knowing the why can lead us to the who. Is he—or she—finished? Or are all gladiators in danger? Is the killer enraged at gladiators? Or fascinated by them? Is he trying to show power over fighting men who could easily kill anyone they face, and yet are killed themselves?"

Such things were beyond me. Cassia was the sort who pondered questions like a philosopher.

She continued, "Why were they given a fine meal beforehand? To relax their diligence? Or is it a ritual of some sort?"

"Gladiators are given a feast the night before the games. The *cena libera.*" I'd never been able to eat much at them, not wanting to dull my senses with meat and wine.

"Interesting." Cassia opened the tablet in front of her and wrote with quick strokes. "It could very well be a ritual. A gladiator's blood is meant to heal, as you told me. They might be collecting such blood to heal a loved one, or for good luck. We never find blood with the corpses. Perhaps they gave Ajax and Rufus a good meal beforehand as a sort of apology."

I was not convinced. "If so, why cut the bodies to pieces, dress them, and leave them for others to find? No, this person is cruel, and crazed."

Cassia released another breath. "I am simply trying out ideas. I still would like a look at Chryseis's warehouse."

I would as well. I did not want Cassia to come with me, but she was already bundling up a few tablets into her bag. I knew she'd find her way there with or without my permission, so as usual, I took her with me so I could keep my eyes upon her.

The rain had ended and the day had warmed slightly, but it was dank as we crossed the wet stones and moved through the crowded Forum Romanum and along the Vicus Tuscus to the

Forum Bovarium. Beyond the cattle market, along the river, lay the Emporium and its vast warehouses.

Boats pulled in and out from the banks of the Tiber as we walked along it, disgorging wares brought up the river from Ostia Antica, shipped there from ports all over the world.

The Porticus Aemilia drew my eye as it always did when I ventured this far down the river. It could not help but draw anyone's eye, as the huge warehouse was one of the largest of such structures in all of Rome.

Fifty barrel vaults ran down its length, with four vaulted levels stair-stepping crosswise up the riverbank. The warehouse had been fashioned entirely of concrete, the ceilings formed by constructing wooden supports inside the walls and the concrete poured over the frame. When the concrete dried and the supports were pulled away, the vaulted ceilings stood.

The master builder I'd worked for had brought me here when I'd been an ungainly lad, explaining the techniques as proudly as if he'd built the Porticus himself.

More warehouses flanked the area, including one that was under construction, workers laying bricks that would eventually be covered with concrete. I wanted to linger and watch, but we needed to find Chryseis's storehouse.

Cassia discovered it by heading for the nearest well and asking a woman who drew water there where it was.

She returned to me, triumphant. "There." She pointed to a smaller warehouse resting on the bank of the Tiber south of where we stood. "Chryseis owns the entire building, but she rents out half of it and uses the other half for her own wares."

Impressed with Cassia's knowledge, I led the way along the river. The area was chaotic, wagons moving from docks to warehouses, small ships and barges being emptied and loaded by shouting teams of men. While deliveries were forbidden to be made within the walls of Rome in the daylight hours, plenty of goods moved to and fro outside them, many to be stored in the warehouses before they were distributed later that night.

Chryseis's warehouse lay near a quieter dock, with no barges tethered there. In fact, the entire area was too silent for my taste. The building we headed for had been built near the tall hill formed by discarded and broken pottery. It loomed high, a strange mound made of used amphorae.

"People have been adding to this pile for the last seventy or more years," I told Cassia as she regarded the hill in wonder. Very likely her previous excursions to Rome hadn't included the Emporium and the area around it.

Cassia stared at the hill of broken pots until I turned her away to Chryseis's warehouse.

The building was a miniature of the Porticus Aemilia. Two barrel vaults led back into the hill, one side of the warehouse open to the river. Men worked in one of the vaults, unloading a wagon. They barely noted us as we walked into the other side of the warehouse, which was mostly empty.

Crates, boxes, and baskets stood on the back walls, with shelves holding smaller items. Amphorae were embedded into the dirt floor, their buried pointed ends keeping them upright.

The air was damp, smelling of mud, river, and rain-soaked concrete walls. Chryseis herself was not there—I was not expecting her to be—but she'd left no guard to keep others out. I wondered if even thieves were afraid to steal from her.

"Leonidas?" A familiar voice sounded at my back. "It *is* you. Well met, well met, indeed. Perhaps you can help me?"

CHAPTER 13

Cassia brightened, and I turned to behold the *architectus*, Gnaeus Gallus.

"Why are you here?" I asked, unsure how to greet him.

Gallus regarded me good-naturedly. He was small and thin, his dark hair thick but graying. He wore a fine linen tunic, and as he had the first time I'd met him, let his loosely draped toga drag on the floor.

"I have been hired to build a warehouse," Gallus said proudly. "Not a monumental one, of course, but one that will sit directly next to this. An importer wishes to expand and needs more space for the goods."

Chryseis's new husband's father was an importer. Had Chryseis decided to build a warehouse for when Daphnus took over his father's business? Or was she trying to wrest part of that business from the family by marrying into them?

"What is the name of this importer?" I asked. From Cassia's expression, she had the same idea.

"Tertius Vestalis Felix." Gallus chuckled. "His cognomen means luck. I suppose he is to have married so much money."

Cassia stiffened. The name was familiar to me, but for the moment, I could not place it.

"Does everyone marry for wealth?" I asked distractedly. Rufus had, but also presumably for beauty. My friend Xerxes had found a woman he loved, and though he'd not been able to marry her legally, they'd called each other husband and wife. They'd been together for affection and joy.

Gallus observed me with amusement. "The wealthy do. They must keep all that lovely money in the family. And hire builders to give them more storage space so that they can make more. It will be a large project." He eyed me in eagerness. "Now, as to what you can do for me. Would you like a place on my construction team? I could use someone who was trained in building. I can try you out, see what you know, perhaps make you a foreman if we rub along well."

A tingle rushed through my body, one similar to that when I'd waited to step out under the shouting masses and begin a fight, but this one was accompanied by a wave of pleasure. I hadn't felt such a thing in so long I had to take a step back.

I wanted what Gallus offered more than anything. To be at a building site, helping plan how the work proceeded each day, watching the structure take shape, knowing my hands had guided the stones or laid the brick ... It would give me a sense of purpose, fulfill me in a way I hadn't been in many years. I'd be a real person again.

At the same time, the idea was terrifying. One of the greatest tragedies of my life had occurred at a building site. Another had taken place in an amphitheater, and both times I'd lost someone dear to me.

I wanted what Gallus offered, and at the same time, wanted to thrust it away with dizzying force.

"Do consider it," Gallus said, noting my hesitation. "I'd be the talk of Rome, with my gladiator who knows all about structural forces."

"I will think it over." I swallowed, unable to explain. "When will you start?"

"A few weeks from now. That is, if we can clear the site.

There are always complications. Owners not giving permission until the last possible moment, marshy patches that have to be drained, any soft soil dug away, and there is always a spot that is sacred to *someone*, or was sacred to them several hundred years in the past. Not that I want to offend a god or the ancestors." Gallus touched the wall he stood next to as though to appease any gods hanging about the place.

A few weeks would give me time to ponder. I could see Gallus was disappointed that I did not accept right away, but he didn't pursue the topic.

"Why are you here, Leonidas?" Gallus asked breezily. "Retrieving a shipment?"

I paused a mere instant before deciding to tell him the truth. Gallus had proved to be trustworthy and helpful in the past. "Discovering if someone was killed here."

Gallus blinked and then glanced about wildly, as though ready to run. "Killed *here*?" He let out a breath. "By the gods, Leonidas, you were looking into a death the first time I met you. Is it your profession now?"

"Gladiators are being hunted. My lanista asked for my help."

"Gladiators ... oh, yes, I heard about the one who was found in the insula. Limbs and blood everywhere. My, my." Gallus wiped his forehead with the frayed end of his toga. "Too awful for me. It's one thing for gladiators to battle each other in the games—which I care not to watch—quite another for one to be killed in a person's home."

Cassia broke in. "Whatever tale you've heard is an exaggeration. There was no blood and the body was quite neat. We are searching for where he actually was killed."

A man of the Equestrian class could strike a slave for speaking to him without leave, but Gallus only regarded her thoughtfully.

"Why do you search here, young Cassia?" he asked in curiosity. "If murderers are lurking about the Emporium, I hardly want to start work on my site in such a lonely spot."

Cassia indicated the space around us with a slim hand. "The dead man's wife owns this warehouse."

"And you think she killed him? Is that likely?" Gallus scrubbed the top of his head, his toga still clutched in his hand. "A woman could hardly murder a great hulking gladiator, could she?" He shifted his gaze between Cassia and me as though trying to imagine her sending me to the ground.

"Not without help," I said.

"Or the killers used this warehouse to point at Chryseis," Cassia supplied in her quiet voice.

"How horrible." Gallus touched the wall in an appeasing way again. "Have you found anything?"

"Not yet." I turned away, wanting to finish the search as soon as possible. The air here chilled me and not because of the cool weather outside.

I left Gallus and Cassia and moved to the far end of the warehouse. Its roof had been formed similarly to the one at the Porticus Aemilia—two vaults stepped up the hill, with an open space at the top of the walls of the second vault to provide light.

Even so, I wished I'd brought a lamp. Flame was dangerous in a warehouse, but with the rainy weather today, it was difficult to see into the corners without extra illumination.

But no matter how much I scoured the floor, I found no damp patches at all, no water, no blood. The shelves were neat and mostly bare, as though Chryseis sold her shipments on as soon as she received them. Goods sitting on shelves brought in no money, I supposed, and Chryseis was the sort who'd demand payment as soon as possible.

Not until I reached a gathering of crates on the left side of the building did I find signs of a disturbance. Mud had been tracked in liberally by workers throughout the warehouse, but this section had been scraped clean. I bent down and lifted from the floor a tiny object pushed against the corner of a crate.

It was a feather, broken and limp. I brushed mud from it with my fingers.

The feather hadn't come from a bird, at least, not recently. The plume was the distinct glossy black of a gladiator's helmet.

Cassia, with her uncanny knack of knowing when something was amiss, was beside me in a moment, her warm breath brushing my arm.

"It is like the other I found," she said in excitement. Different color, but same shape and thickness.

I clenched the feather, trying to remain calm. "Chryseis might have been shipping in plumage to sell to helmet makers."

Cassia sent me a skeptical look. "The chances of a feather dropped here matching the one in the insula, and both matching the ones in Rufus's helmet, are too great to be ignored. Where would the killer find a gladiator helmet, in any case?"

"From Aemil?" I suggested. "He keeps the gear for the games locked away. It's costly."

"Aemil would notice if some went missing, wouldn't he? And know if the ones on Ajax and Rufus came from his storeroom?"

Aemil had said nothing about it, but perhaps he'd been too unsettled to check. The equipment hadn't looked familiar to me, but I didn't pay attention to anyone else's gear except to look for weak spots on my opponent.

"If the armor was stolen from Aemil that would mean someone at the ludus is involved." I felt ill as I said this. We always knew we'd be expected to battle one another in the games, yes, but in a fair fight. Not render a fellow gladiator insensible, kill him, and leave his pieces around Rome. Degraded, dishonored.

"I didn't see Ajax's body," Cassia said. "But Rufus's helmet and greaves looked new, not battered from bouts."

I opened my hand to stare down at the feather. It was crisp and bright in spite of the mud, no sand from the arena caught in its spikes.

Gallus, who'd followed Cassia, peered at the feather with interest. "Where does your lanista acquire all the gear? Or is it donated by whoever sponsors the games?"

"He orders from an armorer called Volteius," I kept my gaze on the black quill. "Aemil tells him exactly what to make to fit each of us."

"You could always pay him a visit," Gallus said. "Find out whoever ordered the equipment, and there is your killer." He finished, pleased with himself.

A good idea, but I wasn't as confident. The killer could hire men to do anything for him or her, and hired men were not always easy to trace.

"Aemil's armorer is in the Transtiberim," I said. "Not far over the river."

"I will walk with you if you are going there now," Gallus said. "I don't fancy staying where a man might have been murdered."

There was nothing to indicate whether Rufus had been killed at this spot or only butchered, if even that. Or perhaps the helmet and greaves had merely been stored here. Lugging Rufus in and out would have involved a large cart and much secrecy.

I did not object to Gallus accompanying us, and we left the warehouse and headed up the river for the Pons Sublicius. No one in the other half of the warehouse noted us leaving or asked our business. They went on with hauling things in and out, oblivious. Not until we reached the Porticus Aemilia did I see guards, but except for a glance at me, they did not stop us.

If this was the usual state of things at the warehouses, then likely no one had paid any mind to those lugging Rufus there the day before. Chryseis's warehouse was out of the way, out of sight of the usual Emporium traffic, and her tenants in the other half of her warehouse seemed content to mind their own business.

The house of the armorer who turned out leg greaves and helmets for gladiators and breastplates for legionnaires lay near the western edge of the Transtiberim, where hills gave way to marsh. The sound of hammers pounding on bronze reached us long before we turned up at the house's gate.

Smoke rolled out from somewhere in the courtyard, and a

bony young man, an apprentice, opened up to our knock. The lad recognized me and grinned.

"Have you come to outfit yourself for exhibition bouts?" he asked eagerly. "You're a champion, Leonidas. You had Regulus without a doubt in your last fight. Say you haven't truly retired."

"I have," I said, then softened my tone at his disappointment. "I still train at the bath houses, though. A man never knows when he'll need to fight."

"I hope you're back in an arena soon. Why are you here, then, if you're not buying armor?"

"To see your master about armor he made for someone else."

The youth gave me a puzzled look but gestured for me to follow him. Gallus shuffled behind me, glancing with interest at the breastplates, helmets, and assorted arm, leg, hand, and foot guards that were lying on benches, shelves, and tables around the courtyard in various stages of production. Men stripped to the waist worked metal both in the courtyard and in open-fronted sheds.

"Beautiful things." Gallus paused to admire a shin guard that had been embossed with the portrait of a reclining goddess. "Made for deadly combat, but works of art."

"My master is the best," the lad said proudly.

I watched a man fashioning what must be a sword. He pounded and pounded the edge with a hammer, then heated the metal in a pit of fire before laying it aside to cool slowly. Unlike iron, which was worked when molten, bronze would crack if the metal was too hot.

The apprentice led us into a room that wasn't much larger than one of the sheds. A thickset man in a tunic was carefully tracing a design with a stylus on a thin sheet of bronze.

"Who is it, and what do they want?" he barked without looking up.

"It's Leonidas the Spartan."

At the lad's excited words, the man, Volteius, raised his head. He had a flat face, the nose also flat as though his entire head had been squashed against one of his own breastplates. Two shrewd eyes peered at me from under a shock of graying dark hair.

"Are you placing an order?" Volteius demanded. "Or picking up one? Did Aemilianus send you? Why are so many people in here?"

"Admiring your excellent work, sir," Gallus said quickly. "I'm Gnaeus Gallus, builder. I may have need of bronze adornments."

"Talk to my scribe, then. What do you want, Leonidas? I'm busy."

Cassia, as usual when we went anywhere public, faded behind me and became an unmoving bundle. She simulated a meek, obedient slave, but I knew she listened to every word said around me, storing them all in her memory, and would ask pointed questions when she noted everything down later.

"I'm not here to retrieve an order," I said. "But to ask about one you filled recently."

Volteius turned an incredulous stare on me. "Recently? You will have to be more precise. Look around you. I am constantly filling orders. Not only for the gladiators in this city but in surrounding towns, plus mending battered gear for men of the legions or the Praetorian guard, or the vigiles, or anyone who needs to swing a sword or protect their chest. The spring games are coming up, and every lanista wants his men to be more grand and posturing than ever."

I waited until his diatribe trailed off into a mutter. "A Thracian and a secutor. The Thracian helmet had black and white plumes."

Volteius shoved his stylus behind his ear. "I don't do the plumes here—I send out for that—but yes, I did finish armor for a Thracian and a secutor. Albus!"

His shout brought the young man instantly to his side. "Sir?"

"When did I do the Thracian?"

Albus stared at a corner of the ceiling as he considered. "About a month ago. Together with the secutor. Leg greaves molded with warriors from the Trojan war. One was Ajax, I think."

I jumped. The dead Ajax's leg guards had held the relief of a warrior on each. I hadn't studied them closely, but they could have been the Trojan War hero Ajax. The specific request meant that the killer hadn't targeted a random gladiator, but Ajax himself.

"Who made this order?" I leaned over Volteius's worktable, my large shadow blotting out the etching of a half-clad nymph.

Volteius's thick brows rose. "Aemilianus did."

"Aemil?" I stared at him in amazement, and I heard Cassia rustle behind me. "Are you sure?"

"Of course I'm sure," Volteius snapped. "I do much work for him—you know that."

"I mean, he came himself to place the order?"

"No, he sent someone." He waved a blunt-fingered hand. "I don't know who. I don't keep account of who all works at your ludus. Man says Aemilianus wants armor, I provide it."

I turned to Albus. "Do you remember who collected it?"

"Big man," Albus said at once. "Never seen him before. He wasn't a gladiator. I thought Aemilianus had hired him to fetch and carry. Thick dark hair, big nose, tall and broad. Didn't hear his name."

"Didn't give a name," Volteius said. "Why should he? Set down the money, took the goods. I usually keep a running tally for Aemilianus that he pays after the games are done, but I didn't mind having the cash right away."

The information helped, but at the same time, the man could have been anyone. It would be difficult to trace him, even with Albus's observant description.

"Anything wrong, Leonidas?" Albus peered up at me as I scowled.

"You've heard that Ajax and Rufus have been killed?" I asked bluntly.

"Of course," Albus said before Volteius could answer. "It's all over Rome."

"That equipment was made for them." I set my mouth in a grim line. "For their deaths."

Volteius lost his frown, his lips parting in disbelief. Albus stared at me in shock.

"Then the man who picked them up," Albus said in a near whisper. "He was the killer?"

"Possibly," I said. "Or worked for him."

"Minerva save us." Albus gulped, but he quivered with excitement. "We talked to a murderer."

"He seemed quiet enough." Volteius's answer was gruff. "As you say, Leonidas, he probably was only running the errand. Might not have known what his master had in mind. But he claimed he'd been sent by Aemilianus."

"He lied. Aemil would never kill his own men."

Volteius's voice turned hard. "I had no idea. Remember that. Nothing to do with the business. I thought I was working for Aemilianus, same as ever." He glared at Gallus, as though Gallus might run to fetch a magistrate at once.

Volteius was right to worry. If any believed he was a conspirator in the murder, he would be condemned with them.

"You acted in good faith." I spoke slowly and clearly for all to hear. "No one could blame you."

"See that they don't," Volteius barked. "Now, away with you. I have many more commissions to fulfill."

He snatched the stylus from behind his ear and bent over the etching again, but I noted that his hand shook, and he could not make a mark.

Albus gestured for us to follow him out. "Have I helped?" he asked me, eyes shining.

"You did." I resisted the urge to pat him on the head like a dog. "Thank you."

"If I see the man again, I'll send word right away," he promised.

"If you see him again, hide from him," I said in alarm. "I don't want him cleaning up after himself."

Albus nodded gravely at my warning, and I hoped he heeded it. He ushered us out the gate and closed it behind us but did not lock it.

"Where will you go now?" Gallus asked in curiosity.

I did not know what I should do next. Scour the city for a large man with dark hair and a big nose? That would be a long and arduous task.

Cassia emerged from under her cloak. "The ludus," she said. "Ask Aemilianus if he truly did order the armor. If so, then it was stolen from him for the purpose."

"Excellent idea." Gallus rubbed his hands together, his toga flapping. "In that case, I will leave you to it. As I once told you, gladiatorial combat makes me shudder, and I might go weak if I stood near an entire pack of gladiators at once. Good day, Leonidas. Young Cassia. Do not forget my question about joining me on the building team for the warehouse. My door is always open to you."

Gallus ebulliently headed off in the direction of the nearest bridge to lead him back to the heart of Rome. Once he was gone, lost in the crowds, Cassia and I turned our steps toward the ludus. I sensed she wanted to ask me about Gallus's offer, and I kept a swift pace to prevent her.

As we approached the ludus' gate, Septimius on guard once again, heavy footsteps sounded behind us.

"Get out of my way, Leonidas."

The missing Regulus abruptly shoved himself past me and stormed in through the gate that Septimius hurriedly opened for him.

CHAPTER 14

I barreled inside after Regulus, Cassia directly behind me. Regulus halted on the walkway next to the practice field where gladiators trained despite the rain. He insolently stretched his arms and yawned.

Before I could ask Regulus where in Hades he'd hidden himself, Aemil rushed across the field at him, fury in his eyes and a wooden sword in his hand. I recognized the sword. We'd named it Nemesis.

"Do you think this is a bathhouse you can wander in and out of at your pleasure?" Aemil roared as he reached Regulus. "Where were you? Don't lie to me!"

Septimius slammed the gate, and I heard the bolt slide across it, locking us in. The gladiators ceased training, turning to watch with interest.

Regulus glanced warily at the wooden sword then pretended to ignore it. "I was with a lady. Where'd you think? I was paid well, don't worry."

"I've explained time and again I'm not running a brothel," Aemil shouted. "You return at curfew or you face the consequence." The sword rose.

Aemil in his day had been the most celebrated gladiator in

Rome. I'd taken over the title, but I knew I could never have bested Aemil. He'd never lost a bout, not even when he'd been a green tiro.

"I'm here now," Regulus growled. "And tired. Can't you beat me later?"

He spoke with bravado, but I heard the uneasiness in his voice.

"I will beat you any time I choose." Aemil advanced on him. "You belong to *me*, not any trollop in the Subura. Get to your cell."

"Not a trollop. Rich woman." Regulus backed away toward the line of arches that fronted the cells.

"I don't care if she was a handmaiden of Venus. You go out only with my permission, and you didn't have it. Rufus and Ajax have *died*. You want to be the next stack of gladiator parts?"

Regulus started. "Rufus is dead?"

"Killed and chopped up. We thought you were too—Leonidas has been scouring the streets for you."

Regulus moved his gaze to me, and his derision returned. "Leonidas couldn't find his own ass."

"Get inside." Aemil smacked the sword across Regulus's abdomen before Regulus could block it.

Regulus grunted with the hit, then he wisely turned and jogged toward his cell. Aemil strode after him, and I followed, keeping Cassia tightly next to me. The other gladiators watched us go with the smugness of men who hadn't earned Aemil's wrath that day.

Aemil was locking the door to Regulus's cell when we reached it. Regulus leaned against the far wall, arms folded.

"I'm not a criminal," he snarled.

"You're a gladiator." Aemil turned the iron key in the lock with a decided *clank*. The cells were bolted from the outside, the gladiators imprisoned inside. "You're in my ludus for one reason —I paid for you."

Regulus rumbled his displeasure, but he remained on the far

side of the cell as Aemil withdrew his key and strode away. Regulus spit through the grating, but I noticed he made sure he had no chance of the spittle hitting Aemil.

Once Aemil had exited to the training ground, his shouts at the gladiators to get back to work floating to us, I moved to Regulus's door.

"Tell *me* where you were," I said. "It might be important."

Regulus eyed me with irritation. "None of your business." He bent down to his bunk and extracted a thin piece of metal from under the pallet. He moved to the door, thrust his hand through the slats, and started working the lock with the pick.

I rested one hand on the iron bars. "Ajax and Rufus were murdered after they'd been treated to a lavish meal. Possibly by a rich woman. So who was she?"

"Go eat your own eyeballs, Leonidas."

I abruptly snatched the lock pick from his hand and threw it down the corridor. The thin iron skittered across the stones.

"Prick." Regulus glared at me and rattled the door. "Open it."

"Aemil can still put me on the ground. No."

"He doesn't own *you*, and you have no reason to be loyal to him. Or is your freedman's cap too tight and you want to run back home to his protection?"

I'd never received the cap a slave turned freedman was given by his former master, nor had I enjoyed a celebratory feast. I was handed the *rudis*, then ignored, which was fine with me.

"He's a better fighter than I am." I could state this without rancor because it was true. "Tell me who the woman was—someone very wealthy is luring gladiators to their deaths."

"Well, it couldn't have been the woman I visited, because here I am. I ate, drank, and took her in every position I knew and some I didn't. She's highly educated."

"I won't betray her, if that's your worry."

"Betray her." Regulus laughed up at the scarred ceiling. "I'm not worried about *her* reputation. She's a widow enjoying herself and doesn't care who knows it. I'm worried about Herakles breaking all my bones. She's his special benefactress. At least, he thinks so."

"Domitiana Sabinus?" I asked quickly. I heard Cassia move behind me, but she remained silent. "Herakles won't learn this from me."

"Such a loyal friend, is Leonidas. Will do anything for his comrade, except kill him when begged to, or help him out of a locked cell."

I regarded him stubbornly. "Both times to save your life."

"So you say. Yes, Domitiana. If Aemil is locking us all in the ludus now, she'll be more than willing to welcome *you*. She likes gladiators. Can't get enough of them."

"Did she put anything into your wine?" I asked, ignoring this suggestion. "Did you feel groggy or lethargic?"

"Only after I used my rod for the seventh time. The woman has stamina. But no, she did not have to get me drunk or lace my sweetmeats with a soothing concoction."

"We believe this is how Rufus and Ajax were felled." I held Regulus's dark gaze. "Given food and drink tainted to make them drowsy, before they were coshed from behind. I only hope they were dead before they were butchered."

I assumed they had been because even a half-conscious gladiator had the instinct to fight. Marcianus said Ajax showed no signs of grappling with anyone, and I wagered Rufus didn't either. But I wanted Regulus to worry a little more than he was.

Regulus's eyes widened slightly, but his words dripped with scorn, "You're not good at terrifying men, Leonidas."

I stepped to the bars, hardening my heart, and sent him the stare that made other gladiators falter when they faced me in the arena.

"I am very, very good at it." My voice was quiet. "Stay in the ludus and live. The gods obviously want you to."

"Either that, or they've cursed me with *you*."

I moved my attention to the remaining two stick figures on

the ceiling, etched too deeply to gouge out. "Why did you erase Xerxes' drawings?"

Regulus glanced at them then away. "I didn't. Aemil did."

That surprised me, but I forced myself not to react. I simply unwound my hands from the bars and stalked away from him.

Cassia scurried a few paces ahead of me, and we emerged into the open air of the practice field. Aemil was bellowing orders at the fighters in training, chivying them with shouts and threats. The gladiators obeyed him without argument, hacking at posts in the spattering rain.

Aemil broke from them and met Cassia and me at the gate. "They're all accounted for now. Regulus was the last. I'll keep them locked in, and there won't be any more deaths." He held me in place with his mismatched eyes. "*You* lock yourself in when you go home. I don't want anyone stumbling over *your* dead body."

I had no intention of letting them. "Regulus claims you scratched out Xerxes' pictures."

Aemil's gaze flickered at my abrupt statement. "I did. Before you strike me, I did it because they were the last things Xerxes drew—the last prank he pulled. Regulus doesn't deserve to look at them."

I said nothing. Aemil kept his emotions close, except for rage at disobedient gladiators, and I hadn't realized until this instant that he'd felt a fondness for Xerxes, and was sorry to have lost him.

Fondness was a lethal thing in our business. Death destroyed every friendship, every love. Gladiators strolled with death every day, and we'd be gutted by constant despair if we let ourselves care.

I sent Aemil the minutest of nods before I closed my hand around Cassia's shoulder and steered her out of the gate ahead of me.

We didn't speak much until we reached our apartment. Cassia shed her cloak and I went out to sit on the edge of the balcony in an attempt to pull my thoughts together. The rain had ceased as we'd walked, the clouds rolling away to let sunlight through. The balcony was dry, shielded from the rain by our wall, and now warm from the sun.

Cassia's soft footfalls sounded, and soon, she sank down next to me, both of us dangling our feet over the edge of the flat roof.

I assumed Cassia would begin discussing all we'd discovered this afternoon at the warehouse and the armorers, but she studied me a moment before asking quietly, "Do you intend to work for Gnaeus Gallus?"

I glanced sharply at her, but Cassia serenely turned her gaze to the street. People milled along this quiet lane, visiting the wine merchant or other small shops tucked nearby. None looked up to see us sitting above them.

"I don't know." As I'd reflected before, I wanted it with my whole being, but the fear of it reached up to choke me. "Would our benefactor stop me?"

"I think not," Cassia answered. "The instructions Hesiodos gave me were that you should employ yourself to pay the rent and feed the two of us until our benefactor is ready to reveal himself and his purpose. Hesiodos did not specify what sort of jobs you should take. You and I assumed bodyguard, because that is what most gladiators do." Cassia spread her hands. "Working for a builder can pay the rent as well, depending on how much he offers."

"Possibly not much." A cloaked woman hurried by beneath us, a flurry of white and muted blue. "When I worked for the builder who apprenticed me, my payment was food and a place to sleep."

"You were in training," Cassia pointed out. "And a youth. From what Gallus said, he wants you as an assistant."

"Which sounds like not much pay at all." I leaned back on my hands, enjoying the sunshine. "Gallus will judge what I'm good at. I barely remember my life from before the games. I'll have to learn about building all over again."

"It will come back to you," Cassia said with confidence. "I think you ought to take the employment if Gallus wants you in truth."

"The last builder I worked for died," I said, the words low but succinct.

"That was not your fault." Cassia regarded me with sympathy.

"I thought it an accident." I tried to push away memories of that horrible day, but the images came to me before I could stop them. The brick structure, not yet finished, along with the roof scaffolding, in a pile of ruins. The broken and bloody body of the man who'd taken a chance on me found under the stones. "Then others discovered evidence of deliberate damage to the building. I was convenient to blame, so I was arrested." I'd been sixteen, defiant, and terrified.

"And sent to the games," Cassia concluded. "The true killer never found."

"Why should they look for one?" I shrugged. "I'd never have hurt my master, but he'd shouted at me the day before when I was slow, and the magistrates said I pulled the building down on him in revenge. Stupid."

Cassia reached a hand toward me then withdrew it before she touched me. "That does not mean it will happen again. Gallus is a gentle man, and clever. I doubt he will anger anyone enough for them to try to kill him."

I rubbed my upper lip, which was growing bristly. I needed to visit the barber. "My builder might not have angered anyone at all. A rival who wanted the site could have had him killed." I'd never learned exactly what had happened, and that had always bothered me.

"The past does not necessarily repeat itself."

Cassia gazed across the rooftops before us. Above the low

buildings on this street, we could just see the hills beyond the river.

I wondered if Cassia reflected on her own experiences. Though born a slave, she'd been raised in some comfort, as her father had been a trusted member of the household. Cassia had enjoyed her father's protection, and he'd taught her everything she knew.

Her exit from that house had been hard on her—her mistress angry for her husband's attentions that had been no fault of Cassia's. A slave, even a learned one, was at the mercy of her master's whims.

I'd made clear from the start that I did not expect Cassia to warm my bed. If I wanted to sate myself, there were plenty of women in brothels up and down Rome's seven hills. I was supposed to take care of this woman, and I felt protective of her, even from myself.

"I believe I will tell Gallus I would like to work with him," I said after a time of silence. "I've found all Aemil's gladiators for him, which is what he originally hired me to do. We should collect our fee, and be done."

Cassia smoothed a thread of her already neat hair. "The killer is still out there. Gladiators from other ludi might be next."

"The urban cohorts will have to find him, then." Though I knew she was right, I did not want to endanger Cassia any more than I already had. She'd been hurt when I'd pursued a killer before.

"Nero instructed *you* to find him, remember? The urban cohorts will simply nab whoever is convenient."

She was reminding me in her gentle but pointed way that my entire life had changed because *I* had been a convenient suspect. I might condemn another to my fate if I gave up now.

I wanted to argue that Ajax's and Rufus's deaths had nothing to do with me. Aemil had asked me to find his missing gladiators, and I'd found them. Regulus had brought himself home, and now he was locked in, his lock pick out of reach.

I knew, though, that if I woke in the morning to hear that another gladiator had been found in pieces and I'd done nothing to stop it, I'd not forgive myself for a long time. Even more so if an innocent was condemned to death for it, as I had been long ago.

I leaned back again, studying the tattered clouds in the blue sky, the storm spent, and let out a long breath. "I will find whoever it is and make sure it stops. But I don't know how to go about it."

"We will think on it," Cassia spoke with confidence, then both of us fell silent as we watched the clouds disperse on the warming wind.

IN THE MORNING, I WAS AWAKENED BY A THUMPING ON THE door at the bottom of the stairs. Cassia, already up and having fetched water and bread, started toward it.

I passed her in my musty tunic and went down the stairs in my bare feet, my knife in the palm of my hand.

I wrenched open the door to find Merope and Gaius on the doorstep.

"Chryseis is preparing a funeral for Rufus," Merope said, her brows furrowed in an uncharacteristic frown. "She will not let us have anything to do with it. Your lanista is providing the funeral pyre for him, but Chryseis is having a funeral of her own. Can you help us, Leonidas?"

CHAPTER 15

Cassia had the two upstairs and supplied with a cup of watered-down wine before I reached the upper room once more. She shared our breakfast with them as well.

I leaned against a wall, folding my arms, as Merope and Gaius plopped themselves on stools and proceeded to heartily eat and drink. Recalling their barren rooms over the popina, and the meager meal they'd offered me, I concluded they hadn't consumed this much in a while.

"What can I do?" I asked.

Merope wiped her mouth to answer while Gaius remained deep in bread and lentils.

"Will you ask your lanista to let us come to the burning? And any feast he has after? We often dance at funeral feasts."

"Do you want him to hire you?"

"Only if he won't let us be there as guests," Merope said. Gaius nodded around his mouthful of food.

"I don't know if Aemil has planned a feast," I told them. "He's not extravagant when it comes to his gladiators."

Gaius swallowed noisily. "Then at least to the pyre. We need to give old Rufus a proper sendoff. He was good to us."

Merope rose from her stool. "We can keep the dance simple, but we want to honor him. Like this."

She shed her threadbare cloak to reveal a tunic of thin, worn linen. Raising her arms, she began to step from foot to foot, her body bending gracefully. Gaius licked off his spoon and started banging out a rhythm on the table with the spoon and his hand.

Cassia watched, enraptured, as Merope swayed, her leg coming up to spin her around in one fluid motion. When I thought she'd overbalance, Merope finished the turn with precision and continued the dance.

I could see that she was very good. Gaius's rhythm was exact, practiced, with the competence of a professional.

Cassia clapped along—she loved music. Merope glided to her, holding out her hands. To my surprise, Cassia took them, allowing herself to be pulled into the dance.

Cassia did not know the steps, but Merope slowed her pace, and Gaius expertly matched their rhythm. Merope demonstrated how to slide and kick, wafting an arm while she held Cassia with the other hand.

Cassia copied the movements, learning them quickly. She'd had training in music, she'd once explained to me. Likely she'd had it in dance too.

She was not as practiced as Merope and stumbled a few times, but always caught herself. Cassia's cheeks flushed, and a smile lifted her lips, her eyes shining.

The reason for the dance was mourning, but I saw Cassia come to life with Merope's tranquil guidance. The dance was to celebrate the man, I understood, to honor him, and there was joy in that.

Gaius sped the rhythm. Merope pulled Cassia around a bit faster, and Cassia soon adapted. The two women dipped and swayed, feet landing softly on the stone floor.

Around the room they went, returning in a sweep to the center. Merope made some signal to Gaius, who sped into a rousing, rushed rhythm that abruptly quieted and died into silence.

Merope spun to a close, drawing Cassia to her. The two ended in a pose fit for a sculpture, and everything went still.

I thumped my hands on my knees, making noise to show my appreciation, as did Gaius. Merope made a graceful bow as though it was her due, but Cassia ducked her head and rushed back to her stool.

My cheeks ached for some reason. I put my hand up to touch them, and I realized I was grinning, smiling harder than I had in a long while, since the days I'd laughed without worry with Xerxes, my closest friend.

I PROMISED TO HAVE A WORD WITH AEMIL ABOUT HIRING THE dancers. Merope and Gaius departed, a bit more hopeful than when they'd arrived.

Cassia, embarrassed by her unrestrained display, opened all her tablets and pretended to be engrossed in them. I wasn't certain whether to reassure her that what she'd done had been beautiful or pretend nothing had happened.

Never good at deciding what to say, I took myself to the baths instead.

The baths I'd recently began frequenting were about forty paces up the Quirinal Hill from our lodgings. They were not as immense as the public baths of Agrippa on the Campus Martius or the complex Nero had recently opened near the Pantheon, but they suited me. There was a charge to enter, one *as*, which I paid over to the man at the front doors.

The baths were small but sumptuous, with high arched ceilings and one large mosaic depicting Neptune among strange sea creatures, another Bacchus and his maenads.

Residents of the Quirinal, including senators and praetors, frequented this bath. They frowned on plebs joining them, but I'd discovered they didn't mind sharing this space with a former famous gladiator. I kept my distance and occasionally suggested routines for the younger men who exercised next to me in the gymnasium. For the most part, people left me alone.

Women were allowed in this bathhouse, though they had separate changing rooms. Today as I handed my strigil to an attendant after I'd been rubbed with oil and sand, a procession paraded past the courtyard on its way to the caldarium.

Procession was the only way to describe it. Two tall, solidly built men—obviously bodyguards—led the way, and two more brought up the rear.

Lady's maids in plain but luxurious tunics bore boxes and bags for shoes, clothing, cosmetics, hairbrushes, jewelry. They surrounded a woman in layers of red and blue silk, her head covered with a shimmering cloth. I imagined a grandly appointed litter waiting for her outside.

Her voice came to me as she strolled. "Slowly, pests. I shall not run to keep up with you. If I have to run, you'll be out on the streets." She laughed, the tone rich and musical, but the words were sincere.

The bodyguards immediately paused, and the attendant women took smaller steps, only one daring to laugh with her, but nervously.

"A moment." The woman in silk had caught sight of me. I couldn't see much of her through the folds of her palla, but her dark eyes skewered me. "Who is that?"

The women began to babble that they didn't know, but one of the male attendants leaned to her. "Leonidas the Spartan," I heard him say.

"Oh, yes?" The woman gave me such a long stare that my skin prickled. I wore a loincloth only, but I might be naked for the lurid interest of her gaze. "Such richness in a lowly bath house. But enough." She clapped her hands, gold bracelets jingling. "Stop dawdling, toads. I have much to do today."

She set off at a brisk pace, and her maids and bodyguards scurried to keep themselves around her.

I signaled the attendant to begin scraping, and he sent me a knowing grin. "Fortunate man. She is very rich."

"Who is she?" I asked.

"Severina Casellius, married to one Tertius Vestalis Felix, an old man who doesn't care what his wife gets up to. She surrounds herself with gladiators and pays them well, from what I hear. You might have a chance to make some coin."

Severina Casellius was Domitiana's daughter, the woman Cassia and I speculated about having killed Ajax. Her bodyguards were massive, and she liked to have gladiators and others at her home.

I watched Severina until she was out of sight while the attendant flicked dirt and oil from my skin.

I remembered now where I'd heard the name Tertius Vestalis Felix. Cassia had told me he was Severina's husband, and Gallus had indicated that the same man was planning to build a warehouse in the Emporium. The building site would give Severina or her servants an excuse to be in the area, and perhaps gain access to Chryseis's warehouse, where I'd found the feather from Rufus's helmet.

I wanted to get closer to Severina and discover if our speculations had merit, but I realized I would have to make it seem her idea. A woman like that would not respond well to demands.

Once the attendant finished, I strode to the frigidarium. After a swim, I pulled on my tunic, and on a whim, headed for the caldarium into which Severina's party had disappeared.

Three of the four bodyguards stood in the arched doorway, forming a wall of muscle, not letting anyone in, not even the slave who fetched and carried towels.

The fourth, a big man with a shaved head and beaked nose, stepped forward out of a niche where he'd been watching over Severina in the caldarium. He folded his arms as he faced me, saying nothing.

I looked the guard over, met his gaze without flinching, then turned and departed.

DAYS PASSED, AND WE APPROACHED THE IDES OF THE MONTH. Aemil kept his gladiators locked in at night, none to be allowed out on pain of death, and he meant it. The gate guards, who had sometimes let us slip away without Aemil being the wiser were threatened until they were too terrified to do anything but obey. So Septimius told me, the large man's eyes tight.

No more gladiators were found cut into bits, none dead at all. When no more excitement came from these events, Rome forgot and found new things to talk about.

I managed to persuade Aemil to allow Merope and her family to perform at the double funeral for Ajax and Rufus. He did it grudgingly, not wanting to make too much fuss.

"If he has to have a grand funeral for those two, he will be expected to do so for every gladiator he loses," Nonus Marcianus told me after I'd finished speaking to a snarling Aemil. "He doesn't like losing them at all."

True, Aemil did everything he could to keep his gladiators alive. He was hard on us in training, because once we were released onto the arena floor, he had no more control. He had to watch us die with the rest of the crowd.

Three days before the Ides, Cassia and I, Marcianus, Gaius and his cousins, and all the gladiators walked out of the ludus and west up into the hills to the place Aemil burned the remains of gladiators who'd fallen.

Others from the *collegia* of gladiators joined us, men from ludi on the outskirts of Rome, ready to send off a fellow gladiator. The *collegia* was footing half the fee for Merope and Martolia, as well as for the cremation. I was part of the organization myself, contributing what sums I could to the burial funds plus the collection for widows and children.

Romans came out to watch as we processed. Gaius carried a drum under his arm, beating it in a sad and slow rhythm. Merope and Martolia, in thin gauzy, pure white tunics, moved in a graceful pace to the beat of the drum, tiny bells on their wrists and ankles jingling.

A mule-pulled cart, led by Aemil himself, bore only the body of Ajax. The day before, Chryseis had abruptly announced she'd take Rufus's body for a private funeral, which she'd conducted yesterday afternoon. She'd burned her late husband with very little ceremony and interred his ashes in her family's tomb, so Cassia had learned. Chryseis of course had not allowed Merope or Martolia anywhere near. They had to honor Rufus, as the rest of us did, in spirit, and from afar.

Ajax's body had been kept cool in a cellar under the ludus while Aemil and the *collegia* made the arrangements. At the crest of the hill, where a bare patch around the fresh stack of wood attested to previous pyres, we halted. Aemil and I carried Ajax's body to the unlit pile.

Gaius increased his tempo. Merope and Martolia swayed and spun, tears glittering on Martolia's cheeks. No one had hired professional mourners, as Aemil didn't like them, but the two young women showed the grief that losing a gladiator, one marked for death by his very profession, could bring.

Aemil lit the pyre. Smoke stung my eyes, the sensation taking me back to the day we'd burned Xerxes. His wife had stood by my side, upright and stiff under her veil, the children she'd had by Xerxes huddled against her. I'd lost a friend, she a husband and lover.

I found my eyes wet, a burning in my heart.

A touch brought me back from the past. Cassia, who'd insisted on attending, brushed my bare arm with her fingers. I glanced down at her, but she dropped her hand to her side, her gaze on the flames.

The pyre would burn for some time. I turned and led Cassia away before long, while Merope and Martolia danced their mourning, Gaius weeping as he banged the drum.

Smoke drifted toward the river, the monuments and aqueducts of Rome glittering in the late winter sunshine.

Aemil and the *collegia* had contributed to a marker, which would be erected outside the ludus with those of other gladiators. The stonecutter had been instructed to write:

Ajax, captured in battle in the borderlands, secutor, lived twenty-two years, won thirty matches, lost five, with six draws.

Rufus, freedman of Rome, myrmillo. Lived twenty-five years, won forty matches, lost six, with ten draws.

We fellow gladiators put up this stone to honor them.

Later, someone would scratch under Rufus's name, *Beloved of M., M., and G.*

THE DAY AFTER THE FUNERAL, WHICH WAS THE SECOND BEFORE the Ides, I was invited to Domitiana Sabinus's villa, along with Herakles, for a banquet.

Aemil took me aside when I reached the ludus that evening and told me I needed to bring Herakles home tonight alive or throw myself into the river.

Regulus was furious that Herakles had been given leave—Domitiana must have paid Aemil well. Regulus's voice echoed through the cells, his language foul.

I ignored him, but Herakles gloated. "Don't wait up, Mother," he shouted at Regulus, laughing in glee as we walked out the gate.

I was not the only person venturing into Domitiana's villa this evening. As Herakles and I reached the front gate, a cloaked figure slipped through the small servants' door in the wall.

I'd argued with Cassia about her accompanying me to the villa, but I'd lost. She'd won me over by pointing out that if Domitiana proved to be the woman sending gladiators to their doom, she and Helvius, her trusted friend, could run for help.

This was only true if Helvius was more loyal to Cassia than to his mistress, and if Helvius himself had nothing to do with the murders. I also knew that further argument was futile, and I reasoned silently that I would be there next to her if anything went wrong.

I finally conceded, *if* she promised to run at the first sign of danger. Cassia had turned away and murmured, “Of course.”

The doorman ushered Herakles and me into the atrium. He barely hid a sneer as he did so, making it clear what he thought of his mistress inviting gladiators to supper.

He shut the gate behind us, the latch clanging into the silence like a cell door closing.

CHAPTER 16

The doorman led us along the colonnaded garden to the villa and through its enormous atrium, the house rising around us. We passed empty rooms that had oil lamps flickering inside them, illuminating wall paintings and floor mosaics. Domitiana was indeed wealthy if she could place lights for effect in dark, unused portions of the house.

A dining room opened from the peristyle garden, screens pulled closed after we entered to cut the night breeze.

The triclinium's walls were painted with floor-to-ceiling murals, one on my left depicting maidens dancing in a landscape that resembled the terraced gardens outside the house. Satyrs cavorted near the ladies, sending them lascivious leers.

The center wall showed a long table laden with food, from whole fish to overflowing baskets of grapes and pomegranates, heaps of bread, and glasses of wine. One glass had overturned, sending droplets of purple liquid to the floor. Under the table, a cat gnawed on fish bones.

The right wall portrayed a beautiful woman in diaphanous silk reclining on a couch, one breast visible through her nearly transparent stola. A naked man with a large phallus knelt at her feet, licking the inside of her bared leg.

I'd seen far more erotic wall paintings and floor mosaics at other villas I'd visited, but I wondered if the lady of the house had commissioned it after her husband had died, or if he'd ordered the painting himself.

Several low, small tables surrounded on three sides by a dining couch took up most of the room. Domitiana, our hostess, lounged on one end of the couch, very much like the painted lady behind her did, except that while her thin blue silk stola clung to her every curve, it covered her fully. Domitiana's only jewelry was a pair of delicate earrings of three gold hoops studded with precious stones, and her wig tonight was a dark brown affair of simple curls.

Possibly she'd chosen modest attire because another woman, a younger version of herself, lazed on the couch on the opposite side of the table. I concluded that this was Domitiana's daughter, Severina. I'd only glimpsed her at the baths, and now I could view her fully.

She was in her very early twenties, I'd guess, with black hair that flowed in artfully arranged locks to the folds of her red silk stola. The fibulae that clasped the stola at her shoulders were beaten gold in the shape of bees, and a strip of gold and green cloth decorated her neckline. Her feet, perched on the couch, were shod in thin gilded sandals, and earrings similar to Domitiana's hung from her ears.

Herakles and I were presented by the doorman, but we halted in the middle of the room, not invited to sit, while the two women looked us over. We both wore clean tunics and sandals, our skin scraped and washed at the baths. I'd visited my barber today and had a smooth face and hair trimmed back to my scalp.

Severina's eyes brightened as she took me in, and she pointed a long finger at me. "I saw you. At the baths on the Quirinal."

I acknowledged this with a nod. I wouldn't speak unless instructed to.

"Sit." Domitiana waved her hand at the expanse of couch next to her. "Drink, my friends."

Herakles moved first, edging me out so he could recline closest to Domitiana. That left me to stretch out on the cushions nearest Severina.

Cups of beaten gold, filled with dark wine, reposed on the tables, well within reach. Herakles lifted one, grinned at Domitiana, and slurped.

I took a more hesitant sip of mine, but I tasted only wine, rich and full. An expensive vintage.

No others were joining us, I saw. Servants materialized to set dishes on the tables our couches surrounded, moving silently and efficiently before they vanished again.

I'd been invited to such meals before. Most often the triclinium would be full, with a dozen or more guests. I'd either be asked to join the meal, or I'd sit waiting until they wanted me to show off my fighting moves or talk about bouts. Sometimes guests would be cajoled by their friends into sparring with me—I'd judge the temperament of the crowd before deciding whether to gently best my opponent or pretend to let him defeat me.

Occasionally I was invited to dine with women alone—though not always for copulation—as we had been tonight.

Bodyguards lurked in the shadows in case Herakles or I decided to rob the house or ravish the two ladies without their permission. One I recognized as Severina's, the same who'd given me a scowl at the baths. None of them had overly large noses or thick dark hair.

Musicians stationed outside the room began to play as the meal was served, sweet strains wafting out of the darkness. The first course consisted of flatbreads and cheese alongside small eggs, boiled and opened, the yolks mixed with herbs and salt. The food was elegant and tasty but nothing like the overly exotic meals Marcianus had found in Ajax's and Rufus's stomachs.

Next came platters of meat formed into balls and stuffed with anchovies; roasted pork; fish stuffed with breadcrumbs; and several different kinds of sausages. I disliked to eat much meat, but I dutifully chewed a few mouthfuls while Herakles happily gorged himself.

While we ate, Domitiana kept up a steady chatter with Severina about people they knew and what they'd each done during the week. Domitiana invited our opinions from time to time, while Severina only watched us with a secret smile as she replied to her mother.

The food continued, as did the wine. Once the main course was disposed of, servants brought out sweets, more to my liking. Fried bits of pastry dough dipped in honey covered the platters, surrounded by apricots, walnuts, almonds, pomegranates, grapes, and other fruits depicted in the mural above me.

With the dessert came the doorman announcing a stooped man in a toga.

"Tertius Vestalis Felix," the doorman intoned.

I studied Severina's husband as I chewed a handful of walnuts. He'd been a senator and a consul, I recalled Cassia telling me, and then a proconsul of a colony on the edges of the empire. Retired now, he had gray hair, a lined face, and an expression of resignation.

Severina's smile never wavered as she rose. "I am honored, husband."

Domitiana made room on her end of the sofa. "Dear son-in-law. Come and sit by me."

The man walked slowly to Domitiana and settled himself on the couch. He seemed in no way dismayed or unhappy that two gladiators reposed next to his wife and mother-in-law. Herakles drained another cup and thunked it to the table as a servant darted forward with wine for the older man.

Severina reclined again, reaching for an apricot. She lifted it to her mouth and ate it with slow sensuality, but her husband only sipped wine and turned to answer a question from Domitiana.

He was deferential to Domitiana and she to him, though as a

paterfamilias and former senator, Vestalis had no need to be so amenable. He could, within his rights, grab his wife and haul her home from this lewd entertainment, and beat her until she begged for mercy. A paterfamilias had the power of life or death over anyone in his household.

Vestalis spoke with Domitiana and paid his wife no attention at all.

Severina, therefore, turned her entire focus on me. She rested her hand on my scarred arm.

"I have so enjoyed meeting you, Leonidas. You must come to my house for a feast." She leaned to me to whisper under cover of the music. "A much better one than this. My mother has forgotten how to be indulgent."

I glanced at Vestalis, who was deep in discussion with Domitiana about a proposed tax being debated by the senate. Herakles, annoyed at being shut out, moved restlessly and emitted a loud belch.

Severina tightened her grip, her pointed nails creasing my flesh. "Never mind my husband. He lets me do as I please. Say you'll come. I'll pay that stingy old Aemilianus plenty for you. I don't care."

"I no longer fight for the ludus," I said. "I'm a *libertus*."

Severina's mouth quirked into a cold smile. "All the better." She dragged a nail across my forearm hard enough to break the skin then lifted her finger to her mouth and licked it.

Her eyes were bright and glittering, lined with kohl, her cheeks touched with rouge. The coloring on her mouth had been enhanced by the blood-red wine.

A hunger lurked inside her, I sensed, one she barely kept contained. I'd been the guest of a number of women who'd wanted to be bedded by a gladiator—eager wives of patricians, Equestrians, or plebs, who believed they wanted to make themselves vulnerable to my strength. It excited them.

I saw that in Severina, but something more, something predatory.

The wine I'd drunk suddenly tasted sour. Was she truly the hunter of Ajax and Rufus—had she lured them to her and enjoyed watching them be killed? Conquering the strongest and ablest fighters in Rome?

I could discover this by accepting her offer, however dangerous it was. If she proved simply to be a woman who wanted to sate herself with novelty, then I would leave her and seek the murderer elsewhere. But if the slayings had happened at her home, then I would expose her and leave her to Nero's mercy.

I leaned to Severina, keeping my voice low. "You humble me with your invitation, lady. I will accept."

"Good." Severina's smile deepened as she lifted her wine. "Mother, why don't we have our guests demonstrate their fighting skills? Leonidas has been given the *rudis*, and we won't see him fight in the amphitheaters any longer."

Domitiana beamed at her daughter. "An excellent suggestion. Herakles, Leonidas ... please." She waved a hand to the open space in front of the tables.

The exchange between the two women emerged like lines spoken in a play. They'd rehearsed this, had probably mouthed a similar request many times before.

I rose, knowing I wouldn't be allowed to refuse. I put aside my wine and joined Herakles, who'd jumped readily to his feet, moving to the area cleared for us.

One of the hovering servants handed me a wooden sword and a small shield, and another brought Herakles a net. He smiled as he tested it—the weight must be to his liking.

Instead of a spear, he was given a long pole with no point. No one was meant to die in this bout, I understood, but we could batter each other with the blunt weapons for our watchers' amusement.

Herakles was a talented retiarius. He had a wicked hand with his net, which could entrap and render an opponent helpless while Herakles finished him off with a swift jab of his spear. In earlier days certain gladiators would only fight certain others—a retiarius against a myrmillo, for instance—but the lines had blurred now, and the audience was happy to watch any pairing.

I would have to keep away from the strangling lines of the heavy net—once I was tangled in it, I'd be hard-pressed to defend myself. I'd only been felled by a net once, managing to roll free because the net had been torn and the retiarius who'd thrown it hadn't used his advantage quickly enough.

Domitiana acted as referee, holding up her hand and saying in a loud, clear voice, "Let the game commence."

"The prizes are worth it," Herakles told me, even as he began to glide around me.

I held my sword and shield ready. The way to win against Herakles was to put myself behind him before he could turn, or make him throw the net and miss me. Once the net was gone, I could deflect or break his spear and bring him down.

Herakles was too experienced to throw early. He stalked me on light feet while I backed away, watching for my opening. The wooden shield had a point on it, with which I could catch the net and fling it away if I could. However, the shield could also snag the net and trap my arm.

Herakles grinned, his light hair gleaming in the candlelight. I kept my face straight, concentrating.

It didn't matter who won this bout. Domitiana would take Herakles to bed with her this night, and I would depart with Cassia and go home. I had nothing to win, and nothing to lose.

As soon as I held the sword and shield, however, my training took over, and the fighting man I'd once been stepped forth.

I saw, not the dining room with its decadent wall paintings of food and sensuality, but the spear and net coming at me in a vast arena. I felt the sand grating beneath my bare feet, smelled the blood and sweat of those who'd fought and died in earlier matches.

My bouts usually were the last of the day, the populace of

Rome on their feet in the Circus Gai or the Saepta Julia, chanting for Leonidas the Spartan to win once again.

Herakles, with his maniacal smile, wanted to best the champion.

I had an advantage tonight, no helmet. The bronze helmet that protected my head from blows also limited my eyesight. I had to keep the retiarius in front of me at all times or figure out where he was by sound and the change in the air at my back.

Tonight, I could turn my head and keep him in sight.

Herakles likewise was unhampered by arm guards or heavy leg greaves. He danced sideways on the balls of his feet, sizing up his opening, enjoying himself.

I moved out of his way without running, slowly drawing him to me. Herakles watched me carefully, not falling into little traps I set that would bring him too close to me to use the net.

He lunged abruptly, and I just as quickly sidestepped, dancing out of the way. At the last moment, Herakles stopped himself from throwing the net, knowing it would be a wasted toss.

The two ladies gasped and laughed, beating the table to show their appreciation. This became the noise of the crowd as I fought for my life.

My heart hadn't been in my finals bouts—I'd long grown weary of the life, fighting only because I had no choice. Even so, I'd won every time. My body had become a machine as mindless as the cranes that lifted massive stones onto new wings of Nero's domus. Once the machine was set in motion, it operated with grim efficiency.

Herakles wanted me to let him win, to impress his lady, and I could have. But my body and my training refused.

Pretending to retreat, I led Herakles quickly across the small floor, my feet brushing a mosaic of nymphs reclining at a fountain. I paused for a moment near a corner of the wall, as though pinned there, out of breath, and Herakles, with a triumphant expression, threw the net.

It hit empty air. As soon as I saw his wrist bend for the throw, I jumped a length sideways, the heavy net brushing my foot as it fell.

I shifted my weight so the cords wouldn't trip me and charged Herakles. He desperately brought up his spear, trying to make me impale myself with it, but I whirled past the spear and spun behind him, knocking my shield hard against his hand as I went. Herakles's weapon wavered, and then I rammed into him with my entire body.

As he staggered, I threw down my shield, grabbed Herakles's head with my free hand, and shoved my sword against his throat. He could do nothing but try to hit me with the side of his spear.

I bore down on his throat, cutting off his air. "Yield?"

Herakles choked out a foul word, eyes full of rage.

"Shall we grant him mercy?" Severina asked in delight.

"He will have to ask for it," Domitiana observed. Her voice was calm, as though she had no interest in whether her lover lived or died.

Herakles snarled, but he held up his forefinger, the signal that he wished to stop the fight and beg for clemency.

I waited, Herakles dragging in strangled breaths. In this room, the two ladies and Vestalis were the sponsors of the games, with the power of life or death over us. Domitiana thoughtfully chewed on a grape.

"I suppose we could let him live." She finished her grape as her daughter laughed.

"Mitte!" Severina called. *Spare him!*

Herakles continued to growl, furious with me for besting him. I glanced at Severina's husband, but the man had slumped down on the couch, head on his chest, eyes closed. He'd nodded off while Herakles and I battled in front of him to the death.

Herakles did not lose his anger at me until Domitiana took him to her side and pretended to fuss over his wounded body. His next look at me was smug, as though he considered this a victory.

Tertius Vestalis snorted awake, blinked at the room, then rose and wandered out. Severina beckoned me to her, but a manservant appeared and deferentially whispered a message to her before I could reach her.

Severina screamed through her teeth and slapped the manservant hard. He came up, the red imprint of her hand on his face, bowed, and fled.

"My tiresome husband needs assistance home," Severina snapped at me. "Or so he says. He is only trying to prove he has power over me. Stupid old fool." A maid hurried to Severina's side and helped her to her feet, straightening her stola until Severina pushed her away.

Domitiana peered up from where Herakles lay with his head on her chest. "And you will be a dutiful wife and go to him. Good night to you, daughter."

Severina glowered at her mother but conceded to let her maid wrap a palla around her. Without returning the good night or saying a word to me, she swept from the room, the maid rushing after her.

Domitiana returned her attention to Herakles. He'd snuggled in closer, ever so slowly and subtly twining himself around her.

No one paid any heed to me. I could not depart and leave Herakles here on his own. I feared I'd find his body in pieces by morning, and Aemil would never forgive me for losing him another gladiator.

I also had no wish to join the two in whatever antics they would adjourn to do. I silently withdrew from the room, seeking the peristyle garden and its quiet comfort.

I decided to find the servants' quarters and search for Cassia. I did not want to betray her presence, but at the same time, I wanted to make certain she was safe.

When I turned to make my way toward the back of the house and the passageway I'd spied under the stairs on my last visit, a large man stepped in front of me. I recognized him as Severina's bodyguard, the one who had stopped me at the bathhouse.

"My lady requests your presence at her house two nights hence," he intoned. "After the Lupercalia. Her home is on the Caelian Hill off the Clivus Scauri, near the shrine of Minerva."

I nodded to his glittering eyes. I'd already accepted her invitation, but he was making it formal.

The bodyguard said not another word. He turned and marched away, his footsteps surprisingly quiet for such a large man.

As I'd suspected, the *culina* and storerooms for foodstuffs lay at the other end of the peristyle, the entrance to them under the staircase. The kitchen I glanced into had a larger stove than most domii—a rectangular stone cabinet with a fire below and tripods on which to set the cooking pots on top. No one was there, the food already finished and served.

Laughter floated from the storeroom next to the *culina*. I stepped inside it to behold Cassia, her eyes shining, laughing in an easy way I'd never heard from her before. A tall and gangly young man stood in front of her, holding her hands and gazing at her in adoration.

CHAPTER 17

"Cassia." The word jerked out of me, and I heard the snarl that came with it.

Cassia turned without starting, her smile fading in concern, but concern for me, not herself. "Leonidas. Why are you here?"

The young man dropped Cassia's hands and stared at me in stark terror. He had very thin limbs that held wiry strength, and a prominent lump that moved up and down his stick of a throat as he swallowed hard.

"I'm not wanted," I said, "but I can't leave without Herakles." I fixed my gaze on the man. He swallowed again and backed a step from Cassia.

"This is Helvius," Cassia told me.

As I'd guessed. The young man possessed the slightly protruding eyes and hunched back of someone who stared at scrolls all day.

"Why are you in the storeroom?" I asked abruptly.

Helvius spluttered, but Cassia replied smoothly, "No servant except a bedroom attendant is allowed in the family's rooms at night. The household staff either gathers here or outside in the kitchen garden behind the house." She peered at me. "Won't they miss you in the dining room?"

"I doubt it." Herakles and Domitiana had been melding ever closer as I'd gone and would never notice my absence. "What do you know of Severina Casellius and her household?" I directed this question at Helvius.

Helvius glanced quickly at Cassia, but she nodded at him to answer. He cleared his throat. "She's married to a retired proconsul."

"I know that. I met him. He joined us for dinner."

Cassia's brows went up, and even Helvius was startled. "Unusual for Vestalis," he said. "He mostly ignores Severina. Perhaps he didn't want her too involved with gladiators, especially when they are being killed."

"You mean he ordered her home to protect her?" I asked. "Seems unlikely. He fell asleep while Herakles and I fought an exhibition match."

"He is nearly seventy years old," Helvius said, his voice tinged with awe. "Most men aren't alive at that age, let alone awake."

Cassia chuckled in appreciation of his humor.

I wanted more than anything at that moment to grab Cassia by the hand and pull her home with me. The feeling startled me —it should make no difference to me if she laughed at a young man's jokes, especially those of a scrawny specimen like Helvius. But the impulse persisted.

Helvius continued speaking, oblivious to my tension. "Severina is Vestalis's second wife. His first died when they lived in the provinces, as did his daughter. Very sad. He never had sons."

Sons were what every highborn Roman man desired. Someone to carry on his name, his business, his honor. Today had begun the nine-day long festival of Parentalia, a tribute to deceased parents and ancestors, sons venerating fathers. Family and heritage were very important, the celebration taken seriously.

Tertius Vestalis Felix must hope to achieve sons with Severina. Perhaps that was why he'd dragged her away from gladiators tonight, to ensure that any child she carried would be his. But if that were the case, then why had Severina dared to extend an invitation to me?

I caught Cassia and Helvius exchanging a glance, as though they shared secrets I was not to know. My irritation rose.

"Where is this kitchen garden?" I asked curtly. "Where the servants gather? I will wait for Herakles there."

Helvius moved to a small door in the back of the room and pulled it open. "Just down the path. Veer to the left, or else you'll go to the main garden, and that is forbidden to all but the family."

Without a word, I strode past him into the night. Cassia stepped out after me, but I turned on her.

"No," I said harshly. "It's too cold."

I marched toward the thin line of trees Helvius had pointed out. From the house, floating loudly over the peristyle to the open air, came a shriek of feminine ecstasy, then another, and another. It might be a while before Herakles was ready to leave.

A COLD WIND WAS BLOWING, AND A HALF-MOON HUNG IN A sky tattered with clouds when Herakles emerged. I'd returned to the peristyle after wandering the kitchen gardens for a time and lounged on a bench under the colonnade, shutting my ears to Herakles's animal-like grunts.

The majordomo of the house ushered us out, and the doorman quickly shut the gate, bolting it behind us.

We were both still alive, our senses not fuddled, and free to go.

"You didn't have to wait for me." Herakles let the thick accent he'd favored during dinner fade. "I know my way back to the ludus."

"I promised Aemil I'd return you whole."

"Domitiana has nothing to do with killing Ajax or Rufus. I could have told you that."

"Best to be sure." I tramped along the road that led to the Transtiberim, fully aware of the light footsteps that followed close behind.

Herakles didn't notice Cassia in our wake, but he was bathing in the aftermath of sating his appetites. To show me they hadn't been quite sated, Herakles suggested we go to the Subura to finish the night.

"No," I said in a hard voice. "Aemil will have my head if I don't bring you home."

Herakles turned surly. "You could have gone down in that fight. You had no need to prove you are and always will be *primus palus*."

"Your lady liked you as a fallen warrior," I reminded him.

"True. She smells like vinegar, but she has endurance. And much money." Herakles wasn't foolish enough to clink a pouch of gold on the dark street, but his satisfied grin told me she'd paid him well. I'd received nothing.

I maintained stony silence as Herakles tried to persuade me to visit a lupinarius with him, but finally he gave up. I waited until Septimius locked the gate firmly behind Herakles before I turned for my own way home.

I paused to wait for the shadow that soon caught up to me. I walked close to her, my hand protectively on her arm.

Our rapid pace through the streets to the lane on the lower slopes of the Quirinal kept us from speaking. The Forum Romanum was silent, the columns of the Basilica Julia and the temple to the divine Julius gleaming in the moonlight.

Only when we reached our lodgings, and I'd shut and bolted the outer and inner doors, did I breathe more easily. Our apartment was dark—the only noise the rumble of delivery carts through the streets.

Cassia immediately divested herself of her cloak, lit an oil lamp, seated herself at the table, and opened her tablets. "What did you learn from Domitiana?" she asked.

She was already writing, the stylus moving rapidly. I sat down heavily and poured myself the last of the wine from the jug.

"I learned that she is a vain, selfish woman interested in her own pleasure. Not much different from many highborn women who invite gladiators into their homes." I turned the cup in my hands. "The difference was that she did not care who knew it. Believes herself too rich and important to worry about scandal."

Cassia wrote for a moment, the stylus making only a whisper of sound. "From what Helvius tells me, Domitiana's husband—Severinus Casellius—expected her to be the perfect Roman matron, in the style of Octavia. Rarely leaving the house, spending all day weaving, and taking care of the home and children, never raising her voice in argument. Humble, chaste, and obedient. An old-fashioned sentiment these days, but some patricians expect their wives to adhere to it."

I'd seen none of these traits in Domitiana. "So once he died, Domitiana decided to be exactly the opposite?"

"It seems so. Helvius said that once Severinus was in the family tomb, she bought new clothes, opened the villa for substantial banquets, and began affairs with anyone her husband would have disapproved of."

"Her son did not object?" Once a son became paterfamilias in his own right, he could condemn his mother or even have her executed for her behavior.

"Her son left Rome as quickly as he could. He also revels in his freedom, having been under his father's thumb as well. He stays in Hispania and rarely visits Rome."

"Leaving his mother and sister to do as they like."

"It seems so." Cassia took on a thoughtful expression. "Severina hides behind the respectability of her husband, pretending to be chaste in public, but at home, she does as she likes. Tertius Vestalis Felix was a very popular consul during his year in office, considered to be a wise senator, and also a just ruler the short time he was in the provinces. People talk about Severina's behavior, of course. Shake their heads and declare that Vestalis is a poor, sad old man, but no one dares rebuke him for his choice in wives. They understand he married her to bolster his fortune, and they ignore her excesses, so he won't be shamed."

I raised my brows as I sipped wine. The vintage we could afford was nowhere near as smooth as what I'd been served at Domitiana's, but it was familiar and comforting.

"Vestalis must be held in very high regard then."

"He is. Helvius tells me he loved his first wife deeply and grieved when she died. Still is grieving, which is why he pays no attention to Severina. She's a means to an end, nothing more."

I recalled my speculations about him this evening. "Is he trying to have a son with her?"

"Presumably. Once she gives him an heir, Helvius is certain Vestalis will lock Severina away to keep her from their offspring. So far, though, she has not shown any sign of being with child."

I studied the surface of my watery wine. "How does Helvius know all this?"

"He talks to Severina's servants whenever she comes to visit her mother. He also transcribes Domitiana's letters to Severina and reads all the documents pertaining to Domitiana's household, some of which involve Severina. Mother and daughter tell each other everything."

And the two shared an interest in gladiators.

I took a noisy sip of wine. "Why does Helvius tell you the secrets of his mistress' household? Not very discreet of him."

"Because he knows I would not ask if it were not important," Cassia answered readily. "Helvius would not chatter about all this to just anyone—he takes his post seriously."

"He tells you, because he is in love with you."

Cassia gaped at me in the ensuing silence, the flame from our single oil lamp flickering in her dark eyes.

"That is nonsense," she said faintly.

I shook my head. "I saw how he looked at you. When you laughed, he became ... intoxicated."

As had I. When Cassia had laughed without inhibition at

whatever Helvius had said, she'd been beautiful. Likewise, when she'd danced with Merope, her face bright, her sorrows fallen away, a beauty had shone from her.

Cassia's expression became troubled. "Oh, dear. What a muddle."

"Why do you say this?" My voice had grown gruff, commanding.

"Because I have no wish to cause him pain. Helvius is a friend. Has been for a long time."

"Why would you cause him pain?" I set the wine cup on the table, hard, and liquid splashed over its rim. "He seemed perfectly happy with you."

Cassia's brow furrowed. "I am fond of him, of course, and can speak to him of things only another scribe would understand, but I have no intention of becoming his lover. Neither of us could do so without permission anyway."

"And if you had permission?"

I didn't understand why I asked the question. All I had to say was that she was forbidden from seeing the man again, and that would be the end of it. Her feelings about it shouldn't matter to me.

"It would make no difference. Are you certain Helvius feels this way?" She peered at me. "I should hate to lose his friendship, but I also do not wish to give him false hope."

"Very certain."

Cassia sighed. She began to make a note, then her hand faltered, and she laid down her stylus. "I claim to be so very observant, but I never realized that Helvius cared for me. I am too close to him, I suppose. It is easier to see the true shapes of things from a distance."

Knots unwound from my stomach. Cassia was a truthful person—except when she was haggling to negotiate a better fee for my work—and I believed her. She'd had no idea Helvius was fond of her, and she didn't return the affection.

I ran my hand over my scalp, the short hair prickling my

palm. "Do not break his heart just yet. He might have more useful information about Severina."

"I cannot use his admiration for my own gain," Cassia said with conviction. "I must be honest with him."

"I know you do, but do not make him hate you. There is a killer living freely in Rome still, and Helvius might be able to help find him."

She cocked her head. "You say information about Severina, not Domitiana. Do you think Severina is the one hiring men to kill for her?"

"Possibly." I lifted the cup again but did not drink. "Domitiana is selfish, but I think she is no more than that. She enjoys herself indulging in gladiators and parties and her gardens, yes, but I saw no cruelty in her. She had Herakles fight me with blunted weapons and little possibility for either of us to be hurt. She fussed all over Herakles when he lost—she'd have done the same if he'd won."

"And Severina?" Cassia asked.

"She has a ruthless streak, I think." I shrugged, not knowing how to put my speculations into words. "I've known many gladiators. Some fight only because they are forced to. They do their best to stay alive, but they kill to survive, and regret those they slay. Then there are those who relish the kill. They go out of their way to win, and they gloat in their victory. You see it in their eyes, their need to gut you, to feel your blood on their skin."

Cassia watched me, her face tight. "Have you fought many such men?"

"A few. Most gladiators want to win, yes, but they prefer an honorable fight. They want the glory and to be known for their skill, even if they lose. I have also battled those who would do anything to make the kill." I ran my thumb over the uneven ceramic of the cup. "I won those bouts."

"I am glad."

Her words were quiet, but the sincerity of them warmed something inside me that had been cold a long time.

"They make mistakes, those men," I continued. "They are so certain they will vanquish that they grow overconfident and underestimate their enemy. Too many wins, and they become careless." My speech grew slower. I was tired, and I disliked thinking back on my life in the arena. "I never believed I was destined to win whenever I stepped out onto the sand. Every fight was different. All the training helped my body make decisions for me when the blows began, but I had to let the fight itself tell me what to do. I didn't think about conquest, or death. It was one move at a time. One blow was never the same as the next. I took what the other fighter gave me and gave back what I learned from him."

Cassia's lips had parted as she listened. "I am vain enough to believe myself wise," she said when I finished. "But I believe your wisdom surpasses any I've ever known."

I shook myself out of my remembrances and gazed at her in perplexity. "You have known some very stupid people then."

Her faint smile returned. She always gave me that particular smile after my jokes, as though humoring an elderly relative.

"You should retire," Cassia said. "It has been a long night."

I rose. "Severina has invited me to her home for dinner," I told her. "After the Lupercalia."

All amusement drained from Cassia's face. "No," she said sharply. "You must not go."

CHAPTER 18

I had started to turn for my bed, but I halted. "Why?" I asked sharply. "What did Helvius tell you?"

Cassia rose from her stool. "Nothing that I haven't already relayed. But you just said that she has the cruelty that could have led to the deaths of Ajax and Rufus."

"Yes, she is predatory. Evil even. But what better way to catch her than let her try to kill me?"

"Are you mad?" Cassia balled her fists but kept them rigidly at her sides. "Think. If she is the one, she lures the gladiator to her home with promises of fine food, wine, and amorousness. Once there, she adds something to his food or drink to put him in a stupor or at least lull him to be incautious. Severina has several large bodyguards—they could do the killing for her, for whatever her perverse reason. She will make certain her husband is out—or perhaps she sedates him too. He'd be no help to you even if he was present."

"I don't plan to eat or drink anything she serves me. I'll spit out the food and wine when she isn't looking."

"If the bodyguards are there watching you?" she argued. "You will likely have to swallow *something*. Some poisons work very quickly, even if only a drop gets into your mouth." Cassia, who had been poisoned herself once, shuddered as she spoke.

"I can think of no other way." My voice grew harsh. "Unless we are there to catch her in the act, who would believe us? A former gladiator and a slave sold in the Forum?"

"Nero might."

"*Might.* He will want proof. If Vestalis is as lauded as Helvius claims, the magistrates will be careful about arresting and condemning his wife. She is not a whore in a lupinarius, but the daughter of a very wealthy man and the wife of a former proconsul."

Nero could always override the senate if he wanted a man executed, and he often did, but he would not do so on the speculations of nobodies like us. Yes, he wanted a culprit for the killings, but even he would be careful.

"What if the magistrates refuse to believe you even if you *do* catch her in the act?" Cassia asked. "In that case, you could be very dead, all for nothing."

I put my hand on the wall to keep myself from stomping back and forth in frustration. "What do you suggest, then?"

"As I suggested once before, I can gain entry to Severina's house and observe what she does. Helvius knows their servants. He can sneak me inside."

"No!" I roared.

Cassia took a step back, but she was in no way submissive. "I will watch and report to someone respected, such as Sextus Livius. Vestalis himself can help—he'd not be happy to learn he has a crazed murderer for a wife."

"Now I must ask if *you* are mad. If Severina or her bodyguards discover you, you will be dead on the spot. *I* can at least defend myself. You cannot." I pushed myself from the wall to tower over her. "You already nearly died once when you got in the way of a killer."

"Does that matter?" Cassia asked in a reasonable tone. "Hesiodos can always find you another slave."

"I don't want another slave," I shouted. "I want *you*."

Cassia went still, her voice falling a notch. "Hesiodos will make certain someone else can do your accounts."

"*Accounts?* I don't give a dog's ass about my accounts." I leaned to her, menace in every line of me. Seasoned gladiators had scrambled hastily away whenever I did this, but Cassia only gazed up at me, her eyes round. "I can't do without you, Cassia. I need you."

She continued to stare, as though what I said confounded her. I straightened, trying and failing to stem my rage.

"You will *not* go to Severina's, and you will *not* spy on her," I said in a harsh voice. "You will go nowhere until this killer is found, even if I have to lock you in here. *I* will go, and *you* will stay."

Cassia did not respond, not to argue or weep or rant. She stood very still, fingertips on the table, the folds of her tunic unmoving.

I swung away from her, but I could not go tamely to bed as I'd planned. I slammed open the door and charged down the stairs and out into the darkness.

I had the presence of mind to lock the door behind me, then I strode away into the Roman night.

CASSIA AND I DID NOT DISCUSS THE INVITATION TO SEVERINA'S over the next day and a half. She had been asleep when I'd returned the night I'd stormed out, and I hadn't awakened her. In the morning, she'd tidied the already tidy rooms without a word and departed to bring home water and breakfast.

We didn't speak about anything at all. Cassia busied herself with her tablets, and I went to the baths, then returned to Chryseis's insula and warehouse in the hopes that I would find something—anything—to confirm who the killer was, but I was unlucky. I found nothing but the scraped-clean floor where I suspected the bodies had been cut up, and perhaps where Ajax and Rufus had been killed in the first place, carted here while stupefied or unconscious.

I questioned those who rented part of Chryseis's warehouse from her, but they'd claimed to never have seen anyone suspicious.

Likewise, the family who'd lived across the hall from Chryseis, who had taken my advice and moved to the next building over, could tell me little. The father, after much persuasion, admitted that a big man had paid him well to vacate the rooms and move upstairs the day Cassia and I had found Rufus. His description matched what Albus, the armorer's apprentice, had given me—large nose and thick dark hair.

This did not help much, though I scoured the streets every time I was on them for a man matching such a description.

The basketmaker had suddenly taken his family to visit his mother in Ostia. This from the coppersmith in the next shop, who also had no information for me.

The Subura revealed even less, and I returned home, discouraged.

The day of Lupercalia dawned.

This festival for the purification of the city was so old few remembered how it began, but the populace, as usual, turned out to celebrate. In front of the cave where tradition had it that Romulus and Remus had been raised in infancy, two young men were anointed with blood from animals sacrificed there. Armed with strips of these animals' flesh, they then began a sprint around the lower slopes of the Palatine, merrily striking out at those they passed.

I had walked to the Palatine to join the crowd for the festivities, but Cassia had declined to accompany me, saying she had things to put in order. I'd simply departed—we'd been stiff with each other since our argument.

Women thrust out hands and arms as the young men ran

past, eager to be struck by the bloody strips, which conveyed fertility. The youths happily obliged.

One of the young men came at me. His eyes were wide under a forehead smeared with drying blood, his red mouth open in laughter. I tried to dodge, but he ran resolutely into me, stinging me on the forearm with his makeshift whip.

The woman next to me flung herself at him as the whip came down, managing to catch the end of it on her hand. She spun away, smiling.

I studied the tiny spatter of blood on my arm from the strip of animal flesh. I'd never thought about my own fertility—my focus in life thus far had been surviving to live another day.

As my skin tingled from the brief slap, I wondered if I would ever have children. A boy, perhaps, to dog my footsteps and listen to me drone on about building walls or traveling around Roman lands in exhibition bouts to cheering crowds. Or a daughter, one to buy pretty trinkets for and to hoist on my shoulders so she could watch the chariot races.

I shut down the thoughts. Children lived perilous lives—accidents and fevers took away so many, not to mention people ready to steal a child for the price he or she would bring. Parents grieved for children all the time, as Marcianus, who tried to save many of them, attested. Small stones erected up and down the Appian Way and other roads outside the walls were sad testaments to short lives.

A man's hope for a child to carry on his name could quickly end in tragedy. Having a family was a frightening business.

And yet. I recalled the boy I'd found not long ago and taken to stay with Xerxes' widow. I'd grown fond of him in the brief time I'd known him and had wanted to protect him. Marcella had children of her own, mites who were so like Xerxes, smiling and laughing as they tumbled about the place.

I told myself it was futile to contemplate having a boy or girl of my own when I was obligated to a benefactor I didn't even know. What would this man or woman do if I suddenly decided to walk away and start a family?

Still, the phantom boy and girl I'd never have rose before me. The boy looked like I had as a youth, and the girl resembled Cassia ...

Abruptly I tore myself from the crowd on the Palatine and went back down the hill, my thoughts tangled.

ONCE DARKNESS HAD FALLEN THAT EVENING, I PULLED ON A clean tunic and trudged from our home to the Caelian Hill. Cassia made note of the time I left—the second hour of night—but she said nothing at all to me as I went, her lips tight.

I did not like Cassia angry at me, but I did not want to argue about this mission again. We needed to learn anything about Severina we could, and Severina had handed me a perfect opportunity.

I crossed the Forum Romanum and headed along the Sacra Via, past the Palatine on my right, and a marshy valley on my left. On the other side of the Palatine, I followed Severina's bodyguard's instructions and found the Clivus Scauri winding upward toward the small shrine of Minerva near the top of the Caelian.

The domii grew more opulent as I snaked up the hill, the homes wider and taller. Finally, they became true villas, surrounded by walls to keep out intruders.

I hesitated before the gate that led to Severina's domus. Would she want her neighbors to see a gladiator knocking at the front door? I saw no other entrance, however, so I bashed at the gate with my fist.

The door quickly opened, Severina's large guard with the shaved head peering out at me. He silently beckoned me inside, then marched me at a quick pace past the atrium and along a wide hall that ran the length of the right side of the house.

This was only one wing of the villa, I realized. The place was large enough to have several of those on both floors, probably divided into public and private quarters. As only Severina and her husband lived here, that meant plenty of unused rooms, rooms in which a gladiator could be secretly killed before being hauled off to the warehouse for butchering.

The bodyguard took me to a triclinium that was several times the size of the one at Domitiana's. Low tables, empty now, stood before three dining couches, which were strewn with cushions and silk throws.

I was the only person in the empty room, no sign of Severina. The bodyguard indicated I should take a place on the middle couch, where the most honored guests were seated.

He walked away before I settled myself to wait, his sandals making almost no noise on the polished mosaic floor.

I lounged on my side, my feet sticking out over the end of the sofa, my legs too long for it. I hoped Severina and any other guests would arrive soon because the comfortable couch made my tired eyes droop. My body seized upon any excuse to sleep.

Servants pattered quietly in, setting dishes of food and cups of wine on the tables. I didn't touch them, remembering my promise to Cassia.

Severina kept me waiting for a long time. Oil lamps burned in holders shaped like flowers or fruit—one was a naked nymph who held the flame between her breasts. Another, I observed idly, was in the shape of a phallus, the flame coming out the business end.

I eyed the food—plain apricots, fried dough cases with unknown content, a salad with torn bread soaked in vinegar among cheese, nuts, and cooked eggs, all drizzled with honey.

My stomach rumbled with hunger, but I smelled garum in the salad, which kept my appetite at bay. I was an unusual Roman who didn't like garum, the salty fish paste the highborn and lowborn alike smeared on everything.

Just as I contemplated taking an apricot away with me to test for poison, Severina glided into the room.

I had expected her to dress provocatively for this tryst, but she wore a modest stola belted under the breasts and at the waist, clasped at her shoulders with silver fibulae. The fabric was silk, full enough to drape over her in many folds. I imagined her maid had spent much time setting every pleat exactly. The tunic beneath bunched over the top of the stola, hiding her breasts.

A wig of tall dark curls arched up from Severina's forehead, her own hair pulled sleekly back behind it, a few curls of it drooping to her neck. No different from what any Roman matron would wear to a formal dinner.

Severina waved away the two maids who'd followed her and faced me alone.

"You," she said archly. Either she'd forgotten my name or did not think I deserved to be addressed by it. "Why have you eaten nothing? Do you believe my food tainted?"

I could not tell what was in her eyes. Did she taunt me? Or was she wary?

I rose from the couch and made a low bow to her. "I thought it rude to eat before you did, lady."

"Oh." She sounded pleased. "Sit. Do. You're too tall for me to look up at. And eat." Once I had reclined once more on the couch, she took up an apricot and held it to my lips.

There wasn't much I could do but open my mouth. I saw the gleam of a lamp on the shaved head of her bodyguard and wondered if she'd have him beat me if I refused. I had confidence I could fight him, but then I'd be thrown out of the house and learn nothing.

I parted my lips. Severina slid the apricot into my mouth, brushing my tongue with her finger. She withdrew, and I chewed and swallowed.

I tasted nothing but apricot, a fine, ripe one. If it held poison, I couldn't discern it.

Severina decided that feeding me was enjoyable. She seated

herself next to me, her silk stola brushing my bare thigh with warmth. Morsels came at me: the pastry cases that enclosed spiced meat; almonds covered in honey; the vinegar-soaked bread. All of it was savory, the sweet nuts and cool bread a good match for the warm well-seasoned meat. Fortunately, she didn't feed me the garum-soaked greens.

"I want you to be full and happy." Severina shoved another almond into my mouth and licked honey from her fingers. "A sated man is a gentle man. You are so strong." She ran a sticky palm over my upper arm, pressing at the muscle there.

Women liked to trace the arcs of my arms, finding the firmness of them pleasing. Usually, I didn't mind, but I wondered if Severina concealed a pin in her hand to scratch the poison into me that way.

I felt nothing but the smoothness of her fingertips. The food all tasted as it should, nothing odd. I recognized that Severina had a talented cook.

The servants slid in to remove the empty dishes and serve the second course. They brought platters of meats with or without sauces; a dish that contained pork, spices, and mint; and pastry cases of all shapes and sizes including one of a phallus stuffed with ground nuts and cream. Severina laughed with excitement when she had me bite the top from that one. To me, it was nothing but fried dough and nuts, but her eyes flared with longing as I ate it.

Eventually, Severina grew tired of feeding me and began to drop food into her own mouth. She lifted the morsels high, parting her lips and lacing her tongue around them to pull them inside. I suppose she meant to entice me. When she obviously wanted me to feed her, I obliged, she licking my fingers at every chance she could.

Severina ate exactly the same food I did. None of it tasted wrong, and none was gilded.

Next came wine. More servants carried in jugs to pour wine

without dilution into a series of cups. It was very good wine, and Severina drank plenty.

If Severina imbibed the same wine from the same jugs as I did, then any poison would be in the cup itself, put there before the servants brought it into the room. Instead of drinking from the fine gold vessel offered me, I seized Severina's half-drunk cup and drained it myself.

She started, rage flickering across her face, then the anger cleared, and she laughed in delight. She called for more wine, which she poured across her neck and expected me to lick it clean.

As I did so, ignoring her pawing hands, jingling bells and the soft but steady beat of a drum announced that entertainment had arrived. A very familiar beating of a drum.

Once Severina finally released me—shoving me impatiently away—I sat up again and swiveled to survey the dancers.

I stilled for one heartbeat before I arranged my face in neutral lines. The musician was Gaius, tapping a wide drum tucked under his arm, and the dancer, clad in thin linen, bells on her wrists and ankles, was Merope.

CHAPTER 19

Gaius never looked at me, only watched Merope, keeping his beat steady. Merope had her eyes half-closed, dreamily following the music.

What were the chances that Gaius and Merope had managed to have themselves hired in this very house this very night? I had the feeling I knew exactly how Merope and Gaius had come by their invitation.

Cassia had been wise, I decided as I imbibed another cup of wine. If Severina sent in her men to kill me as I lay in a drunken stupor, Merope and Gaius could run for help. No one paid attention to dancers when they weren't performing—they could slip out unnoticed.

Very wise.

"Pardon?" Severina was against me, her face near mine. Her breath smelled of garum.

I realized I'd mumbled the words out loud. "Fine," I amended. "The meal is very fine."

"Of course it is. What did you expect?" She sat up and clapped her hands, very loudly, next to my ear. "Clear it off. We're tired of it. Bring the sweets."

Severina collapsed against me as the servants scuttled in to remove the dishes as quickly as possible. The moment they disappeared, another set of lackeys scurried in with platters heaped with fruit and dates, more pastries coated with honey, and nuts broken and whole.

Severina drizzled honey from a pot onto my shoulder. "Let me feast on *you*."

I held myself still while she cleaned my skin with her tongue. Gaius glanced swiftly at me then away.

Severina did this several more times. In between she pressed more wine on me, the rich taste making my head lighter and lighter.

After a time, Severina swung on Gaius and Merope, bringing her hands together in another loud clap.

"Enough," she shouted. "Go. The noise is making my head ache."

The drumming instantly ceased. Merope spun to a halt, gracefully bowing low. Severina took no notice of her. Merope ran out to the passageway, jingling softly. Gaius, with another surreptitious glance at me, followed her.

The room quieted. The servants had gone, except for the bodyguard in deep shadow, his eyes glittering.

Was he waiting for a signal from his mistress? Ready to beat down the drunken gladiator and add him to the dead?

Severina took my cup of wine from me and swallowed the last dregs in it. Her lack of worry about drinking it made me conclude that perhaps Ajax and Rufus hadn't been poisoned after all, only made so drunk on potent wine they'd been unable to fight.

My hostess threw her leg over mine and slid herself onto my body. Her stola hoisted itself to her hips, but her tunic beneath shielded her bare skin from me.

She began to kiss me, then to slither back and forth on my torso, as though she knew the theory of what to do with a man but hadn't had much practice. I realized, as Severina went on, that she was simply drunk. She'd imbibed even more wine than I had.

I clutched her as she started to slide from me, fearing she'd smack her head on the table or the floor if she fell. Severina laughed, believing me amorous.

She covered my face and my neck with honey-sticky kisses, then she laid her head on my shoulder, stilling.

The bodyguard stared from the darkness, unmoving. I tensed under my intoxication, eying the table for any knife I might use for defense. We'd eaten with fingers only, however, the food cut into bite-sized portions in the kitchen, as was done in polite households.

After a moment, Severina began to snore.

I glanced down to find her eyes tightly closed and her mouth half-open, her breathing sonorous. A minute line of spittle trickled from the corner of her lips.

Footsteps sounded in the dark doorway. The bodyguard came to attention, then stepped back, fading from sight.

Severina's husband, Tertius Vestalis Felix, entered the dining room. He approached the tables in a slow shuffle, as though he didn't notice his wife draped over a huge gladiator on the dining couch. A shaky hand, skin almost transparent, reached for the almonds and scooped up a few.

"Sir." I gently untangled myself from Severina and laid her on the cushions as I rose from them.

Vestalis munched his almonds and plunked heavily down on the couch as far from Severina as possible. He peered at me in indifference.

"Never mind, boy." His eyes sharpened as he studied me. "If you get a son on her, though, I will claim it as mine. I need an heir."

I shot a glance at Severina, now curled up on the pillows, sleeping the sleep of the guiltless.

"I do not believe that will happen tonight," I said.

Vestalis slid his gaze to his wife. "She reminds me of a wild animal, like a monkey one brings back from Africa as a pet. She runs about and plays then falls asleep."

Watching Severina now and recalling how she'd behaved at her mother's house, I considered it a very good description.

I bowed, my legs unsteady. "I will go."

Vestalis waved a hand filled with almonds at me. "No, no. Sit down and partake. All this food shouldn't go to waste. She'll simply throw it out."

When a patrician commanded me, I was obliged to obey. I sat next to him and lifted a few grapes from their basket. My belly was full, but I could have a few morsels if he insisted.

We didn't recline, simply sat with our feet on the ground, as we would at an informal meal at a popina. Vestalis's teeth ground the almonds to bits, the crunching sound nearly drowning out Severina's snores.

"You're a gladiator no longer, I hear." Vestalis reached for the dates. "Given the *rudis*. Felicitations on surviving the games. They are brutal. But you were a champion."

"I fought to survive," I said without rancor. "I was glad to leave the life behind."

Vestalis chuckled, his face softening. "Modest too. A gladiator is the very picture of *virtus*, is he not? Strong, powerful, lauded, courageous. Everything the soft-bellied senators want to be."

Virtus—the elusive word meaning honor, courage, fortitude. The highest achievement a Roman man could obtain was to be known for his *virtus*.

"I fought because I had no choice."

"Of course you didn't. But old consuls who haven't led men in battle in these peaceful days envy those in the arena. Wouldn't want to *actually* find themselves there, you know." More thin laughter.

"No, sir."

"I found my glory in the provinces." Vestalis ate dates with a sucking sound, then returned to almonds. He lifted a jug of wine, shook it to see if any remained, then trickled it into a spare cup.

He ate and drank without worry, from which I decided that our idea of Severina's food being tainted was far off the mark.

"You were a proconsul," I prompted, as Vestalis seemed to want to talk.

He swallowed his wine. "Went to several places. Spent a few years in Britannia." He shuddered. "Never go to Britannia, Leonidas. It's cold, damp, and full of howling savages. I preferred Hispania, but only just."

I wasn't certain how he wanted me to respond, so I gave him a polite nod.

"Hispania is where I met *her*." Vestalis gestured with his cup to the sleeping Severina. "Came across her brother there—he's a praetor in a small town among the olive groves. Severina and her mother were visiting him, just after Domitiana's husband died. The brother, Severinus, wanted to get young Severina married off. She was trouble, though he tried to hide that fact. She chased after legionnaires and gladiators like a tart. The family hushed it up, but she was a worry. I sought a fortune, and Severinus sought a husband for his wayward sister. So I married her."

Again, I had no idea how he wanted me to respond. I ate a few more grapes in silence.

"You wonder why, eh?" Vestalis's humor faded. "I never had much money, though I could not complain about my career, or my lineage. But it was empty, in the end."

Helvius had said that Vestalis had lost his first wife and daughter during his years as proconsul. I saw the grief in him still. If his affection lay strongly with that wife, he'd not have expected to form any attachment to Severina. He'd walked into the marriage knowing exactly what Severina was, and did not care.

"I wanted the comfort of a large house and plenty of money to take me into old age," Vestalis went on. "The family is respectable enough, no matter how the women of it try to ruin that. *I* have great respectability. That is what I gave young Severinus in exchange for his sister's wealth."

The gaze Vestalis sent to Severina was one a man might give to an unruly child that he had no intention of looking after. There was unconcern, even detachment.

Vestalis inhaled one more handful of almonds. "Go home, gladiator. She won't wake until morning."

I rose, swaying a little. I moved one step to Severina, intending to straighten her stola over her exposed legs, but Vestalis shooed me off.

"Her maids will attend her. Good night, Leonidas the Spartan. Thank you for speaking with me."

I inclined my head. Out of nowhere, Severina's bodyguard appeared, ready to usher me from the room.

Vestalis snatched the last of the grapes and stepped out to the peristyle, brushing past me as though he'd already forgotten about me. The bodyguard motioned for me to follow him.

I left the massive, quiet house. Gaius and Merope were nowhere in sight—I assumed they'd been escorted out a servants' entrance. The bodyguard said nothing at all, only opened the front door at the vestibule and stood aside so I could depart into the night.

As soon as I was on the street, the door shut with a bang, and I heard the bolt being dragged across it.

I was alone at the top of the Caelian Hill, having learned absolutely nothing from the one person I'd most suspected of the crimes. No one had tried to poison me, strike me, kill me, or butcher me.

I drew in lungsful of the cool night air, preparing for the long and unsteady walk home.

I WAS NEARLY ROBBED SEVERAL TIMES AS I STUMBLED TO THE Quirinal. I carried little money, but this did not stop a burly, smelly man trying to push me into a wall and another from attempting to garrote me. My body came alive to elbow the garotte man hard in the gut until he retched in pain and for the burly man to be smashed face-forward into the wall for his trouble. In the darkness of the Vicus Compiti Acili, a third man came at me with a knife, only to stop short a few paces away.

"Aren't you Leonidas the Spartan?" His tone held admiration. "I've seen many of your bouts. Won coin on you."

I supposed he wanted me to congratulate him. I growled like the fierce fighting man I had been, and he chortled in delight. "Good night to you then."

Before I left him, I grabbed his knife and threw it across the stones, where it skittered into a sewer. He'd not be able to rob another with it tonight.

He tottered away, laughing. "Bested by Leonidas the Spartan. No one will believe me."

I kept a wary eye out the rest of the way home.

The aftermath of the fights was crashing me toward sleep on top of all the wine and food. I had to hold on to the walls as I climbed the stairs to our apartment, and this after fumbling with the outer door's key for a very long time.

I found Cassia still awake. She hummed to herself as she bent over her scrolls, a lone oil lamp flickering in the darkness. The point of light stabbed into my eyes, my head aching.

I shut the door after I nearly fell into the apartment and leaned against it, wondering how I would reach the far side of the room and my bed.

"You." I pointed a wobbling finger at Cassia. "You found a way to go after all."

Cassia rose, setting aside her pen, and regarded me in all innocence. "I never left the apartment, I promise you. You were wise to tell me to remain out of danger."

I kept jabbing with my finger. "You sent spies to watch over me."

"You mean Merope and Gaius?" She flushed. "I might have

mentioned their names to Helvius and suggested they be hired for Severina's dinner tonight. Did they perform well?"

"Spies," I said this with conviction as I stumbled on the uneven floor.

Cassia was beside me in an instant, her cool touch balancing me. I reflected that her gentle fingers were far more pleasant on my skin than Severina's groping, honey-sticky ones.

"Guards," Cassia contradicted softly. "They were to run for help at the first sign of trouble. But as you are home, and safe, then we must be wrong about Severina."

I tried to tell Cassia what had happened—about the feast and wine, Severina's flirtation and attempted seduction ending with her falling asleep, and my conversation with Vestalis. Banal events that were nothing like the intrigue and danger I'd expected.

My words came out slurred and garbled. Cassia towed me to the bed and nudged me down to it. I didn't need any coaxing—my body fell onto the reed mattress in an ungainly heap.

I kept trying to explain my story, but Cassia only straightened my limbs and removed my sandals.

"Hush," she said, her voice tranquil. "Sleep now. We'll speak in the morning."

I saw the sense in this and closed my mouth and my eyes. I felt a blanket ease over me and Cassia's touch on my shoulder.

"Thank all the gods you are well, Leonidas." The words were a low murmur, but I heard them as I slid into a deep and numbing sleep.

WHEN I SWAM AWAKE THE NEXT MORNING, THE SUN WAS WELL up, the apartment warm. Cassia sat at the table, writing as usual. The street outside was very quiet, which meant I'd slept through the time when nearby residents lined up to buy their daily supply of wine.

I raised my head and immediately regretted it. The rich food and drink I'd taken at Severina's table roiled in my stomach and pounded through my skull.

Cassia glanced up. "Good morning," she said brightly.

"Is it morning?" I mumbled, or thought I did.

"Nearly afternoon. I've mixed something for you to drink." She pointed with her stylus to the copper cup that usually held my wine.

I never wanted to eat or drink anything ever again. With great effort, I heaved myself to a sitting position, realizing I smelled of old sweat and Severina's cloying perfume.

Standing came next. That took a while. Finally, I was on my feet, staggering toward the table.

How I reached it without bringing up everything that was in my stomach, I never knew. I held on to the thick boards of the table and lowered myself gingerly to my stool while Cassia watched me without expression.

She slid the cup to me, and I peered down into gray-green sludge. "What is it?" I croaked.

"A mixture to make you feel better. Nonus Marcianus taught me how to prepare it."

Marcianus's concoctions usually resembled something an animal had spat up. But I trusted him and trusted Cassia, so I lifted the cup to my mouth, closed my eyes, and swallowed what was inside it.

The mixture tasted as foul as it appeared. The liquid oozed down into my stomach where it settled like lead.

"When you are up to it, I have bread and eggs for you to eat," Cassia said.

"I don't want any food."

Ignoring me, Cassia rummaged in one of her boxes and pulled out what looked like a small, flat board. "I bought something for you yesterday."

She set the wooden board in front of me, which had a polished surface with letters carved into it. I recognized a few as the letters in my name, but they were in random order, and I could not put them together. Cassia laid a stylus next to the board.

I lifted a puzzled gaze to see Cassia beaming at me, as though she expected me to know what to do.

"What is this?" I asked, touching the smooth wood.

"It is a writing board." Cassia lifted the stylus and fitted it between my fingers. "A tutor at a street school sold it to me. You will use it to learn your letters."

CHAPTER 20

I stared at the board in perplexity. The marks on it ran from side to side, top to bottom, neatly inscribed in straight lines.

I'd seen a tutor near the ludus the day Aemil had first asked me to find his gladiators, the man admonishing the half dozen children around him while they hunched over boards like these, small faces screwed up in frustration. It was a common sight on Roman streets.

I clutched the stylus in my fist. "How will this teach me letters?"

"Like so." Cassia pried the stylus out of my hand and ran its point through the first letter on the board, then the second. "You trace the letters, again and again, so your hand gets used to forming the shapes. Similar to training with your sword and the posts, except now you are using a pen and letter board."

She handed the stylus back to me as though she'd explained everything. Bemused, I studied the stylus—about as long as my hand, the thin bronze stick had a point on one end, the other flattened. I'd watched Cassia rub out letters on the wax with the flat end.

I held the stylus between my thick fingers and drew it down the angled straight side of the first letter on the board.

The stylus caught on the wood and started to bend. Cassia quickly put her hand over mine. "Not so exuberantly. A light touch."

I gazed at our fingers, hers slim and elegant, nails trimmed and clean, mine blunt, scarred, unwashed. Her touch was cool, like silk, yet her hand was warm.

I did not realize how long I stared at her hand on mine until she lifted it away.

"Try again," she said, as though nothing remarkable had happened.

I carefully traced the first letter, two angles and a crosspiece. I tried to start with the crosspiece, but Cassia directed me to trace the two angled lines first. I had no idea why.

"That is the letter A," she explained. "It begins all kinds of words. Aqueduct, *architectus*, *amicus* ..."

I glanced up at Cassia, she composed, with a small smile on her face. How she expected me to remember all this I didn't know, and I had traced only one letter.

The next had a long stem and two humps.

"The letter B," Cassia told me. "*Bene,* Britannia."

"Vestalis—Severina's husband—had been in Britannia," I said as I went on to the next letter, a continuous curve. "So he told me. Also Hispania."

"Did he? That is interesting."

I raised my head again. "Why is it interesting? We already knew he met Severina in Hispania."

Cassia regarded me thoughtfully. "That he told you his history at all."

"I think he needed someone to talk to. He only has Severina and all his servants. The house is large. Echoing. Full of furniture and nothing else."

"A cold place, yes. So Merope told me." Cassia leaned her folded arms on the table. "That is the letter C. Many words begin with it—*canis*, *carus* ... Cassia."

An important letter. I would not forget it.

We continued along the board. Cassia gave me words for each letter that promptly dissolved in my head. After a time, I drank a cup of wine she passed me and nibbled on a chunk of bread.

"How long did it take you to learn to read?" I asked when we'd reached the middle of the board. The letter M—*medicus, mitte*, Marcianus.

"I don't remember. I was a tiny child. A few weeks, I suppose."

"A few weeks?" I stared at the board and the letters I still didn't comprehend, except *L* for Leonidas and the powerful *C*. "I'll be a few years at it."

"That doesn't matter. As long as it's clear in the end."

She was humoring me. I also realized that while I'd labored, my stomach had settled, and I was eating and drinking without discomfort. Marcianus's tinctures worked miracles.

I'd begun the next letter when a banging on the door gave me the excuse to toss down the stylus. I rubbed my hand, which hadn't cramped like this since the days I'd first begun to use a sword, and went down the stairs to open the door at the bottom.

Merope pushed past me without greeting, scampering up the stairs to find Cassia. She had been out almost as late as I had, and dancing, yet she raced upward on light feet while I plodded heavily behind her.

"The vigiles arrested the basketmaker," Merope said breathlessly when she reached the apartment. "The one who lives downstairs from Chryseis. They were waiting for him when he returned home last night and nabbed him. Martolia saw it happen." Merope's usual smiles were gone, her brows drawn in anger. "That woman killed Rufus, I know it, even if she didn't strike the blow herself. We can't let someone else pay for her crimes."

I wasn't certain the basketmaker was innocent and Chryseis guilty—the man was hiding something—but I agreed he shouldn't be condemned out of hand.

Cassia was already on her feet, reaching for her cloak. "Yes, we must go. The poor man."

"Wait." I stepped in front of the doorway as the two women rushed for it. "Merope, go home. Cassia and I will find the basketmaker." I pictured Merope in her grief and anger trying to drag the basketmaker to freedom and only being arrested with him.

Merope scowled, but Cassia said, "It is best. Do you know where they took him?"

"Watch house on the Aventine, Martolia told me. She danced at a house nearby last night and when she was walking home, she saw the vigile captain take the basketmaker away."

I'd wondered why Merope had come alone with Gaius the night before. Likely the sisters each took different jobs so they could make more money in one night.

Cassia clasped her shoulder. "We will find him and help him," she promised.

Merope quieted, but only a trifle. "I don't understand why Chryseis isn't locked in the Tullianum."

She'd been released on my conviction that she hadn't murdered Rufus. "Because she had no reason to kill him," I said.

Merope turned her frown on me. "Of course she did. Spite and vengeance on me and Martolia. *She* did it, mark my words, not that silly idiot you were trying to seduce last night. Severina fell asleep," Merope told Cassia with a snort of laughter. "Such were the charms of Leonidas the Spartan."

Severina had been trying to seduce *me*, but I decided not to argue. I stood aside and gestured Merope out the door. Cassia wound her cloak around herself and stepped past me to descend the stairs. Whatever she'd thought of Merope's last declaration was lost in the folds of wool.

We headed toward the Aventine. Rome was at its height of activity, and the markets were thronged. Soon people would drift home to eat their midday meal and head to the baths, but at the moment, the crowds were thick.

It was the middle of Parentalia now, and the occasional small procession of a family honoring their ancestors snaked through, blank death masks on the faces of the family members. Cassia and I would honor our deceased parents, and I would add Xerxes, who'd been as close as a brother, with a small feast on Feralia, the festival's final day.

Merope slipped away from us at the Basilica Julia, making nimbly for the Tiber and a bridge to take her home. I hoped she'd stay there.

I led Cassia through the masses around the cattle market and on past the Circus Maximus, where races would be held at the beginning of the next month in honor of Mars.

We reached the fountain of the three fishes on the Aventine. A right turn would lead us to Marcianus's, but we went left to find the house of the vigiles, which lay near Chryseis's insula.

As it was midday, only an idle guard sat in the lower room of the house. When I strode inside without knocking, he nearly fell off his stool. He was up quickly, however, a sharp sword pointed at my chest.

"Where is Vatia?" I demanded.

"Asleep," the guard growled. He was a different man from the guard I'd spoken to when I'd come to inquire about Chryseis, and less affable. "Out. I don't care if you are Leonidas the Spartan. I'll not let you wake him."

"Where is the man you brought in last night? The basketmaker?"

The guard lowered his sword in confusion. "What do you want with *him*? We had to bring the whole family. His wife kicked up a big fuss."

"Where is he?" I leaned to the man, putting plenty of menace into my words.

The guard backed a step, but perplexity overrode his fear. "You can't talk to them. They don't even speak a sensible language."

A weary male voice rolled from above as I moved in on the

guard. "It's all right. We have him in the cellar, Leonidas. Won't say a word in any language at all."

Vatia clattered down the stairs, his tunic rumpled and his face unshaved but his boots in place. "Truth to tell, I'd be glad to be rid of the man, so if you can make him talk we can either turn him loose or send him to the cohorts."

He reached the ground floor, combing fingers through his thick hair as though trying to force it into some sort of order, and unbolted a door at the back of the room. Vatia waved at the guard to lead us down a narrow set of stone steps, he bringing up the rear.

I suppressed a shudder as I descended, Cassia close behind me. I didn't like underground spaces, having spent too much time first in prison and then in cells deep inside amphitheatres, waiting for my turn to battle on the sand. Not good memories.

The cellar was larger than the house above us, but that did not make me feel any better. A wide central hall ran its length with cells on either side, complete with the stink of sewage and unbathed prisoners.

The basketmaker and his wife and daughter had been crammed together into a cell at the far end of the corridor. The guard unlocked the door, holding his sword ready, but the three inside were not about to rush him and try to make their escape.

The wife glared at us, though the daughter huddled in the corner, and the basketmaker sat dejectedly on the floor, staring at nothing. When the wife spied Cassia, she stiffened.

Cassia stepped around me and began speaking before Vatia or the guard could force the prisoners to their feet. Rapid and fluent Aeolian Greek flowed from her lips. The basketmaker jerked his head up, eyes rounding as he recognized her.

"What's she saying?" Vatia asked me in bewilderment.

I shrugged. "I don't speak Greek."

Neither did the guard, obviously, who watched Cassia with a blank expression.

When Cassia finished, the basketmaker began to weep.

Broken sentences tumbled from his mouth, his hands moving shakily. The daughter drew into an even tighter ball, hiding her face in her knees.

The wife, on the other hand, sprang to her feet and started shouting in Aeolian, first at her husband, then at Cassia, then her husband again.

Vatia strode forward. He carried no sword but balled his big fists, which could easily break bones.

"What is he telling you?" he demanded of Cassia.

Cassia turned to him, shrinking slightly in on herself, a stance she took when she wanted to appease another. "He says ..."

The wife lunged desperately at Cassia, but Vatia seized the woman by the tunic and jerked her back.

Cassia tucked a lock of her hair behind her ear and continued, "The basketmaker says he is ashamed. He saw a man go into the insula, who he now realizes was the killer. He thought nothing of it—men visit tenants of the insula all the time. The basketmaker is cut up inside for not understanding that the man was a murderer, and realizes that if he'd stopped him, he might have saved the life of another."

The wife hung silently in Vatia's grip, her mouth dropping open. Cassia did not look at her, keeping her gaze on Vatia.

"Oh, yes?" Vatia growled. "Why didn't he say so when we came for him? Or why didn't *she*?" He shook the woman.

"She didn't know," Cassia said quickly. "She wasn't certain what her husband saw." Cassia asked the basketmaker a question, and he replied without hesitation, tears in his eyes. "He did not know how to explain, and he was confused," Cassia told Vatia. "He doesn't understand much Latin."

The daughter now peered fearfully from her knees. The wife continued to stare at Cassia, lips parted. I shook my head at her ever so slightly, and the woman snapped her mouth closed.

"Will he swear that on his ancestors?" Vatia asked in irritation. "I'm not giving the cohorts a man who weeps and can't answer their questions. They'll torture him and throw him out. If he can describe the man he saw ..."

I read sympathy in Vatia. A man with a wife and daughter who happened to be in the wrong place at the wrong time would not drive him to cruelty. He'd prefer a real culprit with the word *murderer* branded on his forehead, carrying the exact evidence to convict him, to stop by the vigiles' house to give himself up. I sensed that Vatia preferred fighting fires to arresting people.

Cassia again spoke to the basketmaker. I knew the man was far more involved than what Cassia had told Vatia, but he'd be safe as long as Vatia didn't understand him. If the wife and daughter remained silent, all might be well.

"He describes a large man, broad of shoulder," Cassia said after she'd finished her chat. "With a large nose and wiry black hair, quite a lot of it. This man entered the insula alone before the eleventh hour, but the basketmaker doesn't remember seeing him come out. He was busy in the back of the shop. As he says, many come and go from the insula."

"What about them?" Vatia jerked his chin at the wife and daughter. "What did they see?"

"Nothing at all. They were quite focused on their tasks, as it was a very busy day."

Vatia heaved a sigh that came from the bottom of his boots. "Any number of men might have large noses and a full head of hair, but at least it's something."

"Others have described this man," I put in. "He is very likely the killer of both Ajax and Rufus."

As Vatia gave a signal to his guard to lead the three prisoners out, I suddenly wondered if the basketmaker, or Volteius the armorer, or his apprentice Albus, would recognize the big man if he'd shaved off his memorable head of hair. Would he then resemble Severina's lead bodyguard?

"I believe you," Vatia said, cutting through my pondering. "But searching every street for a man with a pile of hair and a big nose will be tedious. My commander may tell me to leave it. The dead men were only ..."

He broke off uncomfortably, stopping short of saying *They were only gladiators.*

Scowling, Vatia stomped out after his guard. I took Cassia's arm and led her after them.

Once we were all back on the street, the basketmaker lost no time in herding his wife and daughter home. They hurried close together, the basketmaker peering fearfully over his shoulder at us before they rounded a corner and were lost to sight.

I thanked Vatia for his help—he grunted a response but appeared relieved that he didn't have to deal with the basketmaker and family any longer.

I turned our steps to Marcianus's, wanting to seek his opinion of my ideas. I needed his steady head in all this.

Marcianus was in but seeing a patient, a woman who jabbered at him in his back room. Marcianus's calming tones rolled to us, cut off by the woman insisting she needed a charm to heal her festering hand, not Marcianus's paste. We glimpsed Marcia in another room, grinding something in a stone mortar, probably the concoction Marcianus was trying to prescribe the woman.

I sat on the bench just inside the cool front room to wait, Cassia sinking down beside me.

"What did the basketmaker really say?" I asked her in a low voice.

Cassia glanced outside the open door to make certain we wouldn't be overheard.

"He was paid to let the man into the building," she murmured. "Paid quite a lot, though the basketmaker did not specify how much. This man came not long before we arrived the first time. He was lugging a large bag, and paid the basketmaker and his wife to say nothing. The basketmaker took the money, believing the man simply there for a secret liaison. This happens all the time, and a few coins are always welcome. When the basketmaker learned about the murder, he realized the man who'd paid them was the killer, or at least he'd lugged in Rufus's body after the fact. The basketmaker feared that if anyone found out he took the man's coin he'd be arrested as part of the conspiracy and possibly his entire family condemned for it. Hence, his sudden trip to Ostia. When no one came after him, he thought it safe to return to Rome, but a vigile saw him and Captain Vatia hauled him in for questioning."

If the basketmaker had no friends among the magistrates, then he'd been right to worry about himself and his family.

"This is not what you told Vatia," I said quietly.

Cassia moved her shoulders in a shrug. "Does the man deserve to die because he welcomed a few sestertii from the wrong man? Does his wife or daughter deserve to be sold into slavery for it? I told Vatia what he needed to know."

I studied her, a small woman with a crooked nose and soft eyes. "That was good of you."

Another shrug. "The basketmaker is not a bad man."

"And he speaks Aeolian Greek."

"It was pleasant to hear it again."

There was a faint quaver in her voice. Cassia probably hadn't spoken much of that language since her father had died.

I rested my hand on hers. Cassia turned her head and met my gaze a brief moment, one that revealed her loneliness, which she covered every day with her determination to get on with life. She bared herself in that one instant, before she blinked, shutting out her inner self as thoroughly as she swathed her body in her cloak.

I squeezed her hand gently and released it.

Running footsteps drew my attention outside. I spied Septimius, the bulky gate guard from the ludus, approaching Marcianus's place in a hurried shuffle.

I assumed he was rushing to bid Marcianus to tend an injured gladiator, but when Septimius saw me, he ducked inside and heaved a sigh of relief.

"Leonidas, thank the gods. You weren't home so I came to tell Marcianus to help me find you. Aemil is asking for you. Bellowing for you, more like."

I was on my feet. "Why? What's happened?"

"Regulus is gone." Septimius rested his fists on his hips, trying to catch his breath. "He vanished last night and didn't turn up this morning. Aemil is livid. And afraid he's going to be a corpse like the others. Come and calm Aemil down before he beats us all."

CHAPTER 21

I left Cassia at Marcianus's and jogged with Septimius back to the ludus.

By the time we reached it, I could hear Aemil shouting. He usually ran the school with gruff efficiency, but today, his rage filled the space like wind-tossed waves. He was, at the moment, beating the second gate guard with the flat of his wooden sword.

"Leonidas!" Aemil broke off and charged at me. I prepared myself for him to strike *me* with Nemesis, but he halted an arm's-length away. "This lout says he never saw Regulus go. But he must have let him out, the oaf."

I was happy I'd persuaded Cassia to remain behind. She'd argued, but I hadn't wanted her near a furious Aemil. He was a dangerous man who kept himself contained by great effort. Marcianus had agreed with me, and Cassia had consented, reluctantly, to stay.

"I never saw him." Plinius, the second gate guard, lifted his bruised face. "I swear it on all the gods. On my ancestors."

"Regulus could easily have slipped out," I told Aemil. "He knew how."

"I know he did!" Aemil's bellow betrayed fear behind his

anger. "Where would he go, Leonidas? You knew him better than anyone."

Which was hardly at all. "Was he locked in his cell?"

Aemil's eyes flared with rage, the different colors of them blazing. "Of course he was. I took his lock picks too. The one you threw away from him and the other three I found tucked under his mattress."

"Even a wooden stick could have helped him," I said. "He's good at locks."

"I should have put a cobra outside," Aemil snarled. "Find him, Leonidas. Before he becomes a pile of gladiator parts. He can't fight for me like that. He's my best, and I've already promised him to the games at the equinox. The fee is too much to lose."

Aemil blustered about the money, but I knew this was to cover his terrible worry of finding another of the men he'd trained, fed, clothed, and cared for as the victim of a brutal murderer.

"Do any of the other gladiators know where he might have gone?"

"Hmm, I never thought to ask a one of them." Aemil glared at me, his sarcasm cutting. "None have any idea, useless pillocks. He never confided in anyone but you."

Regulus had rarely told me anything personal about himself. We'd become drinking comrades, turning to each other because it was better than drinking alone. I'd destroyed that comradeship when I'd refused to release him to death during our last bout.

Had Regulus sought that death by stepping squarely into danger? Or, more likely, did he think so much of himself that he believed he could best the killer? Find him when I could not?

I strode past Aemil to Regulus's cell. The last of Xerxes's drawings were cheerful reminders of his sense of humor and brought a distracted pain to my heart.

Regulus lived simply, as all gladiators did. His cell contained a bed, a stool, spare tunics, and a small box of his belongings.

Inside that, I found a rope belt, a rough-carved statue of a god I couldn't identify, and a smaller box. Opening this, I lifted out a gold earring, delicate and masterfully crafted. Only one, and it would have been costly.

"Lady must have given him that," Aemil said, gazing over my shoulder. "Or he stole it from her."

I studied the earring. Three gold hoops, wire-thin, hung from a clasp, with tiny chips of emeralds decorating each tier. I knew where I'd seen a similar style, and recently.

I clenched the earring in my hand and marched to the practice area. "Bring all the men out here," I told Aemil.

He bristled at my command but went back into the cells and barked orders. Most of the gladiators were already in the training yard and drifted my way in curiosity.

"Regulus's woman gave this to him." I dangled the earring once all were assembled, the gold and emeralds flashing spangles of light. "Can anyone tell me who that woman is?"

Most shrugged, neither knowing nor caring. Praxus, his arm in a sling, bent to peer at it. "Woman in a villa on a hill."

"Domitiana?" I asked sharply. She'd worn earrings like these the night she'd hosted me and Herakles at her supper. Regulus had confessed he'd been to her, but I had to be sure he'd gone there again tonight.

"No." The sharp answer came from Herakles. "Domitiana likes only me."

Guffaws sounded behind him. "Oh, she loves you, barbarian," one gladiator laughed. "She'd never stray."

Herakles swung on him, and the man backed a step. "She knows what I do to bitches who cross me."

"Shut your gob, Herakles," Aemil growled at him. "You'll not touch a highborn woman, because I won't save you when they drag you to your crucifixion."

"Not Domitiana." Praxus's scoffing tones broke through as Herakles subsided to a glower. "Not at that villa. On a hill in the city."

"Which hill?" I stepped to Praxus, meeting his unnervingly light blue eyes. "The Caelian?"

He nodded with certainty. "That is what Regulus said."

My headache increased as my blood pounded. Was Severina the killer after all? Why then, had she decided to spare me last night?

"How do you know this, Praxus?" Aemil demanded. "And why didn't you speak up before?"

Praxus pulled at one of his ears. "I hear all talking. They think I am the stupid oaf from the north and don't understand. And you didn't ask before. You just shouted *Where is Regulus? Tell me now.* I don't know where he is. But I know he likes this woman on the Caelian who gives him gifts."

"Thank you, Praxus," I said. "You've helped much."

He'd known about Domitiana in the first place, I remembered. I observed his ingenuous expression, the man young and confident, believing himself ready to take on the toughest gladiators.

Did he know more than he was saying? Had *he* sent gladiators to the house where they were given opulent meals and then slain? Was I looking into the eyes of a merciless killer?

I had no idea. Cassia read people far better than I could. Praxus was very likely exactly what he appeared to be, a young man ready to take on the world, using the fact that people dismissed him as a barbarian to his advantage.

Praxus's face split with a grin. "How about you give me that bauble as a reward?"

I closed my hand around it. "Regulus would kill you to get it back. I'll keep it safe."

Praxus brayed with laughter. "Of course, the great Leonidas will keep it safe for his friend. He is honored among men."

The other gladiators laughed with him. They liked Praxus, I could see, even if they underestimated him.

"If you're right about where Regulus is, Praxus, I'll give you a better reward," I said.

Praxus made some very lewd suggestions for this reward to the glee of the men as I left them and headed for the gate.

Aemil strode beside me. "Want me to go with you to pull him out?"

Aemil would be a formidable ally if I had to storm Severina's fortress, but the two of us could be arrested for bursting into the home of a well-respected former consul and his wife.

"I'll look first," I said. "Regulus might just be rutting her and in no danger. I was at that house last night, and no harm came to me."

Aemil poked a blunt finger into my chest. "If he's there, you drag him out and bring him home. Understand?"

"I do."

Aemil held me with his gaze, then he growled and jerked his hand away. "I'll be ready to help if you need it. They will be as well." He waved at the men, who'd taken the opportunity to have a rest, talking in clumps or stretching out on the ground to enjoy the sunshine.

Even a killer of gladiators would be no match for all of them together. However, if I led an army of gladiators to storm a patrician's home on the Caelian, we'd be the ones gutted. I needed to alert the cohorts and vigiles, not bring in a horde of Aemil's fighters. Spartacus's revolt had occurred more than a hundred years ago now, but the fear he'd engendered still lingered in Roman imaginations.

Clutching the earring in my fist, I left the ludus, striding past the pillar of Septimius, back at his post. Plinius, the other guard, had taken advantage of my arrival to disappear, away from Aemil's beatings.

I turned my steps not toward the Aventine to find Cassia, or to the Caelian, but to the workshop of Volteius the armorer.

"WILL YOU LEND ME ALBUS FOR A TIME?" I HAD TO RAISE MY voice over the sounds of hammers on metal in the courtyard when I entered the shop.

Volteius ceased scowling at a bronze helmet with a large crack on its crest and stared at me incredulously. "Albus? What for? He can't pound out a nutshell. I'll be reduced to using him to keep accounts."

"I'd like him to help me," I said. "He has an eye for detail and a good memory."

Volteius grunted. "I'll give him that. Yes, take him away for an hour or two. I might have a little peace and quiet."

The hammering around us increased, the *clang, clang, clang* deafening.

Albus joined me with the energy of youth. He was probably sixteen summers, ungainly and thin with tangled brown hair, but he was old enough to begin a profession. Maybe he *would* end up being Volteius's accountant.

"Where are we off to? A bout? Do you want me to fix a sword? An arm guard?" He exuded eagerness.

"We're going to the Caelian Hill," I said.

I couldn't tell him more than that as we made our way through the crowded Transtiberim and across the river to the Aventine, where I fetched Cassia from Marcianus's. I told Marcianus to keep an eye out for Regulus, then I led Albus and Cassia around the end of the Circus Maximus and up the Caelian Hill.

About twenty paces from Severina's large home I found a popina that was cleaner and less crumbling than those on the lower streets. I ushered in Albus and Cassia for a cup of wine and fetched pastries from the shop across the street.

"Very nice." Albus munched a fried sheet of dough folded around walnuts and honey, gazing with interest around the wine shop.

The walls were painted with bright depictions of overflowing fruit baskets and tall amphorae of wine. Patrons ate and discussed business, family, friends, and the latest races without compunction. In deference to Parentalia, plates on an empty table contained bread soaked in vinegar, a handful of almonds, and a glass of wine, should anyone's ancestor decide to drop in to refresh himself.

Cassia removed a wax tablet from the bag at her side and began to make notes in it.

"Is she writing down the price of the meal?" Albus asked in curiosity. "I wish I had a scribe. I'd not spend so much money without realizing it, I think."

Cassia gave him a wise smile and continued to mark her tablet. I knew she was noting the time we had entered the popina, the fact that Albus was with us, where exactly we were, and what we waited for. I hadn't told her, but she'd likely guessed.

"The man who ordered the gladiator helmets." I shoved my wine cup aside, though the wine was quite good. "Would you recognize him again?"

"Absolutely." Albus spoke with confidence.

"Even if he shaved off his hair? Or wore different clothes?"

"Of course. A man can't change his nose, can he? Or the shape of his face, or his ears."

"Even though you only saw him once?"

"Once when he made the order, once when he came to collect it." Albus tapped the side of his head. "I remember everything, me. But I'm not as good at bronze work. So Volteius tells me, every day."

"Perhaps your master will realize your true skills," Cassia said kindly. "You said the man made the order and then collected it. How many helmets did he ask for?"

"Four. Four helmets, four sets of leg greaves, three arm guards, a couple of swords, a spear." Albus rattled this off without having to think about it. "Said Aemilianus needed to outfit new gladiators and replace some broken equipment."

Four. A knot tightened in my stomach, and Cassia and I exchanged an uneasy glance.

I feared Regulus would be the third gladiator the man meant to kill. The fourth—any of them. Praxus, Herakles, me.

"Why are we here?" Albus asked, noting our tension. "If you wanted to give me a cup of wine, we didn't have to walk all the way up the Caelian."

"The man who ordered the gear might be in that house over there." I gestured with my wine cup, keeping my voice quiet. "When he comes out, I want you to tell me if it's him."

Albus's eyes rounded. "You brought me here to identify the killer?" Alarm warred with excitement in his voice.

"Maybe," I said.

I had no evidence but the hardness I'd seen in the large bodyguard's eyes, coupled with the fact that he protected Severina without the disgust or apprehension I'd observed in the rest of her servants.

We waited for several hours. The proprietor of the popina didn't mind as long as we continued to order wine and bread. His luncheon customers had long gone, and the popina quieted. Cassia glided to the pastry shop and returned with more crushed, sweetened walnuts in a pastry shell stamped to look like a whole walnut.

Albus grew restless by the afternoon and worriedly said he should get back to Volteius before he was dismissed. I was about to relent and send him off when the gate of Severina's domus opened, and a litter emerged.

Two muscular men with the blank faces of those assigned the heaviest tasks bore the litter, and Severina's head bodyguard walked closely beside it, his gaze watchful.

I moved into the deepest shadows of the popina and gestured with my chin. "Him. Is that your man?"

Albus leaned forward to peer at him, almost falling from his stool. His wine cup teetered, but Cassia caught it before it tumbled over. Albus did manage to sweep an empty plate to the floor, where it shattered, earning him the glare of the proprietor.

The bodyguard paused a step and gazed straight at Albus. His eyes flicked past the young man without recognition and then landed on me, and stopped.

CHAPTER 22

I tried to conceal myself, but a large champion gladiator could only be so hidden. I decided to brazen it out, met the bodyguard's gaze, and gave him a nod.

He stared at me in grave suspicion for a few heartbeats, then he decided, like me, to pretend there was nothing unusual in me sitting in a popina a few strides from his mistress' gate. He returned the nod and walked on.

Cassia let out a long breath. The bodyguard had not noticed her, but Cassia was excellent at effacing herself.

Albus turned to me in disappointment. "I thought you said he was the one killing gladiators."

It took me a few moments to understand what he meant. "He didn't order the armor?" I asked.

"No." Albus drained his wine cup. "Not the same man."

Cassia craned to watch the litter and bodyguards disappear around a corner. "Are you certain?" she asked Albus. "Imagine him with a full mop of hair."

Albus was already shaking his head in negation. "He's big, yes, and has a large nose, but otherwise not at all like the man who came to Volteius. This one's face is wide, but our man's was long and narrow. Like a horse's. And his forehead stuck out, even through all his hair. This bodyguard has a smaller head with a more pleasing shape. And his eyes didn't make me shiver and want to clutch a charm."

I leaned against the wall and tried to stem my disappointment. I'd been so certain that Severina's bodyguard and the man Albus and the basketmaker had seen were one and the same.

Now I'd have to start hunting for him one street at a time, just as Vatia the vigile captain mourned he'd have to do.

I also had to find Regulus. Maybe Praxus was wrong, and Regulus had gone to Domitiana after all, or to some other woman on the Caelian.

I scowled in frustration. I was no closer to discovering answers than when I'd started.

Albus, restless, leaped to his large feet. "Thank you for the wine, Leonidas. And the holiday. If I see the man again, I will lock him in Volteius's shed and run to fetch you."

"If you see him, you will stay far from him," I said sternly. This murderer would have no trouble felling an untrained apprentice. "But send word to me if he returns to make another order."

Albus grinned at me without promising anything, then he loped off into the street, heading back down the hill to drudgery. The afternoon out had cheered him considerably.

"Return home," I said to Cassia.

She regarded me in surprise. "Where will you go?"

"To discover if Regulus truly is in that house. Severina is the sort of woman who'd leave him to sleep while she went off to visit her mother. If he is not there, I'll see if he's in any of the other domii." I hesitated. "Can you ask Helvius if Regulus is a regular guest of Severina? Or of any of her friends?" I dug into my pouch and produced the earring I'd found in Regulus's cell. "This might be one of Severina's. She either gave it to Regulus, or he managed to filch it."

Cassia studied the earring with interest. "Severina has no friends, from what I hear. I'll enter her house with you, and maybe talk to the servants. They'd know if the earring was truly hers. I can say I found it and am returning it ..."

I was already shaking my head. "I haven't yet dismissed Severina as the one ordering the deaths. The head bodyguard might not be the man doing her fetching and carrying, but that doesn't mean she hasn't hired another to help her."

"Exactly." Cassia closed her tablet and slipped it into her bag. "The servants can tell me if the man Albus describes has ever been there. I know how to be discreet."

"No." Fear made me short-tempered. "If you poke around in a patrician's house without their permission, you can be flogged, or arrested, or killed. You will go home and send word to Helvius."

We spoke in low, rapid tones, keeping our argument from the curious proprietor.

"But *you* will be safe? You're a freedman, not the son of a rich senator. You could also be arrested, flogged, or killed."

"Not as easily as you," I returned stubbornly. "Gladiators are welcomed for exhibitions. I can say I was summoned to perform and got the house wrong, or the day wrong. We're expected to be stupid too."

Cassia took in my rigid stance, my clenched fists, my adamance. She usually did exactly as she pleased, no matter what kind of orders I gave her, but this time at least, she seemed to recognize the danger.

"Very well," she said with the air of one conceding with great reluctance. "I will speak to Helvius and try to locate Regulus. Helvius and I between us likely know every servant on this hill, and we will encourage them to gossip. Have your peek in Severina's house, but be careful. Her husband was courteous to you, but he might object to you bullying your way inside."

"Asking politely to go inside," I countered. "To pay my respects to the paterfamilias and his ancestors. It is Parentalia."

"I know it is." Cassia's insistence died away, and the sadness I'd observed earlier again entered her eyes.

I gentled my tone. "We will light candles to your father on Feralia. And Xerxes."

Cassia lifted her bag over her shoulder. "Hurry home, Leonidas," she said softly.

She turned to go, every line of her sorrowful. I hated when she was dejected, but I'd buy some trinket or sweetmeat that we could lay on the altar for her father.

I waited until Cassia had trudged her way down the hill, out of sight, before I turned to Severina's home.

The domus was quiet as I approached. No Regulus lounging on a balcony above or peering from a window, annoyed to see me coming for him.

No one lingered near the domus. This late in the afternoon, most people on the hill would be at the baths, including many of Severina's servants. I might not be able to gain entry at all.

As I squared my shoulders, rehearsing my speech about paying my respects to Vestalis, Severina's door slave appeared in the vestibule and sleepily inquired my business.

I asked to see the master of the house. I hoped I could poke around the atrium and the rooms off it for signs of Regulus while the doorman trotted away to inquire, but he immediately admitted me and waved for me to follow him.

The great house was silent and empty. My footsteps echoed, ringing against beams high above me. The walls held paintings of domestic scenes or garden vistas enclosed in borders of red and yellow, and tapered Egyptian marble columns supported the gallery on the second floor.

I saw no one as the doorman quietly led me through the wide space. A soft trickle of water sounded from a distant fountain, but there was no other noise.

The doorman took me to the tablinium, which opened from the far side of the atrium. Vestalis dozed on a chair there, but he snorted awake when the doorman announced me.

Vestalis rubbed his watery eyes and peered at me in puzzlement before rising in apparent delight.

"It is the gladiator who has honor. Welcome. Bring us wine," he ordered the doorman, and the young man scurried off. "Why have you come, Leonidas? My wife is out."

"To see you." I kept to my planned excuse. "To thank you for your hospitality and your courtesy. To see if I can do anything for you, perhaps say a prayer for your ancestors on this day of Parentalia." This was the sort of thing clients said to a patrician.

"How very kind." Vestalis appeared to be flattered, which had been my intent.

Another servant brought wine in elegant bronze cups. The wine was not as strong as what Severina had served me but still very good.

"I import it from Campania," Vestalis said when I praised the drink. "I have a share of a vineyard there, though I let my partner do all the raising and growing. I know very little about viticulture. Hispania has decent vintages as well, and even in far-off Pannonia, they grow good grapes. Not Britannia." Vestalis shuddered. "Never go there, Leonidas." So he'd warned me before.

It was not likely I'd travel to Britannia, so I nodded.

Vestalis bade me sit on a stool while he reclined on his comfortable chair and stretched out his legs. "Glad to return to Rome after my many years of travel. I can at least live out my days in ease."

I wasn't certain what else to say to him, but Vestalis was happy to talk about inconsequential things, asking me about my life in the ludus. He found the tedious rounds of training, exhibitions or bodyguard work, eating and sleeping to wake to more training interesting.

"And then you were freed," he said. "Quite a coup."

"Yes." I did not mention my secret benefactor, not knowing whether he or she wanted that information to be spread.

"So what will you do now? Become a trainer yourself?"

"No," I said abruptly, then softened my tone. "I might start working for an *architectus*." The one planning Vestalis's own warehouse, but I kept that detail to myself.

Vestalis's gray brows rose. "An *architectus*? How extraordinary. I suppose a strong man like yourself would be good at hauling blocks about. Or whatever it is he'd have you do."

"I apprenticed to a master builder before I became a gladiator," I said. "I miss that work."

"You are an interesting young man, Leonidas. I must ask, why have you succumbed to the charms of my wife?"

Vestalis watched me, eyes alight, truly wanting to know.

I shrugged, as though I'd had no hidden reason for visiting her. "It was a meal, and I'd hoped for some money. I no longer win prizes in the games."

Vestalis chuckled. "I suppose you hoped for some coin today as well. I do not blame you—it is difficult to be poor. Do not look surprised. My family never had much money, and I was required to spend much of it traveling and keeping up a home in the provinces. It's why I married Severina. She has more money than any woman ought." He broke off and unlocked a box that reposed beside his chair, extracting a few denarii from it. "There you are, my boy."

I did not reach for the coins. "I truly did not come here for that."

"No matter. Men hire gladiators to entertain them, and you have done that for me today. Listened to an old man natter on. Besides, you deserve it for putting up with my wife."

I sensed that Vestalis would be offended if I did not take what he offered, and so would Cassia. Our coffers were never very full.

I held out my hand, and Vestalis dropped the three denarii into my palm. As I closed my fingers around the cool metal, I decided to take a chance.

"Your wife hasn't invited another gladiator to see her today, has she?" I asked as though offhandedly interested. "One called Regulus?"

Vestalis moved his gaze past me as he thought. "I haven't heard that name. But then, I don't know every man she drags in here. None have been to visit today, as far as I know."

"Do any other ladies of the neighborhood ... invite in gladiators?"

Vestalis snorted. "Possibly. So many are scandalous these days. My own dear wife—my first wife, I mean—was quiet and serene. A joy to have her enter a room. All praised her—she was beautiful, intelligent, modest, kind, and funny too. She could make me laugh. And my daughter—as beautiful as a goddess ..."

His eyes grew moist as he trailed off. He stared at nothing for a moment, as though he'd forgotten my presence, then he buried his head in his hands. "Forgive me," he said brokenly.

I rose and stepped out of the room, waving for the doorman, who scurried to us. When he saw his master weeping, the young man took on an expression of great sympathy.

"I'll look after him," he said. "He misses his lady and his daughter something terrible," he confided in a whisper.

Losing them must have been a grievous blow, and I could see that Vestalis hadn't recovered from it, probably never would. His loss was much more on his mind than the indecorous behavior of his frivolous second wife.

I again thanked Vestalis, who did not respond, and followed the doorman out.

I STILL HADN'T FOUND REGULUS, AND MY IDEA THAT Severina's bodyguard had ordered the gladiator equipment and hauled Rufus's body into the insula was wrong.

I needed to think, and for that, I needed Cassia.

I trudged home through a Rome settling down for the evening. More family processions wended their way along the streets. Groups walked together, some carrying small shrines, honoring the deceased members of their families. I paused to buy a small bag of nuts from a vendor to lay on our own shrine.

Cassia had returned to the apartment as she'd promised, but I found a throng inside.

I recognized Helvius, and Martolia and Gaius, but not the others. By their garb, they were slaves or freed servants.

Cassia spoke animatedly with a woman I didn't recognize while Helvius watched Cassia with admiration. Gaius sat on the floor and beat one of the stools like a drum, and Martolia swayed idly to the rhythm on the balcony.

I stood in the doorway for a long moment before anyone noticed me. Then Helvius caught sight of me and gasped, and attention turned my way.

"Leonidas." Cassia turned in eager welcome. "What have you learned?"

I gazed across the sea of faces, some trepidatious, others fascinated. Oil gleamed on limbs, and some of the group had damp hair. They'd taken their turn at the baths, I guessed, and then stopped by to see Cassia before continuing to their master's homes.

"Regulus was not there," I said. "I saw no sign of the man Albus describes."

"Ah." Cassia's disappointment was short-lived. "No matter. My friends will inquire about him as they go about their duties. As well as search for Regulus."

"Too dangerous," I said quickly. Slaves poking about where they had no business faced dire consequences with no recourse.

"No one notices servants," Cassia said with assurance. "My friends know how to discover things unobtrusively. Evening is coming," she announced to them. "Time to return home. We will meet again tomorrow, and you will tell me what you find."

Gaius gave the stool—mine—a final thump as the crowd began to disperse and heaved himself from the floor. "Martolia is dancing on the Caelian tonight. We'll ask if any servants there know which senator's wife is hosting a gladiator."

Before I could argue, he was following Martolia out, his voice raised in song as he clattered down the stairs.

It took some time for all to leave, but finally, I shut the door on the last straggler.

"How did you summon them all here?" I asked Cassia as I restored the stools to the table.

"I sent the boy who works for the wine merchant to Helvius, and he spread word to the others." Cassia seated herself in front of her open tablets and neatly lined-up scrolls. "Between them, they'll find Regulus, I am certain."

"Or be killed," I pointed out.

"I believe the servants will be safe. You and Regulus and others at the ludus are the ones in danger." Cassia's confidence did not bolster mine. "Now, what happened on the Caelian?"

I described to her my foray into Severina's house and the conversation with Vestalis.

"He is a sad old man." I pulled out the coins he'd given me and laid them on the table. "Says he doesn't care about Severina, but he'd no doubt be happier with a kinder wife and a son or two."

"Very likely. Children should mourn and honor their fathers, not the other way around." Cassia's gaze moved to our ancestor shrine, decorated once more with a vase of flowers. I added my handful of walnuts to it before I took my seat at the table.

"He is still in great pain, which explains why he barely notices Severina," I told her. "His wife and daughter died in Hispania, I think. Or perhaps Britannia. He is the most bitter when he speaks about Britannia."

Cassia studied two tablets laid out side by side in front of her. "What I don't understand is why Ajax and Rufus? They are very different men."

"Maybe to this man gladiators are all the same. Fighting bodies in the arena."

"But they are *not* the same. I have seen the drawings on walls all over Rome—people sketch the gladiator they like best, adding what makes him distinctive. The Thracian helmet. The net and spear of the retiarius. The sword and shield of the secutor."

"True." I traced the shape of a helmet on the table with my finger. "Ajax was a secutor, Rufus, a myrmillo. But the killer dressed him as a Thracian."

"Which means he was vague about which type of gladiator Rufus was. There are other differences between them, though. Ajax was a captive, sold to the games. Rufus was a free person, who became a gladiator voluntarily."

"Rufus took a wife, while Ajax had no permanent lover," I added.

"Ajax also isn't Roman." Cassia ran a fingertip along the wax in her tablet. "Rufus is from Latinium and grew up in Rome. Ajax was a soldier in Pannonia."

Cassia's finger halted. I don't know what she pointed at, though I recognized the P from the letters I'd traced. I felt a small trickle of pride that I remembered it.

"Pannonia." Cassia's voice went quiet. "Great Minerva. Is it that simple?"

CHAPTER 23

I saw nothing simple about our life these past days. "What are you saying?" I asked impatiently.

"Ajax is from Pannonia." Cassia held my gaze with her adamant one, as though I should understand everything. "He was a soldier, you said."

"Not in the Roman army. From a tribe called the Quadi. So was Herakles. Ajax and Herakles call it something different, but I don't remember what. They were captured in a battle, or during a raid."

Cassia hurriedly opened tablets and unrolled scrolls, leafing through them. "Vestalis lost his wife in the provinces."

"In Britannia ..."

"No, no." Cassia ceased her searching and sat back, tapping her stylus to her notes in triumph. "His wife died when he was proconsul of a small settlement in Pannonia. Killed in a raid, Helvius told me."

I regarded her quizzically. "You think Ajax was part of that raid?"

"Possibly. Herakles too. When did Aemilianus bring them into the ludus?"

"Three years ago. I remember they did well in the Saturnalian games not a month after they joined us. They did not speak Latin, and they'd never had a bath in their lives, but their ferocity drew the admiration of the crowd. That was three Saturnalias past."

Cassia began to scan her notes again. "Three years ago, yes—Vestalis's wife and daughter died. He was moved to a post in Britannia, then asked to be transferred to Hispania a year or so later, a warmer clime. There he met Severina and Domitiana, while they were visiting Domitiana's son."

Helvius, secretary to Domitiana, would have learned of Vestalis's sad story.

"You are saying Vestalis killed Ajax?" I asked. "In revenge?"

"Very possibly. Hiring a man to do it for him, of course."

Her conclusion did not match the frail elderly man I'd shared a cup of wine with today. He'd been heartbroken, not full of the fires of vengeance. "Why have Ajax cut up and left in the Subura?"

"That, I do not know." Cassia sat back, fingers resting on the edge of the table. "From what Helvius told me, the raiders were not kind to Vestalis's wife and daughter. They were brutal. Perhaps Vestalis was returning that brutality."

"What you say could explain why Vestalis would want to kill Ajax. But why Rufus?"

Cassia deflated. "Perhaps his hired man mistook Rufus for Herakles."

"But Vestalis knows Herakles, who has become Domitiana's lover. He'd have pointed out the right man. Herakles and Rufus are nothing alike, we've just decided."

"True," Cassia conceded.

"And why is Regulus gone? He's from Etruria and had started at the ludus well before Aemil acquired Ajax and Herakles."

"There is no reason to believe Regulus has been taken," Cassia said. "He might simply be out enjoying himself. You say he is good at freeing himself from confinement."

"Doesn't like to be ordered about, no."

"I suppose we can't know if Ajax or Herakles had anything to do with Vestalis's wife." Cassia let out a little sigh. "They might have been on the same raiding party, but nowhere near Vestalis's family. Or in another raiding party altogether. Or have been captured in an entirely different part of Pannonia."

I rose to my feet, the stool skittering away. "We *can* know. I will go ask Herakles right now."

"It's dark," Cassia said with an apprehensive glance at the balcony.

"None will waylay me." I could not wait tamely until morning to discover answers.

"Take your cloak." Cassia's soft voice touched me. "It's gone chilly."

Somewhere under my anger and impatience, I felt a sense of wonderment. I'd never had someone worry, for my own sake, whether I'd take cold or return home unhurt.

I lifted the cloak she'd neatly hung on a peg and went out the door.

WHEN I REACHED THE GATE OF THE LUDUS, SEPTIMIUS admitted me without hesitation. Aemil, emerging from a line of cells, strode to meet me.

"We found it," he said grimly. "The curse."

I'd forgotten I'd suggested he search for a curse. Perhaps it was to blame for all the trouble, and Cassia and I had been rushing about Rome for no reason.

"It was in Rufus's cell." Aemil's face was hard. "A bit of leather rolled up, inscribed with a venomous spell."

"Wishing his death?" I asked quickly.

"Wishing him misfortune. Boils on his body. Breaking a leg. The usual thing to keep a gladiator out of the ring. But it worked all too well, didn't it?"

"What did you do with it?"

"Took it over the bridge to the temple of Hercules at the Circus. Had the curse neutralized and the leather burned." Aemil's anger had stamped weary lines on his face.

"Who had a chance to put it in his cell?"

"Anyone." Aemil waved his arms. "Another of the gladiators. I've threatened to flog the whole lot, but none will confess. His bitch of a wife. A fan of a rival ludus."

I readjusted my conclusions. The curse could have lain in Rufus's cell for a long time, and true, his wife might have put it there so he'd be injured or die in the arena, and she'd be free to marry Daphnus. Daphnus himself could have had it smuggled in to make Chryseis a widow.

None of which had anything to do with Ajax.

"Where is Herakles?" I returned to my original purpose.

"Dining. Do you have Regulus? I thought you knew where he'd gone."

I couldn't find the words to explain, so I strode past Aemil and into the long room where the gladiators took their evening meal. New gladiators weren't allowed to eat there until they'd proved they'd accepted their fate, and those who caused trouble at training were locked away to consume their meals alone. The rest gathered around a communal dining table.

Praxus, who'd obviously won Aemil's trust, busily shoveled food into his mouth with his good hand, the other still in the sling. "Leonidas," he sang out when he saw me. "Too bad you aren't allowed to join us. Aemil's a stingy bastard and won't let us share."

I knew the rules. Aemil kept a close eye on his provisions, and uninvited guests went hungry.

"Leonidas has a slave to get him meals now." Herakles grinned smugly. "She's a tender thing. Wish Leonidas would share *her*."

He barely had the last words out before I was lifting him by the tunic and dragging him across the table. The gladiators near him grabbed their bowls and wine cups and scrambled out of the way.

Herakles struggled mightily, but I transferred him to a headlock as his feet flopped over the table's edge. None tried to help him. I didn't often grow enraged, but when I did, the other gladiators had learned to stay out of my way.

I hauled Herakles across the floor, and when he gasped desperately for breath, I slung him against a wall and held him there. "What did you do? In Pannonia?"

"What did I ...?" He trailed off, coughing.

"You and Ajax. To a woman and her daughter. Wife and child of Vestalis."

Herakles stared at me in shock. "Vestalis?"

"Domitiana's son-in-law. *That* Vestalis. He was a proconsul in Pannonia. Did you kill his wife and daughter in a raid? The raid that got you captured?"

Herakles's mouth hung open, but when I finished, furious scorn flashed in his eyes. "I don't know. I did many, many Roman women. Maybe they belonged to Vestalis—who knows? I didn't care." His voice filled with venom. "Roman soldiers, they came to *our* lands, took what they wanted, violated *our* women, and then said we must be grateful that greedy Roman bastards had bullied their way into our territory. I and the brothers of my tribe took from them what they took from us. Yes, I had Roman women under me, and I sliced their throats when I was done. But there were too many soldiers, and they captured me. Flogged me, branded me, and sold me *here*."

He tried to jerk away as he said the last word, but my grip was too strong, too practiced.

The silence from the other gladiators was heavy. They listened, none intervening.

"Ajax too?" I asked in a low growl. "He did what you did?"

"Yes." Herakles sneered. "He gave back plenty."

"And now he's dead for it."

"You think *Vestalis* did that?" Herakles's laughter held derision. "That feeble old man? Sits and watches while I do everything but stick myself into Domitiana? He's the kind I crushed with my bare hands—soft Roman whoreson."

I slammed his head back against the wall. "Vestalis's wife and daughter did *nothing* to you. A man who kills innocents is not a man."

"And Roman soldiers who plow through a camp and stamp little children to death under their boots show *virtus*, do they?"

I couldn't argue with him about soldiers acting brutally, because I knew they did, all the time. Barbarians were savages to them, needing to be conquered by any means. Herakles and Ajax had taken vengeance for that, and now vengeance was visited upon them.

I swung Herakles around and tossed him away from me. By the time he regained his balance, I was out the door into the cool night, across the training courtyard, and out the gate. From there, I turned my steps once more to the Caelian Hill.

DARKNESS HAD FALLEN COMPLETELY BY THE TIME I REACHED Severina's house. Moonlight gleamed here and there through scattered clouds, but otherwise, the night was black.

The doorman answered my impatient pounding and gaped at me when I demanded to see Vestalis.

"The master's gone to bed," the doorman said. "He goes early most nights. The mistress is at her mother's."

"It's very important." I barely restrained myself from simply shoving him out of my way and storming inside.

The doorman sensed this. "I can ask his manservant."

"Yes." I stepped swiftly past him into the huge atrium. "I'll wait."

If I had not been a welcome guest earlier today, the doorman would likely have shouted for help, but as it was, he simply shut and bolted the door and then pattered off into the dim recesses of the house.

I studied the opulent scenes in the atrium, paintings of people lounging on sofas or in gardens, while birds posed on trees and deer calmly grazed. Everything was serene, peaceful, manicured, bathed in moonlight from the open roof above the atrium. The perfect Roman life.

Though my fury burned at Herakles for what he'd boasted of doing, I knew he had a point. The Roman army had always pushed their way into the frontier, drawing the lines they controlled farther and farther out. Behind them came the permanent army camps and then towns, with aqueducts, amphitheatres, baths, and colonnaded markets. The barbarians were told to be humble and thankful for the civilization forced upon them, no matter how mercilessly. I could not be surprised that men like Herakles had tried to punish their invaders.

I heard a step behind me and turned quickly.

"You have a message for Tertius Vestalis Felix?" a voice came to me from the shadow of the passageway.

A man stepped into the moonlight and the feeble flicker of the oil lamp resting beside the atrium's square pool of water. He was tall, with a long face, a large, fleshy nose, and a thick quantity of black hair.

We studied each other for a long moment. He took me in, his nostrils flaring as he realized who I was, and what I knew.

I lunged at him at the same time he came at me. We grappled on the mosaic, on top of nymphs dancing under spreading trees. He was big and strong, but I was fast, skilled, and experienced.

I soon had him in a headlock, as I'd done with Herakles, ready to kick his legs out from under him. I'd beat him senseless then haul him to Vatia or maybe to the Praetorian Guard on the Palatine.

Something sharp pricked my arm. The stab was not deep, but in the next moment, my arm grew numb, and my torso and legs quickly followed. I kept the man in my grip until my knees buckled and I fell to the floor.

As I landed on my back, he stood over me holding what looked like a comb, the kind that held lady's hair. The poison, whatever it was, must have been on its tines.

The atrium blurred, then the man bent to me, his long face and thick hair blotting out the silvery moonlight and the idyllic paintings of a family enjoying their leisure in a perfect garden.

CHAPTER 24

When I swam awake once more, I found myself flat on my back on a hard slab, the dank chill of stone walls around me, no light anywhere. I might be in a tomb.

My heart beat wildly as that thought took hold. I'd lived in cells a long time, but I'd known that someone would eventually open the door and let me out, even if that release might lead to my death. It wasn't the same as being walled in.

I needed to rise and discover if I were entombed or simply in a room with tightly shuttered windows.

I tried to swing my legs over the side of the slab and realized I couldn't move. I could twitch fingers and toes, open and close my mouth, and blink my eyes, but not much else.

"Hades," I muttered. At least my voice worked. When my throat ceased being so dry, maybe I could shout for help.

"Who is that?" The croak came from my right, not far away. I sensed another presence—smelled him, in truth. The rank stink of sweat and urine didn't rise only from me.

I recognized the snarl. "Regulus?"

"Oh, the luck of all the gods is upon me." Regulus's sardonic drawl cut the air. His voice was hoarse and weak, but his anger was plenty strong. "I'm penned up for my last day on earth with the great Leonidas. Fortuna loves me."

"Last day?"

"I wasn't thrown down here so I could be garlanded and fed sweetmeats and honey. That prick, Silvanus ... pricked me ... and dragged me to this place underneath his master's house."

"Silvanus." I worked through my confused thoughts. "The slave with the big nose?"

"He's a freedman, but stayed on to laud and worship his master."

"And murder for him," I murmured.

"The brilliant Leonidas has figured that out, has he? I am next into the pot, unless they decide to start with you. I hope they do. If I help them butcher you, maybe they'll let me go."

Regulus's voice was strained, bluster covering fear. He must not be able to move any better than I could.

I smelled, over the odor of both of us, the distinctive stench of death. Muted, as though it had faded over the last days, but there. I had a feeling I'd found the place where Ajax and Rufus had been felled before they'd been taken to the warehouse to be cut to pieces. Silvanus must have dragged them here after they'd feasted with Severina for the killing blow so the other servants and Severina wouldn't be aware of it.

"They have no reason to kill you," I said to Regulus.

"I disagree. Silvanus stabbed me with his poisoned comb as I left his mistress' bedchamber. Rufus was probably sticking it to her as well, and we know *you* were." Regulus huffed a laugh. "Though if the lofty Vestalis is murdering every man who ruts his wife, he'll have to chop up half of Rome."

"Rufus wasn't her lover. Neither was I."

"It doesn't matter," Regulus returned. "Silvanus is a madman, and so is Tertius Vestalis Felix." He spat the name.

"Maddened." I stared up into the darkness. "Not mad."

"What does *that* mean?"

I told Regulus, my tongue thick in my dry mouth, the theory

Cassia and I had formulated that Ajax and Herakles had raped and murdered Vestalis's family, and Ajax's death was Vestalis's revenge.

"Huh," Regulus grunted when I finished. "Then why kill Rufus, and now us?"

"I don't know," I had to admit. "It's one idea."

"I spit on your ideas," Regulus rumbled. "Take a dump on them too."

"Right now, I'm not worried about why." I tried to move my legs again, but only my toes obliged. "I'm more interested in how to get away."

"At least you haven't lost all your senses. What are your wonderful ideas on how to escape?"

"I wonder what poison he used." I ran my fingers over the slab I rested on, finding rough-hewn stone. "Marcianus would know."

"Yes, the chattering *medicus* would be useful about now. Except they'd probably poison him too."

"I plan to ask him."

Regulus groaned. "You always did decide you were master of life and death. No matter how much someone wants to die, you spare him because you think it's best."

An old argument. "Do you want to die now?"

"No," Regulus snapped. "But I don't think we have a choice."

"There is always a choice."

Regulus made a growling noise and returned to muttering to himself.

He had at least relieved my mind that we'd not been put into a tomb. We were in a room in the cellars of Vestalis's Caelian Hill home. That gave me hope. The walls might be stone, but wooden doors would break. Regulus and I were two of the strongest gladiators in all of Rome, and Regulus was skilled in picking locks. A mere door would not pen us in.

If only we could move.

Regulus had been down here longer, probably since last night after he'd slipped from the ludus and lain with Severina for a while, so the poison would wear through him first. He was a very good fighter. Even if he chose to save only himself, his engagement with any guards would give me a chance to escape with him.

But not until the feeling came back to my body.

We lay in darkness for a long time. An hour might have gone by since I'd been caught. Maybe two. When the moon set, the city would be fully dark. The lanterns of delivery wagons would light the lower streets, but no wagons would come to the top of this hill near its prestigious villas.

I had regained some movement of my feet and hands when the door scraped open. An oil lamp stabbed light into my now-sensitive eyes, and Regulus grunted a curse.

"I want to see Vestalis," I said clearly.

The burly Silvanus's horse-like face came out of the shadows, the lamplight mottling his skin.

"He doesn't talk to gladiators."

The statement wasn't true, as I'd had several conversations with the man.

"Tell him I want to speak to him about Ajax and Herakles. The tribesmen from Pannonia."

Silvanus went motionless, the flame sputtering in the oil. "You know nothing of Pannonia."

His Latin was perfect, with no accent other than that of Rome. He was no foreigner, but Roman born and bred.

"I know what happened to Vestalis's family," I went on. "I know he blamed Ajax. I understand why. I'd have wanted to kill him too."

Silvanus fell silent. Regulus breathed heavily from the other bunk, only a few feet from mine.

After a long moment, the bulk that was Silvanus turned and stalked out of the cell. He slammed the door and scraped bolts across it from the other side.

I'd seen, in the flicker of the lamp, that the door was simple, two wooden cross pieces over vertical boards. The room was shored up with bricks rather than stone, unfinished. It could have been meant as a storage room, or maybe whoever had originally built this house had put in his own cells for disobedient slaves.

"The door is flimsy," I said to Regulus. "You are good at opening doors."

"Yes, when I can move," he snapped.

My feet were now free of the paralyzing poison, but that didn't help me when I couldn't shift my legs. Feeling had returned to my hands, and my wrists tingled.

"Did you eat or drink anything before you were carried down here?" I asked.

"Of course I did. Severina showered me with food and drink. I was dizzy and drunk after I climbed out of her bed, which is why I couldn't fight that lout, Silvanus. I've been down here ever since."

His food or wine must have been laced, not with poison, but with some kind of soporific. Once Regulus was staggering with that, in addition to his lethargy after lying with Severina, Silvanus had struck with the poison, coated on the tines of the comb, possibly snake venom. Again, Marcianus would know.

I'd taken no food and only a little wine with Vestalis earlier. Maybe both poisons together kept the men immobilized and unable to fight when Silvanus killed them.

"Was any of the food gilded?" I asked.

"What? Yes—the cakes and some of the fruit. Stupid waste of gold. Why?"

I did not answer. Ajax had eaten his last meal here then, prepared by the same cook, Rufus as well. Rufus must have accepted Severina's invitation, wanting to be with a rich woman who'd actually bestow the luxury on him that Chryseis would not. Or possibly Silvanus had lured him to dine with her, promising payment.

I wondered if Severina knew what had happened to them,

and Regulus. Possibly not. She was not the most observant of women of anything outside her own world. I also wondered why my food had not been doctored or gilded, why I'd been allowed to leave freely. But Vestalis had enjoyed speaking with me, so he'd said. Perhaps he'd instructed Silvanus to spare me.

I could feel much of my arms again. Once I regained my strength, I would rip the door from its hinges if I had to and find my way out.

Before more sensation returned, the door scraped open again. Silvanus stepped inside, the stooped Vestalis shuffling behind him.

"This is the other?" Vestalis asked.

"Yes, lord." Silvanus flashed the lamp briefly at Regulus, who glared back at him. I couldn't see much of Regulus, just a gladiator in the dark.

Vestalis spat on Regulus. Regulus rumbled his fury but remained immobilized.

"No," I said. "This is Regulus. He's never been to Pannonia."

Vestalis swung to me, his dark eyes widening in surprise. "Leonidas? Why is he here?" Vestalis demanded of Silvanus. "I said he wasn't to be touched. He is an honorable man."

Regulus snorted his derision, but Silvanus's face didn't move. "He came to stop us carrying out what we need to do," Silvanus said. "Your ancestors will only be appeased when the murderers of your ladies have been slain."

"Then we must do it soon," Vestalis said. "We only have a few days."

"A few days for what?" Regulus demanded, but I thought I knew.

"Feralia," I said. "The final day of Parentalia. By the end of the festival, they want the deaths to be avenged. As their gift to his wife and daughter."

The way Rufus's and Ajax's bodies had been cut up and displayed made more sense now, in a way. They were offerings positioned in the same fashion a person might put together a plate of oranges and walnuts, neatly stacked for the ancestors' enjoyment.

Tears glittered on Vestalis's cheeks. "It shall be so."

"Regulus was not one of the men who killed them." I strove to keep my voice steady. Vestalis should understand this—he was acquainted with Herakles—but he seemed to have moved beyond reason. "Silvanus made a mistake. He made a mistake with Rufus too. Rufus was Roman-born, not of the Quadi."

Vestalis's brow knit in confusion. "Is this true?" he asked Silvanus.

"It was not a mistake," Silvanus returned quickly. "If I killed only the two Quadi, the deaths might be traced to your door. But if random gladiators die, no one will suspect anything of you. They believe it is a madman who hates gladiators, maybe another gladiator himself. You retain your honor and gain your vengeance."

Vestalis did not argue with Silvanus's logic, which chilled me. Vestalis stepped toward me, his expression one of great sorrow.

"Must Leonidas die too?" he asked Silvanus. "He is a good man."

Again, Regulus snorted, but the sound was softer this time.

Vestalis halted very close to me. I'd regained control of my arms now—I could reach out and trap him in a death grip, use him as leverage to free us.

But if I did so, Silvanus would have time to draw a weapon. I saw nothing in his hands, but he might have another poison-dipped comb with him, or some other thing he could scratch us with. I had no doubt another dose would kill us.

"The more gladiators found dead, the less likely you will be blamed," Silvanus explained to Vestalis.

Except people had noticed Silvanus with his distinctive face and hair, and it was only a matter of time before a vigile or a cohort matched Silvanus with the description the basketmaker had given Vatia. The apprentice, Albus, of the good memory, and

Volteius the armorer, and the family who'd lived across the landing from Chryseis, would know him too.

I kept this to myself because I did not want Silvanus, a loyal servant and merciless killer, to hunt those innocents down.

"Did you cut them up in Chryseis's warehouse?" I asked.

Silvanus started, surprised I'd realized that. "It is a large space, not much used."

"And you'd have an excuse to be in the area, as Vestalis is having a warehouse built there."

"My wife is," Vestalis rasped.

I wondered why, but that was beside the point. "An easy place to lug things in and out of with a cart or large baskets—no one would question such a thing at a warehouse. But why leave Ajax in the Subura?"

Silvanus shrugged, his eyes glittering in the lamplight. "He loved the whores there. Why not give him to them? Besides, there was a shrine to Juno at the end of that lane, on the other side of the wall. It was an offering."

I hadn't known about the shrine, but it made a sort of twisted sense. "How did you lure Ajax here? He wasn't fond of patrician women."

Silvanus took on a smug expression. "He came readily enough when I explained my master had taken a fancy to him and wanted to reward him for his prowess in the games."

"Ajax." Vestalis spat on the floor. "It is an abomination that he used such a name. Silvanus thought that if I took a rich wife, I could live out my days in comfort, but it has not been a comfort. I am still alone and grieving. Then, at this past Saturnalia, when Domitiana persuaded me to join her at the games at the Circus Gai, I saw them. The men who'd broken into my house and dragged out my wife and daughter. Parading proudly through the sand, lauded and cheered as champions, given the names of heroes. Ajax and Herakles. It was monstrous."

"So you took your revenge," I said quietly.

Vestalis had moved even closer to me, and Silvanus edged

behind him watchfully. They believed me immobile, which was to my advantage.

"Silvanus explained how I could," Vestalis said. "We would do it for them. Those two, killed and offered at Feralia to appease the spirits of my poor wife and my beautiful daughter. She would have married the next year."

I understood his grief and his outrage. Ajax and Herakles had come to the ludus full of anger—at the Romans for invading their territory and then capturing them, at Aemil, at all of us. Then they'd realized they could release their aggression in the arena and be cheered and acclaimed, which had rendered them arrogant and conceited. Herakles even now showed no remorse for what he'd done to Vestalis's wife and daughter.

I flicked my gaze to Silvanus. "Why would you kill for him?"

Silvanus answered with scorn. "I have worked in the house of my master since I was born. His family raised me, then he freed me. I will avenge his lady wife and daughter as I would my own mother and sister."

"I had no sons," Vestalis said, as though this explained things. Silvanus, the loyal freedman, had done what a son would do.

"Then you aren't truly alone," I said. Throughout the man's loss and grief, Silvanus had been at his side, looking after him. Going so far as to murder for him.

Vestalis shook his head. "It is not the same."

Silvanus would never be anything more than a servant, he meant, no matter what the man had done for him.

Silvanus did not seem upset by Vestalis's statement. He nodded, as though Vestalis spoke wisdom.

Vestalis now stood very close to me. I felt the brush of his tunic, woven of the finest linen, smelled the expensive oils on his skin.

I lunged for him. As I'd hoped, Silvanus immediately sprang forward. He shoved Vestalis out of my reach, and I closed my hands around Silvanus's shoulders and jerked him down to me.

Vestalis let out a rasping shout and rushed for the door, no doubt to summon help.

"No you don't, old man," Regulus growled. Out of the corner of my eye, I saw Regulus grip Vestalis by the tunic, his hand even in a paralyzed body strong enough to halt the elderly man's steps.

That left me to grapple with Silvanus. I could have bested him at my full strength, but while my arms mostly worked, I was still immobile, and he had command of all his limbs.

I twisted his wrist as he reached for a weapon, found the knife in his belt, and closed my hand around it. Silvanus jerked wildly in my grasp and the knife, coming free, fell from my still-clumsy fingers, clattering to the floor. Regulus jeered.

I grabbed Silvanus before he could dive for the knife. I yanked him across my body, twisting him around to lock my arm around his neck. He flailed and struck out, and I began to squeeze.

Silvanus coughed and swore as the crook of my arm cut off his air. I wasn't certain what to do next though, because my entire strength had not returned. Silvanus might faint, but I still could not move enough to get off the slab and carry Regulus out with me. Vestalis was yelling hoarsely, and it was only a matter of time before other servants heard and investigated.

Silvanus beat my torso with one fist. He got in a lucky blow high on my abdomen, whooshing air out of me.

I was transported back to a bout more than five years ago, in a time when I was still gaining my prowess. A myrmillo had knocked me to the ground, his foot connecting with my stomach, sending all breath from me. I'd been almost as transfixed, there on the hot sand, as I was now.

I saw the myrmillo standing over me, gloating, ready to kick me again, his sword rising for the killing blow to my exposed chest.

My instincts took over. I rolled on the sand, tangling my legs with his, sweeping him from his feet. The myrmillo tried to retain his balance but fell heavily, arm out to stop himself. The arm broke, and I barreled him to the ground to the screaming delight of the crowd.

My shoulder met solid ground as I fell from the bunk, wrenching me back to the present. Silvanus came down with me, and I felt the knife cold beneath my side. I rolled again in the tight space, my hand landing on the knife just as a panting Silvanus's did.

A sudden bright light showed me the bronze knife blade rising high, both of our hands clenching it, the blade heading straight for my chest.

CHAPTER 25

The cell filled with noise. I managed to deflect the blow from the startled Silvanus, but the blade sliced my skin, and blood ran from the wound.

Silvanus was ripped from me by a pair of enormously strong, weathered, and rock-hard hands, accompanied by a snarl of rage.

I knew those hands, and that snarl. Aemilianus, who'd terrified the condemned youth I'd been long ago, held the tall Silvanus in his hard grip, and began bashing the man's head against the ceiling.

Regulus roared with laughter. "About time you got here."

Vestalis was weeping, surrounded by people I couldn't make out. One slipped past him and flung herself onto me.

I was half on my side on the floor, my legs knotted in the small space, back jammed against the stone bunk. Now a woman in a woolen cloak clung to me, her shoulders shaking as her hair spilled to my face.

"What are you doing here?" I managed to croak.

Cassia raised her head, her cheeks damp in the glow of too much lamplight. "You didn't come home. I went to the ludus ..."

"By yourself?" I asked in alarm.

"No, no. I found help. At the ludus Septimius said you

rushed off toward the Aventine, and that you'd been asking questions about the lady of the Caelian Hill. I told Aemilianus you were in grave danger."

Aemil was busy bashing Silvanus's head into the bricks, the tall Silvanus slumped and groaning.

"Be careful," I called to Aemil. "He carries poison."

"Has he poisoned you?" The voice of Nonus Marcianus came around Aemil, and the thin man stepped into the light. "With what?" His tone held eager curiosity.

"I don't know." I lay in a tangle, stroking Cassia's hair to soothe her. I noted that it was soft and warm. "I can't get up. Regulus can't either."

"Interesting." Marcianus bent over me, touching my legs with a professional hand. I felt only a tingle.

"Interesting, is it?" Regulus still had hold of Vestalis, who hung dejectedly in his grasp. "What about a cure? Don't you have some vial of a potion that will let me move again?"

"Not until I know the exact nature of the poison. How was it administered?"

I told Marcianus the tale in a mumble. He listened avidly, taking a seat on the stone bunk as though we were in a comfortable tablinium instead of a dank cell beneath a patrician's home.

"Very likely snake venom of some kind, as you suspect," Marcianus said when I'd finished. "Or perhaps spider. As you are already regaining feeling, and you can breathe, I suspect it will eventually wear off. It must be a subduing poison, not a killing one, at least in small doses."

"Delightful." Regulus shook Vestalis. "See what kind of man your lackey is?"

"He meant to help me," Vestalis said in a weak voice. "I am proud that he did."

I gestured to Silvanus, who lay in a half-insensible heap across Regulus's feet, where Aemil had finally dropped him. "He is the man who murdered Ajax and Rufus."

A shriek sounded. "*He* killed Rufus?"

Martolia bounded into the cell, a knife gleaming in her hand. She broke from Merope and Gaius, who were trying to hold her back, and hurled herself at Silvanus.

"I *loved* him," she screeched as she stabbed.

The knife was stopped at the last minute by Aemil, who took it away from her. Martolia fought him, but she was no match for the strength of the seasoned Aemil.

"Help me bring them out," Aemil ordered as he removed a struggling Martolia from the room. He nudged Silvanus with his foot. "We'll take this one to the cohorts."

The sound of tramping feet, followed by shouts, cut through Aemil's orders. Most prominent households employed their own guards, from lictors to ex-soldiers and former gladiators, and I'd known hazily that it was only a matter of time before Vestalis's bodyguards searched for him.

The hulking men reached us. One grabbed Silvanus and hauled him up and over his shoulder. Aemil backed away warily, but Vestalis only stood still—Regulus gripping him—resigned.

I expected to see the large men who surrounded Severina, but these guards wore leather breastplates and carried swords, and I didn't recognize any from Severina's household.

One big man leaned down and hauled me up and across his back as though I weighed nothing. Unnerving.

Cassia stayed close, following me out of the cell as I hung over the man's shoulders like a sack of turnips. I had a view of rough-hewn steps as he jogged up them, which became polished stone steps and then segued into the mosaic tile floors of Severina's giant house.

The man carried me all the way out into the night before dumping me onto a bench next to the villa's front door. I was on the street, a cold breeze on my face. The air smelled damp—rain was coming.

Regulus fell heavily to a bench next to mine, unloaded there by another guard who'd carried him. Cassia sat down beside me and pulled out her inevitable tablet.

One of the guards seemed familiar. I couldn't quite place him until I saw his master walking toward me with an easy stride, moonlight glittering on the gold wristbands he liked to wear.

"Sextus Livius." My voice was a weary scratch.

"I am glad to see you alive, Leonidas." Livius halted before me, his cloak hanging in pristine folds over a fine linen tunic. "When I received the message that you were in great danger, I feared the worst."

"You sent for him?" I asked Cassia in surprise.

"I sent for everyone." Cassia sat very close to me, her tunic-encased leg touching the length of mine, her warmth permeating my numb flesh.

I wasn't certain what she meant by *everyone*, but I was glad she'd decided to disobey my orders to stay home. When she'd said *I found help*, I assumed she meant the boy who worked for the wine merchant who fetched the dancers and Marcianus.

I didn't realize the extent of her network until the street outside the villa again rang with footsteps, and this time, men of the Praetorian Guard marched to the door. With them came the small form of Hesiodos.

I'd seen the lead guard at the Palatine before, and he knew me. "You are to come," the guard told me. *"Now."*

I'D NEVER BEFORE RIDDEN IN A LITTER, AND I DECIDED I didn't like the experience. The stuffy tent that stank of perfume swayed with the out-of-step stride of the men who bore it, bumping me along from the Caelian Hill to the Palatine. Livius had decided it was the best way to convey me, and purloined one of Severina's for the purpose.

By the time I was lowered in a marble courtyard, I could stand, if shakily. The journey up the steep Palatine had been the worst part, the bearers struggling and swearing. One had stumbled, and I'd been certain we'd all go tumbling back down the hill.

Hesiodos, the man as neatly dressed and shod as ever, watched critically as a guard took my arm and walked me into the domus. The sturdy guard conveyed me through open courtyards and closed ones, past fountains and gardens, and along vast colonnades.

Cassia walked beside me. I heard her quiet footfalls between the thump of Praetorian boots and was glad of her presence.

When she'd clung to me as I'd lain on the floor, I'd gathered her close, letting her softness comfort me. She'd been crying, a fact I viewed in wonder. I had command of her, life and death, yet she'd been distressed enough to pull in every favor of every person who'd promised them to me or to her, in order to find me. She had saved my life tonight.

I'd never been to the chamber we ended up in. Porphyry columns lined its length, their gilded capitals complementing the gold-touched friezes on the walls. Floor mosaics depicted a lavish garden with birds so lifelike I expected them to take flight. Lamps flickered everywhere, making the gold shimmer.

Nero stepped into the room not long after the guards halted. I'd seen the *princeps* dressed in a plain tunic with purple toga, in a charioteer's togs, and in luxurious clothes to dine with important guests.

Today, he wore the most opulent things I'd seen so far. A white silk tunic flowed over his somewhat portly body, covered with the flowing folds of a purple toga. Over that was a red silk cloak trimmed with a gold braid that caught the lamplight. A crown of gold laurel leaves sat on his light brown curls, with golden spikes protruding from the crown here and there to suggest the sun's rays. He wore fine leather shoes rather than sandals this evening, which were turned up slightly at the toes and capped with beaten gold.

The clothes had been made for him but didn't hang on him well, making him look like an expensive grain sack.

I tried to bow but swayed like a tree. The guard who'd brought me in held me up by the back of my tunic.

"You have found the killer?" Nero demanded. "Who is it?"

"A servant called Silvanus," I said, my voice strained.

"Who?" Nero fixed a perplexed gaze on me. "Who owns this servant?"

"Tertius Vestalis Felix," Cassia answered in her quiet voice.

Nero started then his eyes narrowed. "Vestalis? The proconsul nearly worshipped in the senate? His servant has been murdering gladiators? What for?"

Cassia, her head bowed, began to tell him all of it. She was much better at explaining and keeping a story straight than I was, so I remained silent while she spoke.

"All that to avenge the death of his wife?" Nero asked after Cassia concluded the tale with my adventure tonight on the Caelian Hill. "It's heroic. Almost fit for a ballad." His voice had begun to soften in admiration, but then he stiffened and flicked his gaze back to me. "But not in *my* city, killing *my* gladiators, and terrorizing *my* people."

He waited impatiently for our response, and Cassia and I agreed with him obediently.

Nero fingered the slight indentation in his chin. "But I can't put Tertius Vestalis Felix to death. He has far too many friends and is too highly regarded. A brilliant career even I remember as a child. No, I need someone else."

His gaze lighted on me, and for a frozen moment, I thought he'd suggest I could be executed in Vestalis's place.

"We'll have this servant arrested," Nero said decisively. "After all, he is the one who committed the actual murders. We'll have a trial so all will hear of his heinous crimes, and we'll have his body cut up and displayed as he did the others. I will show the people of my city that they are safe from him." He paused and drew a breath. "Excellent. It shall be written up how I discovered the identity of the killer, and this news will be read out by the criers."

I stole a glance at Cassia, but she stood absolutely motionless, not reacting to Nero's proclamation.

Did it matter? I pondered silently. If Nero claimed credit for finding the murderer while Cassia and I had no recognition, did it truly matter? Silvanus had been stopped, and Vestalis would be watched.

Nero couldn't touch Vestalis without angering powerful men—men who would likely agree that Vestalis had every right to go after the barbarians who killed his wife and daughter. But Nero could make certain Vestalis had no opportunity to cause more trouble, perhaps by ordering him to retire deep into the countryside. I wondered if Severina would bother to go with him or be glad to have her tiresome husband shunted aside.

Vestalis might have his vengeance in the end, in any case. Herakles was a gladiator and could die in the arena at any time. If Aemil paired him in the next games against Regulus, who was not happy about being poisoned and imprisoned, his life might indeed be short.

Nero took on the tone of a grateful ruler. "You will be rewarded for your services to me, Leonidas. Go now."

He waved a pudgy hand at us then turned and wafted toward the back of the room where he disappeared through a pair of silk hangings, likely forgetting all about us.

Guards closed on us once we were alone, and Cassia slipped her hand into mine.

"Time to go home," she whispered.

HESIODOS STOOD NEAR THE LARGE FOUNTAIN IN THE MAIN courtyard, staring moodily into the dancing waters. I broke from Cassia and the guards, my legs obeying me once more, if weakly, and approached him.

"Have you asked about what I wanted?" I inquired without preliminary.

Hesiodos regarded me coolly. "I have. The answer, unfortunately, is no."

Rage flashed through me, erasing the last vestiges of the poison.

"Why?" I demanded. "What difference does it make whether Cassia belongs to me or whoever is this benefactor?"

Hesiodos moved his slim shoulders in a shrug. "I did not ask his reasons. I only do what I am told."

He was the perfect servant, having no questions or curiosity beyond what he was ordered to do. My fury rose.

"When will he reveal whatever it is he wants of us?" I asked in a harsh voice. "And once he does, and I do what he wishes, will we then be dust to him?"

Again the shrug. "That I cannot say, because I do not know." To his credit, Hesiodos's expression held some sympathy. "Until that day, Cassia is to look after you, and you, her."

I glanced at Cassia, waiting for me near an arch in the colonnade, her cloak wrapped about her, her inquisitive eyes on me. She was interested in everything around her, always, no matter what she had gone through.

"Which I will do," I told Hesiodos. "But he had better reveal himself soon."

Hesiodos fixed me with a stern gaze. "Do not confront him or defy him, Leonidas. I warn you for your own good. And for Cassia's. Be patient. That is the best thing."

I tamped down my anger with effort. If this benefactor decided to punish me, it was true that Cassia would share the punishment. At best, she'd be sold again, to who knew what sort of man.

I gave Hesiodos a final scowl, then turned and left him.

CHAPTER 26

We were not allowed to lock ourselves into our apartment and recover from what happened—I badly wanted to down a flask of wine and fall asleep—because Cassia's retinue waited for us there.

After Cassia told them about what had happened on the Palatine, Martolia danced in triumph that Rufus's murder would have justice, the bells on her ankles ringing frenziedly. Gaius drummed with enthusiasm, and Merope happily twirled her sister out onto the balcony. I remembered that Martolia with Gaius had been hired to dance at a house on the Caelian, which explained how Martolia had reached Vestalis's so quickly. She and Gaius must have noted Aemil and the others rushing to the villa.

Sextus Livius had withdrawn his guards when the Praetorians had come, not wanting to be anywhere near Nero's functionaries. He'd also sought our rooms and now thumped me on the shoulder, holding a cup of the wine he'd brought with him for all.

"I was happy to help, Leonidas," he said when I thanked him. "As I stated, you have done me a good turn. I admit I worried much for you when I received Cassia's message."

"Your arrival was timely. He'd have killed me."

Livius sobered. "No doubt. I can supply a guard for you always if you need it. My men are well-trained and loyal."

His men looked like bandits turned partly civilized, but this was not unusual. Many mercenaries took on bodyguard work when there were no wars to fight or cities to raid.

"You are kind," I said. "But I am supposed to be doing the guard work."

Livius chuckled. "That is true. However, if you continue to hunt killers through the streets, you will need help. My offer stands."

I thanked him again, having no intention of tracking any more murderers. I would seek Gallus and become a builder, leaving death and murder behind me.

Livius finished his cup of wine then departed, his men closing around him as they marched off into the darkness. I listened to their tramp of feet fading, Livius never having to fear the Roman night.

Marcianus had arrived to make certain the poison had worn through me. He gave me a thorough examination, peering into my mouth and eyes, sniffing my breath. This to the fascination of Helvius, who'd also turned up.

When Marcianus finished with me, I took Helvius aside.

"Thank you," I said. "For helping Cassia. And me."

Helvius ducked his head. "I'd do anything for her." He glanced at Cassia, resignation in his eyes. "But I know she won't have me." He sighed. "We've been friends for years, and I will take that bond if I can have no other. I will always make certain she is well, even if she can't give me what I want."

I clasped Helvius's shoulder in new respect. Of all the players in this drama, Helvius probably possessed more *virtus* than any of the others.

Aemil had come with Marcianus, who'd been at the ludus when a frantic Cassia and Helvius had arrived.

"Always glad to see you back from the Palatine in one piece," Aemil said, lifting his cup to me. "And this time, the Caelian."

He frowned. "But I can't believe that a former proconsul of Vestalis's prestige bothered to slip a curse into Rufus's cell. He hadn't even planned to kill him, had he? That was his servant's idea."

"I believe the curse came from Daphnus, Chryseis's new husband," I said with conviction. "Maybe he paid someone to tuck it there, or maybe he pretended to be an admirer and gave it to Rufus himself, telling him it was a good-luck charm. If I see Daphnus again, I will ask him."

And shake him. Would Rufus have been unlucky enough to come under Silvanus's power and killed if Daphnus hadn't cursed him? Curses were tricky things, not to be undertaken lightly.

Regulus was the only one who hadn't stopped by. He'd been helped back to the ludus by Livius's guards to sleep off the poison and his adventure. He'd no doubt blame me for the entire episode.

But I'd forgive him. Regulus had saved us tonight when he'd kept Vestalis from rushing for help while I battled with Silvanus. I'd thank him later and be amused when he spit at me.

As dawn neared, Cassia shooed everyone out. They left cheerfully, the ladies still dancing after they'd hugged and kissed Cassia and then me goodbye. Gaius led them away, and Helvius went with them, the lot accompanied by Aemil and Marcianus, who'd see them home safely. Aemil was already growling at the girls to cease their prancing and pay attention to where they were going.

Cassia closed the door and leaned against it, letting out a breath.

We studied each other for a time. There was much to say, and yet much I should not. We had spoken all the words, and Cassia had written many of them down.

I made for my bunk and fell upon it. I closed my eyes then snapped them open when I was instantly transported back into the cell where I lay immobilized in the dark.

Cassia removed my sandals and draped a blanket over me, setting the burning oil lamp on the windowsill above me.

"We'll keep this lit for a while." She straightened a fold of the blanket. "Good night, Leonidas."

I mumbled something in response. Cassia drifted off to put the room to rights, singing under her breath.

I didn't need the light, I realized as I closed my eyes again. The lamp would burn out in time, but it didn't matter. Cassia's voice would carry me through any darkness.

IN THE MORNING, WE ATE BREAKFAST AS THOUGH NOTHING had happened, breaking the bread Cassia had fetched from Quintus the baker.

Afterward, she drew out tablets and scrolls, as usual, ready to make her notations for the morning.

"What will you do today, Leonidas?" she asked, pen poised.

"Visit Gnaeus Gallus." I shoved in the last of my bread and washed it down with very diluted wine. "And tell him I will join him in whatever building job he wishes."

"I thought you might." Cassia smiled in satisfaction. "Will you have a reading lesson first? I think you are ready to write out the letters on your own."

I set down the wine cup and flexed my hand. "I know how to wield a sword, not a stylus."

"You did fine with the board. Now you will simply trace the same letters on the wax."

I was doubtful, but I let her set an open, unused tablet before me, the leather hinges uncreased, the yellowish wax pristine and unmarred. Cassia pulled her stool beside me and laid the wooden board with the alphabet nearby so I could refer to it.

"We'll start with something simple. You can learn to write *Leonidas*."

I studied Cassia in her plain tunic, neatly belted, her black curls caught at the back of her neck, every thread of them in place. The curve of her cheek, her crooked nose, and her dark eyes had been a beautiful sight as she'd burst into the cell last night, crying out when she'd seen me struggling to move.

"No," I said in a quiet voice.

Her brows went up in perplexity. "No?"

"Teach me how to write the name *Cassia.*"

Cassia gazed at me for a long moment, her lips parted, then she flashed me a sudden and warm smile and guided my hand to form the letter *C*.

AUTHOR'S NOTE

Thank you for reading! I hope you enjoyed this foray into Ancient Rome and the continuing adventures of Leonidas the Gladiator.

I had the idea for this book while writing Book One *(Blood of a Gladiator)*—I was curious about Aemil and the other gladiators of the ludus, and wanted to write more about them. Gladiators came from all walks of life and all corners of the empire, whether captured in battle (e.g., Ajax, Herakles, and Praxus), sentenced to the ludus for crimes (Leonidas), or voluntarily joined the life either to pay debts or in search of fame (Rufus). They usually served a term of five years, after which time they could stay on if they wished or leave as a freedman. Most chose to remain at the ludus, either fighting more bouts for prize money, or as trainers. Many, like Aemil, opened their own schools.

While it's popularly believed that gladiators fought each other to the death on a daily or weekly basis, in reality, the games were few and far between. A gladiator in Imperial-era Rome might fight only twice a year, usually at Saturnalia and one other seasonal festival, such as the spring equinox. Games were costly and elaborate productions, and if anything went wrong, such as the riots in Pompeii that shut down gladiatorial games for a decade, the aediles who sponsored them were held responsible.

Also, most gladiators survived their matches. Evidence from tombstones and other inscriptions show gladiators often losing or fighting to draws and living to fight another day. A well-trained gladiator was expensive to replace—the sponsor of the games had to pay lanistas like Aemil a high price for each gladiator who died. Gladiators did die in this combat, of course, but the average number of deaths has been put to around 16 percent.

Even so, gladiators were expected to fight hard and put on a show, risking death in the course of the entertainment. A life Leonidas readily walked away from.

We will see more of Aemil and the other gladiators in the ludus as the series continues.

I decided to set this book in February, which led me to research on the month itself: The word February derives from *februum* (plural *februa*) which means an object used in a purification ritual. February saw many such purification festivals, as this had once been the last month of the year. (Julius Caesar reformed the calendar to have the year begin January 1, but he kept the length of February to its traditional 28 days). Lupercalia purified the city for the coming year and brought fertility, Parentalia honored deceased family members, Terminalia honored the god of boundaries, and Fornicalia blessed all the grain ovens. A very busy month for Ancient Romans!

Again, thank you for reading. Leonidas and Cassia's adventures will continue.

To stay informed of when new books or audio editions will be released, sign up for my email alerts here:

http://eepurl.com/5n7rz

or check my website for updates:

https://www.gardnermysteries.com

ALSO BY ASHLEY GARDNER

Leonidas the Gladiator Mysteries

Blood of a Gladiator

Blood Debts (novella)

A Gladiator's Tale

Captain Lacey Regency Mystery Series

The Hanover Square Affair

A Regimental Murder

The Glass House

The Sudbury School Murders

The Necklace Affair

A Body in Berkeley Square

A Covent Garden Mystery

A Death in Norfolk

A Disappearance in Drury Lane

Murder in Grosvenor Square

The Thames River Murders

The Alexandria Affair

A Mystery at Carlton House

Murder in St. Giles

Death at Brighton Pavilion

The Custom House Murders

Kat Holloway "Below Stairs" Victorian Mysteries

(writing as Jennifer Ashley)

A Soupçon of Poison

Death Below Stairs

Scandal Above Stairs

Death in Kew Gardens

Murder in the East End

Death at the Crystal Palace

Mystery Anthologies

Past Crimes

ABOUT THE AUTHOR

Award-winning Ashley Gardner is a pseudonym for *New York Times* bestselling author Jennifer Ashley. Under both names—and a third, Allyson James—Ashley has written more than 100 published novels and novellas in mystery, romance, historical fiction, and fantasy. Ashley's books have been translated into more than a dozen different languages and have earned starred reviews *Publisher's Weekly* and *Booklist.* When she isn't writing, she indulges her love for history by researching and building miniature houses and furniture from many periods.

More about her series can be found at the website: www.gardnermysteries.com. Stay up to date on new releases by joining her email alerts here:

http://eepurl.com/5n7rz

CPSIA information can be obtained
at www.ICGtesting.com
Printed in the USA
LVHW101058021222
734414LV00002B/248